HAUNTED OHIO II:

More Ghostly Tales from the Buckeye State

CHRIS WOODYARD

Kestrel
Publications

1811 Stonewood Drive
Beavercreek, OH 45432

ALSO BY CHRIS WOODYARD

Haunted Ohio: Ghostly Tales from the Buckeye State
The Wright Stuff: A Guide to Life in the Dayton Area

First Edition 1992
Printed in the United States of America
Typesetting by Copy Plus, Dayton, OH
Cover Art by Larry Hensel, Hensel Graphics, Xenia, OH
Author photo by Rosi Mackey, Xenia, OH
Library of Congress Catalog Card Number: 91-75343

Woodyard, Chris
Haunted Ohio II: More Ghostly Tales from the Buckeye State/ Chris
Woodyard.
SUMMARY: Old and new ghost stories from around Ohio.

ISBN: 0-962847216
1. Ghost Stories — United States — Ohio
2. Ghosts — United States — Ohio
3. Haunted Houses — United States — Ohio
I. Woodyard, Chris II. Title
398.25 W912 H
070.593 Wo
Z1033.L73

To my husband John—with my undying love and thanks.
Without you, this book could never have materialized.

ACKNOWLEDGMENTS

Many people have contributed their stories and their support to *Haunted Ohio II*. In particular I want to thank the following: "Anonymous;" Dorothy Philips Amling; Vicki Art; Diane Bachman, Miamitown Historical Society; The Barberton Herald; Jane Beathard, The Madison Press; Michael Berger; Marjorie Brissey; Eric Brothers, Lighter Than Air Society; Wilma J. Brumley, The Adams County Historical Society; Jenifer Burns and her classes at Stivers Middle School; Amy Canadee, Ritter Public Library, Vermilion; Carol A. Carey, Fayette Co. Hist. Soc.; Bryan Public Library; Mrs. Evelyn Cozatt, Eden Hall, Xenia; Richard Crawford, Cincinnati Suburban Press; Dennis Dalton, Historically Speaking; Linda and Sean Durbin; Dale and Becky Edwards; Frank Evans; Henrietta C. Evans, Our House Museum; Jim Flanagan; Michael Follin; Martha S. Foster; Audrey Gilbert, Preble County Historical Society; Elizabeth A. Goodan, Madison County Hist. Soc.; Brian Hackett, Ross County Hist. Soc.; Helen M. Hansen, Curator, Follett House Museum; Vivian Harris; Joyce Harvey, Fairfield Co. District Library; Heterick Mem. Library, Ohio Northern; Cal Holden; Barbara Kemper, Our House Museum; Alan Liming; Brian Liming; Duff Lindsay; Vicki Logue; Lorain County Hist. Soc.; Kate March; Ron McCarty; Kim and Mark McMillan; Martha Mechel, Maumee Valley Hist. Soc.; Betty Miller; Sigie Minge; Morning Sun United Presbyterian Church; Muskingum Co. Library System; Nina D. Myatt, Curator, Antiochiana Room, Olive Kettering Library, Antioch University; The National Archives; Mr. and Mrs. Orville Orr, Linda, Cecil Snow, The Buxton Inn; Joseph Owens; Roseanne Patterson; Ted Peters; Gin Phillippi; Patty Ramsey; Mary Lou Raye; Tom Riley, Mgr., Goodyear Airship Operations; Anita Sarkar; Beth Scott; Shelley Seaver; Janet Senne, Erie County Hist. Soc.; Mary Sikora, Dayton Daily News; Brooksany Steed, Xenia Daily Gazette; Becky Stockum; Linda M. Swartzel, The Mary L. Cook Public Library; Bob Thompson; Dr. A. Dale Topping, Lighter Than Air Society; Myra Turner; Vivian Vanausdal; Robert L. Van Der Velde; Ellen Van Schaik; John Walker, Reference Librarian, Sinclair Community College; Jolene Wallace; Warren Co. Hist. Soc.; Jennifer Wilhem; Brian A. Williams, Assistant Archivist, Oberlin College Archives; Tammy and Gary Wilson; Craig and Nanette Young, Harmony Hills Stables; Mark Young

I would especially like to thank Rosi Mackey, friend, editorial assistant, and the perfect ghost-hunting companion. Thanks too, to Anne Oscard, one of the people I would most like to have along when confronting a ghost, and to Susan Durtschi, Linda Marcus, Michael Norman and Beth Scott, who reviewed the manuscript (favorably, D.G.). Beavercreek reference librarians Jo Ellen Fannin, Susan Griffin, and Mary Ann Reese not only started the whole thing, but rose to every challenge and cheerfully filled an entirely unreasonable number of Interlibrary Loan requests. They, along with the entire supportive Beavercreek library staff, have my deepest appreciation.

TABLE OF CONTENTS

Introduction

Prelude: The Ghost Car

INTRODUCTION

All argument is against the appearance of the living spirits of
the dead; all belief is for it...
-Dr. Johnson-

The young girl stood there shivering in the sunlight as she clutched her copy of *Haunted Ohio*.

"Can, can I talk to you?" she stammered.

My heart sank. I wondered if her parents were upset about her buying the book at my Beavercreek Popcorn Festival booth the day before.

Her eyes darting back and forth nervously, she continued,

"I read a couple of chapters of the book last night, and then put it down on the sofa and went to bed. In the morning my Mom asked me if I'd read any of it. I looked over at the sofa and there was this torn-out page lying on top of the book."

She showed me the page, the title page of chapter three. It had indeed been torn out; the rest of the pages were still firmly in their binding.

"Did your mother object to your buying the book?" I asked cautiously.

"No! She was the one who pointed it out in the first place and said I should buy it."

"Who else lives in your house?"

"Just me and my Mom."

"No pets?"—a foolish question since the page had been neatly torn out, not chewed.

"Just a dog and he stays outside."

"Do you walk in your sleep?" I asked desperately. It was all I could think of to ask because otherwise, there was only one other conclusion: that *something* in her house was trying

to communicate. The page came from the chapter on Thomas
Edison's attempts to build a machine to talk with the dead....

While I was writing this book, it often seemed that
something was trying to communicate with me. I have been
haunted by odd coincidences and anomalous events. One
October morning Brooksany Steed, staff writer for the *Xenia
Gazette*, called me for an interview. "I told my boss I was
going to call you this morning, and I was thrilled when she told
me you were already set to come in at 3:00 p.m. Monday."

"I am?"

"Sure, Mrs. S.* made your appointment."

"Who's Mrs. S.?" I asked blankly.

"I thought she was your agent."

No one showed up at 3:00 p.m. Monday, but I wonder if a
cold wind blew through the newspaper offices. I still don't
have any idea who Mrs. S. is. Brooksany figures she's a ghost.
I'm a ghost writer, why shouldn't I have a ghost agent?

When I wrote about the ghosts of Dayton's Victoria
Theatre in *Haunted Ohio*, I tried unsuccessfully to track down a
group of high school students who spent the night at the theatre
and tape recorded the ghost. When I mentioned the story to a
group of University Women, one of the ladies, whom I've
known for eight years, told me that her son was one of the
chaperons that night and that she had heard the tape.

While it seemed at times that stories were materialized out
of nowhere, in other instances it seemed that *something* did not
want its story told.

My files, in fact *all* of my notes from *Haunted Ohio*—a
large boxful—have vanished. One story—"A Real Jaycee
Haunted House"—disappeared from my computer twice. The

NOTE: Names with one asterisk mean that the name was
changed 1) by request of the person involved or 2) because I couldn't
find the person and ask permission to use their real name. If you are
one of these persons and are surprised to see your story here, please
contact me.

first time I searched subdirectories in vain. The next morning the file reappeared. The second time, the file simply vanished and never came back. I had sent a copy to the man who told me the story; when he tried to return it to me, it vanished in the mail.

One fascinating aspect of writing *Haunted Ohio* has been people's reactions after reading the book. I have to admit that it is perversely gratifying to reach out and terrify someone, like the woman who said that she had to sleep with the lights on for a week after reading it. One journalist, Lisa Fatzinger of the *Tiffin Advertiser-Tribune* boasted, "I've covered gruesome murders, I've covered organized crime, I've gotten death threats. I'm not afraid of *anything*!" Then she added sheepishly, "But after I read your book I had to sleep on the couch because I couldn't bring myself to go up those long, dark stairs."

One reader called me from Columbus to tell me his story. I had sent him a review copy. He received my book on Friday the 13th and immediately sat down to read it. Later in the evening, he finished the book and had just drifted off to sleep when his burglar alarm went off. He emphasized how state-of-the-art his alarm system is: it's never malfunctioned, never goes off during storms, etc. etc. Sleepily, he punched in the code to stop the alarm. The panel showed an intruder in zone 5, which was his back hall. He checked. No one there.

The alarm company called. "We show an intruder in zone 12" they told him.

Puzzled, he replied, "I don't even *have* a zone 12."

"Now it's moved to zone 7," they told him. He went to the back bedroom, where, he told me, he had nursed his father through his last illness. He checked the windows—all tightly locked.

"We show a window open in that room." said the alarm people. Whatever it was, it continued to move around the house, leaving him baffled. He says it's just coincidence that the zone numbers corresponded with the numbers in his late father's birthday.

Many theories have been advanced to account for spirits. In studying the phenomena we call ghosts, it becomes apparent that there are several spectral species:

1) Ghosts with a purpose, who come to warn, punish, give advice, say "Goodbye," "I love you," or "I left the insurance papers in the desk drawer."

2) What I call "Video-tape ghosts" who repeat some action or appearance over and over as if replaying a film. They give no indication of being aware of anything around them.

3) Ghosts who don't know that they are dead—what Arthur Conan Doyle called "Invisibles." He says, "They are not wicked for the most part, though you get a mean one now and then. They are simply ignorant. They don't know where they are and they can't believe they are dead. They're dreadfully puzzled and worried like people in a wild dream."[1]

3) Poltergeists: disembodied, randomly destructive energy usually caused by a disturbed adolescent.

4) Time-warps, where people seem to glimpse the past or, rarely, the future.

Why do we like ghost stories? Michael Sadleir says that they provide, "the pleasurable shudder—a horror which we know does not—but none the less conceivably might—threaten ourselves." It is a way of being frightened without risk, a safe way of getting the adrenalin rush that makes us feel truly alive—and never more alive than when we are reading about the dead.

Never in my worst nightmares did I think I'd find so many Buckeye ghosts. When I wrote *Haunted Ohio*, I hoped I could exorcise my ghostly fears and lay them to rest. Instead, hundreds more have swarmed out of their graves to haunt my dreams and—I hope—yours as well. For just as "a sorrow shared is a sorrow halved," a ghost story shared is one less waking nightmare for me.

I present these horrors to you now—direct from that state of terror I call Ohio. Sleep well.

PRELUDE

THE GHOST CAR

Late one winter's night in 1926, members of the Skinner*
family of Lancaster saw a car coming down the road towards
their house. It turned off the main road, fishtailing a little in
the snow. The car crossed the bridge over the creek through
their property, then stopped at the gate. A man in a dark
overcoat got out, opened the gate, then drove the car through
and turned it around at the barn. They watched him get out of
the car, open the gate to the house, and walk up to the house,
his head bent against the snow. A knock came at the door. But
when they opened it, there was no one there.

They went out onto the porch and looked, but there was no
car parked by the gate. Mr. Skinner and the boys got a lantern
and followed the tracks in the snow. They could clearly see
where the car had turned around and driven down the drive.
Baffled, they went back to the house.

The next year the very same thing happened again at the
very same time of night. And it happened exactly the same
way each year until 1930. In 1930 the youngest Skinner boy
died, his death heralded by three owls who hooted and flew
away one by one. Almost a month later his brother fell sick.
The younger sister saw seven owls this time, who hooted and
flew away one by one, until none was left. That night the boy
died.

Mr. and Mrs. Skinner mourned and wondered if the car
had come for their boys. They hadn't seen it yet that year, and
prayed that it would never come again, but sure enough, late
one night, the car came back.

When the knock came, they froze in their chairs and stared
at the door. Out on the porch they thought they heard a faint
chuckle. And then came the voice none of them could describe
later, saying, "Soon no one will occupy this farm but the owls."
The voice went on to prophesy disaster.

And that spring, at planting time, Mr. Skinner fell under the teeth of the harrow and bled to death before help could reach him. After the funeral, Mrs. Skinner took her remaining daughter to the neighboring farm, went home, and swallowed carbolic acid.

The farm hasn't been occupied since, except by the owls. But if you happen to be there late some snowy night, you might hear a knock at the door and see the ghost car, with its dark driver, Death.[1]

WOMEN IN WHITE
Ghostly ladies

Ghosts, like ladies, never speak till spoke to.
-R.H. Barham-

When thinking of ghosts, many people automatically picture a beautiful, if transparent woman, in filmy white robes. The ghostly nun flits through the pages of countless British ghost stories. Americans see ghostly brides or women in white nightgowns like the negligee-ed starlets menaced by architectural nightmares on the covers of gothic romances. Elsewhere in this book you will find ghostly ladies clad in shades of black, blue, or grey, but here are the Women in White, a color so flattering to the ectoplasmic complexion. Watch closely or you may miss them as they drift by in the mists of twilight.

THE THUNDERSTORM GHOST

Just at the turn of the century, on a fine early summer day, young Mrs. Frances Thompson* went berrying. Drowsy after eating her lunch, she lay down for a nap, but was startled awake by a thunderclap and the chill spray of raindrops in her face. Frances sprang to her feet. A bolt of lightning sizzled from the clouds. Her hair stood on end. She rushed under a huge oak tree, the wind whipping her hair across her eyes.

There was a blinding explosion of light then a great wave of heat swept through the young woman's body. Paralyzed, she saw that her fingertips were on fire before the optic nerves burned away.

Her husband and a search party found her late that night. The wind had swept away the clouds, leaving a clear, pitiless moon. Frances stood crucified against the oak tree, her arms rigidly outstretched. Her mouth was open in her last scream. In the lantern light the searchers could see her blackened tongue, like a lump of coal.

Frances Thompson was buried in the Christian Church cemetery near Beattytown. It was whispered that the undertaker had to break her arms to get them to lie down flat in the coffin. That he had to use carpet twine and a darning needle to close that dreadful screaming mouth. Everyone shuddered and then went on with their lives.

Then one night a dry goods salesman who regretted not having stayed in Springfield, found himself caught in the middle of a ferocious thunderstorm. His horse shied and plunged as the lightning illuminated a huge oak tree. The next flash revealed a young woman in a white gown standing by the tree, her arms flung up like lightning rods to the heavens. She seemed to be screaming, but he heard no sound. There was a smell of roasting flesh.

The salesman whipped up his horse and never looked back until he got to the Neff Hotel in Glen Helen at Yellow Springs and gasped out his story in the bar. His listeners heard his story gravely for he was a temperate man, not given to wild stories.

They would hear other stories from other travelers who reported seeing the "thunder-storm ghost"—a young woman in an ash-white gown, frozen in her last death-agony. It got so that if it looked like rain, timid travelers would take the Clifton Road.

One night Dr. William Haffner driving home from attending a patient in Springfield, found himself near the oak as the wind was rising. Haffner had always ridiculed the story. "Show me one single reliable witness," he always said. He chuckled to himself, "Well, if I get a glimpse of the ghost, I'm as reliable a witness as they come."

There was a hiss and a crackle and a smell of brimstone. Dr. Haffner and his horse were blinded by the white-hot light that flooded the clearing by the oak tree. When his eyes cleared he stared. There she was—her arms outstretched in an agonizing longing for life. With a doctor's precise eye, he noted the flames playing about her fingertips, saw the worm of smoke rise from her mouth.

"She was as real as any woman I ever saw in the flesh," he said afterwards, his hand shaking over a stiff drink at Neff's.

And if you are traveling that way during an early summer thunderstorm and mistakenly take shelter under the same huge oak tree, you may see the woman in white, her tortured image burned into Eternity.[1]

THE HANGED LADY

There is a house in the heart of Woodland in Mansfield that belonged to one of the most prominent families in town. The house was up for sale and one Sunday evening a realtor, Mrs. Hugo*, brought a couple by to see it.

She ushered them into the master bedroom, which had a dramatic cathedral ceiling. While the wife exclaimed over the closets, the realtor casually glanced upwards. She froze in horror as she saw a smoky white figure in a long gown hanging from a noose at the point of the ceiling. Miraculously the couple didn't seem to notice anything and she ushered them out as quickly as she could.

Mrs. Hugo spent the next day at the historical society digging up old records and newspaper stories. In reading between the lines she found that the wife of the original owner had hanged herself in that bedroom at that same hour. The next Sunday Mrs. Hugo stood watching anxiously in the bedroom. And at the same hour, the exact hour of her hanging, the ghostly white figure appeared again.

THE GHOST OF LITTLE SUGAR CREEK

Around the bend of the twisting road overhung with trees, I came upon a dismal little park. There was some playground equipment—rusty cages filled with weeds. Beyond them, the stream had bitten sharply through the soil. There was an unnatural stillness in the air, and the shadow of an old sorrow. Even on the sunniest days, darkness hangs under the trees at Magee Park on the banks of Little Sugar Creek.

In the 1880s, the highly respectable and very married mayor of the village of Bellbrook seduced a young servant girl. He was well-to-do and handsome in a fleshy kind of way. He had a plausible way about him—and an invalid wife. The young girl dreamed impossible dreams of replacing the sickly mistress of the house. When she found herself pregnant, she went to the man. He turned white, then ordered her from the house. He told his wife that the girl had—hem—gotten herself into a scrape and it would oblige him if the subject was never mentioned in his house again.

But soon everyone in town knew that she'd done what she shouldn't have even if they didn't know with whom. Her family lived on a farm up near Piqua. She had no money to go to them; they would have barred their doors to her anyway. Friendless, despairing, she welcomed "admirers," who at least paid for enough food to put off starvation until the child was born.

The midwife was called a month earlier than expected. She came, expecting to take her fee in a juicy bit of gossip, but even in her agony, the girl bit her lips until the blood ran, rather than name the man who'd gotten her into trouble. The midwife did all that was necessary, but no more. After all, why should she trouble herself for nothing? And nothing certainly described that puny scrap of humanity who had come silently into the world.

The young woman only went out with the baby after dark. It was whispered that the child resembled its father so much that she didn't dare expose its face to the light of day. She took to wandering about on the banks of Little Sugar Creek, crooning at the little bundle of rags. She grew thin as a skeleton.

One night she went to the back door of the mayor's house, hoping for something, anything to keep her and her child alive. Perhaps she even hoped to show *him* his child, who had something of his features. The door was slammed in her face by the cook, leaving a ghostly smell of roast beef hanging in the air.

She wrapped the still baby closer to her. She no longer felt the pain in her stomach. The June night was unseasonably cold and damp, with a thick fog creeping up behind. She stumbled over the Little Sugar Creek bridge, then paused and looked down. There was no water, only clouds—like the fluffy white clouds of Heaven. She could walk on those clouds to Jesus, she thought, He would give her baby something to eat. Suffer the little children, He'd said....

No one heard the splash and she did not cry out.

Two boys playing hooky from school found her a week later. Her arms were still wound around a tattered shawl, but the child had been washed further down the creek. After the foxes finished with it, there was little enough to bury.

It is said that on certain foggy nights in June, the pale young mother walks the banks of Sugar Creek. Softly she croons a lullaby to that which lies so quietly in her arms. Then the fog closes around her like a shroud, stilling her song.[2]

THE SORROWFUL MOTHER

Professor Louis North*, who had recently moved to the Cleveland area, was delighted with the room he'd chosen for his bedroom. It had a fireplace with an elegantly carved mantelpiece and rich tilework. Quality work, just like the rest of his beautiful turn-of-the-century house with its broad verandah and large windows. Yet his dream house quickly became a nightmare when he was awakened one night by a woman's sobbing.

The night was chill and North had built a fire. He was used to the sound of popping logs, but they had never sounded like *that*. Then he saw a woman in a long white gown sitting by the fireplace. Her long hair covered her face as she buried her face in her hands, sobbing violently.

North was sure he had locked his doors. And no burglar would just sit there crying. He looked over at the door. It was still closed. When he looked back, the woman was gone. The only noise was the sleepy murmur of the fire.

North searched the room, but decided it had all been a dream—until he saw the woman several more times in the next months. He told a few friends about the woman and one of them suggested that she was a ghost. North scoffed at the idea. He didn't believe in ghosts.

Then North met parapsychologist Rick Klaben* at a faculty party. Klaben agreed that the woman might be a ghost and urged North to find out more about the history of the house. So North went to the local historical society and spent hours pouring over old deeds, newspapers, and wills. The only thing he discovered was that the house was built by a man named Paul Whitmore.

One night as the ghost sobbed by the fire, North seemed to hear the name "Victoria" repeated over and over. Klaben suggested that North address the ghost by name and see what happened.

A few nights later the ghost reappeared. Over her sobs, North called, "Victoria!" several times. For the first time, the ghostly woman looked up. Then she walked across the room, stopping every few steps, as if listening. Then she disappeared.

North continued his research. Finally, in a Cleveland newspaper, he found a wedding announcement. The groom's name was William Whitmore. The bride's name was Victoria. The historical society curator told North about an elderly Whitmore cousin who might shed some light on the mystery.

The trouble all began (said the cousin) when William Whitmore, son of the town's richest man, married a schoolmarm named Victoria. An aristocratic enough name, but she was *only* a *school* teacher, said his mother bitterly, with disdainful patrician emphasis. A Whitmore does not marry a person who *works.* Victoria became, in turn, "that person," then "that creature." But William married her anyway and brought her home to his parents' house to live.

It must have been a hellish arrangement: the barely civil breakfasts *en famille,* the tightlipped evenings around the fire. The strain on Victoria was immense. And it became even more so, when it was found that she was going to bear the family an heir. Dear Victoria had breakfasts brought up to her on a tray, then lunches, and then her dinners, as she was strictly confined to bed. "Indifferent health," murmured Mrs. Whitmore senior to anyone who inquired after the young mother-to-be at her Saturday afternoon teas. "Blood will out, you know. So kind of you to ask...."

Some days, lying in bed, listening to the soft clash of teacups downstairs, the distant waspish murmur of voices, Victoria thought she would go mad. But then the child would stir and she would try to be more cheerful, for a happy mother makes a happy child.

The child was born in October, near Halloween, which is perhaps why his grandmother thought involuntarily of jack-o-lanterns when her new grandson was presented to her by the nurse. She ordered him unwrapped. He started convulsively at the chill and began to mew.

"Like a sick cat," she muttered, observing the deformed head, the shriveled limbs, and the misshapen eyes, slanted like a goblin's.

"What's wrong with his head?" she demanded.

The doctor, hovering not far behind, murmured something about a difficult birth...mercifully they don't live long....

If it had been a dog, she would have had it chloroformed.

When "dear Victoria" was recovered from the dreadful shock, Mrs. Whitmore thoughtfully suggested that she and William go for a drive. She provided her own carriage and told them not to hurry back.

They were gone only a few hours, yet it was enough. Mrs. Whitmore was in her boudoir when she heard William carrying Victoria into her room. There was an undercurrent of conversation, like waves clashing on the shore, then loud, ugly screams.

Like a fishwife, thought Mrs. Whitmore wearily. And she settled herself for her afternoon nap.

The baby had disappeared, banished to a hospital for the incurable. His cradle, his furniture, even his tiny clothes so carefully sewed during those interminable evenings under Mrs. Whitmore's censorious eye—all were gone. White-faced, William stood behind Victoria and said, "Why did you do it, Mother?"

"Because Victoria is not well, nor is she capable of taking care of—that—properly."

And because this is my house and I chose not to have it fouled with your misshapen brat, went unsaid, but she saw Victoria blanch. She chose her next words carefully.

If Victoria had a breakdown, she pointed out sensibly, they'd have to send her away too. She'd heard the doctor—he said the child couldn't possibly live. This was the best solution for all concerned.

And she refused to tell Victoria where the child was.

But the tiresome creature *would* keep crying. She wept and she wept until she was quite ill. And then she became confused.

"I hear my baby crying!" she cried, "Won't you let me go to him? He needs his mama! And she would run about the house, looking everywhere for the child. It was a great trial, Mrs. Whitmore admitted to sympathetic callers.

Early one morning, at the time when babies wake and are hungry, Victoria rose from her bed in the darkness and went to the adjoining room where the cradle had stood. There she sat and wept while her child's cries rang in her ears.

Her husband called from the other room, "Victoria, come to bed!"

She rose and stumbled on the rocker. Victoria fell heavily against a corner of the mantelpiece, cracking the delicate bone at her temple. She died on the floor of the nursery—North's room.

The elderly cousin even remembered the name of the asylum where they took the child. North checked the records of the institution and found an entry for the death of "William Whitmore Jr.", age four. He had lived longer than they ever expected, North mused.

Klaben urged North to talk to Victoria. She needed to know she was dead, that the child was not there. She must leave the house and go to find her child in the Light. North felt foolish talking to a sobbing ghost. She didn't even seem to notice him. Yet, she appeared less often and one day she was gone. North still doesn't believe in ghosts, but he hopes that somewhere Victoria and her baby are together.[3]

DIE FOR LOVE

Beaver Creek threads its way through the steep hills and thick forests of Beaver Creek State Park. During the canal boom of the 1880s the area prospered, but today it is an area of deserted logging camps, ruined canal locks, and ghost towns. One such town, Sprucevale, is accessible only by bridle path. And all that remains of Sprucevale are the three walls of Hambelton's grist mill—and the legend of Esther Hale.

On the morning of August 12, 1837, Esther Hale was happily preparing for her wedding. The table in the parlor was decorated with flowers and greenery; the cake was in the kitchen, covered with a cheesecloth veil to keep off the flies. The wedding was set for ten in the morning. By half past ten the guests were beginning to fidget and smile behind their fans. By half past twelve they climbed into their wagons and drove away. The messenger Esther sent could find no trace of her lover. The cabin was deserted, he said, the ashes in the stove were cold.

When her friends tried to help her to bed, Esther quietly rebuffed them until they left her sitting alone in the dark by the window of the parlor. When they returned the next morning, the curtains had been drawn, as if in a house of mourning. They were never again opened in Esther Hale's lifetime.

All summer Esther moved like a ghost through the house. In the kitchen, beetles tunneled through the cake. The flowers withered in the parlor while the spiders spun their gossamer hangings. Her friends coaxed her to eat and drink a little, but when they tried to get her to change her dress or remove the wedding decorations, she flew at them with claw-like fingers. Eventually they left her alone.

Broken hearts kill slowly. Four months later a neighbor noticed that the door to Esther's house was open, banging back and forth in the December wind. He notified the sheriff and the doctor who took a party of men to the dark house. Snow had drifted throughout the rooms like a white shroud. Esther was slumped over the parlor window sill, her veil over her face. Someone held up a lantern. The doctor drew back the shredded lace. Esther had been dead for several weeks. When they saw the horror beneath, they silently covered her over again. She was buried so, shrouded in her wedding clothes.

You can still see her dressed in white looking for her lover. It is said that she haunts the bridge over Beaver Creek, waiting there every year on August 12, a hideous figure in tattered white satin and lace. If she touches you, she will become young and beautiful again—but you will die.

Nanette Young of Harmony Hills Stables enjoys taking people on trail rides, and telling them the ghost stories of the area, especially the tale about the ghostly bride. Local people say they've seen Esther run in front of their headlights. Nanette says that her car shuts off every morning by the grist mill. Other people have had the same experience.

"One Christmas I was out looking at the Christmas lights with my mother. I told her 'This car is going to shut off as we pass that building. My girlfriend who was with us said, 'Yeah, it happens every morning.' My mother didn't believe me, then it shut right off. When this happens I just coast down the hill. There are forty thousand hills out here. But the car doesn't shut off on any of the others."

On August 8th, Nanette took a group of riders out on the trail. It was a clear night, but a mysterious fog rose from the creek up to the horses' legs. As they passed Esther's house and rode onto the bridge, the last man in line said, "I feel a *cold force* pulling on my sweat shirt!" Nanette could see nothing, but when they reached the safety of the barn, the hood of his sweat shirt was torn.

If you are in the area in early August, drive through quickly with your windows rolled up. And keep a sharp lookout for a skeletal woman in a wedding dress stained by the grave for she will lunge at your car, her bony fingers scrabbling at your windows, desperate as Death to touch and claim your living flesh.

THE GHOST WANTED HELP

Dorothy Phillips Amling told this story in the *Madison Press*, October 31, 1991:

"Late on a foggy autumn night, about thirty-seven years ago, my older brother, who was twenty at the time, was driving home on the Van Wagener Road, south of London.

"About one mile west of the Madden-Higgins Road, where Van Wagener makes an abrupt bend, he saw what looked like a person in the road. As he drew closer, the figure, a woman in a white nightgown appeared suddenly in front of his car's headlights. She was waving her arms and crying. "My brother slowed the car and the figure drifted around to the driver's window. She was only five feet away when he realized that the figure was transparent and floating, rather than walking. He was terrified!"

"I need help...please help me," the figure implored.

"What do you need?" stammered the frightened boy.

"Help me, help me, I need help." the woman kept repeating.

"What's wrong?"

But she never answered.

"Certain he had seen a ghost, my brother sped home to tell our family of the vision."

His mother was waiting up for him. When he came in, as white as a ghost himself, she realized he looked scared to death as he told her the story.

"At first, my mother doubted my brother's tale and asked him if he'd been drinking. But when she saw how truly shaken he was, she went with him back to the site to check out the situation herself.

"The place where he'd seen the woman was about a mile and a half from our home. Everything was dark and still. Even the ramshackle tenant house sitting near the road's bend appeared quiet. My mother was still a little disbelieving, but she didn't think he would make the story up.

"My father heard from a sheriff's deputy a few days later that the woman who lived in that tenant house was missing. Apparently there had been marital problems and the rumor was that she had left her husband and run away. The police questioned the husband, but he said he had no idea what had happened. He claimed she'd been at home when he went out to work in the fields and when he came back at dark, she was gone. He didn't report that she was missing for a day or two, because he thought she would come back.

"They were a quiet couple, always kept to themselves and she didn't have any friends to ask questions. Nobody ever stopped or visited. We knew of them, but they were too far away to be neighbors and they had only lived there three or four months.

"After a week passed and she hadn't returned, they searched the area and found her body, clad only in a white nightgown, in a well right beside the house. The coroner said she'd been dead six or seven days.

"Whether she drowned by accident or by foul play was never determined. No one was ever charged with a crime.

"But my brother is convinced to this day that he encountered the drowned woman's spirit just seconds after it left the body in the bottom of the well.

"I often wonder if the ghost of that woman is still walking the Van Wagener Road on autumn nights, looking for help from a passing motorist."[4]

THE GHOST OF MORNINGSTAR ROAD

Mrs. Sigie Minge has an affinity for kids. Teenagers feel comfortable drifting in and out of her house, confiding in her, treating her like a second mother.

"There was a kid, I'll call Tim*," she recalled "although he really wasn't a kid, who used to call me Mama. He pulled up here in his pickup truck and brought in six-pack of beer and set it down on the table and said, 'Mama, do you have time to talk to me? Look at that beer,' he said, shaking. 'That package has not been broken into. Not one. I wasn't drinking when this happened, I want you to know that.'

In that summer of 1973 he had gone down Morningstar Road after work with a couple friends, planning to sit along the creek with a six-pack.

Tim told her, "I walked to the back of the truck to get the beer and one of the fellows says, 'Who's the lady?' Mama, she was as solid as you. She was wearing a high-necked, long sleeved, long nightgown, like you."

The woman didn't say anything. She just went on wringing her hands and beckoning them. Her hair was hanging in a long plait down her back like she was ready for bed.

Thinking that the woman was real, Tim told the apparition, "Well, all right, we'll help you."

"We started to follow her. We had to walk real quick to keep up with her. She came to a big tree and vanished. We made better time back to the truck," Tim reported.

Back at the truck the young men reconsidered, "We're just plain stupid," Tim told them. "That's one of those ghosts!" So they went back up the hill "We called and we pleaded for a good half hour. If she'd just show us what she needed, we'd help her. But she did not come back. Now, Mama," he concluded "do you know what went on on Morningstar Road and why there is a ghost?"

Minge did some sleuthing. She visited the site and found the remains of a house the boys had overlooked. "There's nothing to indicate there was a house there. The foundations are all buried in the brush." Then she talked to two elderly Germantown residents and got the same story.

In the late 1800s there had been a big isolated brick house on Morningstar Road. The gentleman who built it belonged to a social club in Germantown. One summer evening he went into town for a meeting, leaving his wife at home with their four children.

She put them to bed, then went to the back of the house to do some chores. While she was there a storm blew up. The windows were open and the wind blew a lace curtain over a kerosene lamp. It knocked over the lamp and set the front of the house on fire. By the time she discovered the blaze it had engulfed the staircase and the hall, blocking the only way to her children.

Crazed, she tried to beat a way through the flames with a quilt. Choking on the smoke and badly burned, she ran from the house to the road trying to find someone to help her. As the roof caved in with a roar, she began racing through the woods. As she ran, screaming, insane, she rammed into the forked branch of a tree with such force that her neck snapped. She died in the woods as her children died in the flaming house.

Minge told this story to the boys who had seen the woman.

"Mama, did we help her?" asked Tim. "She vanished so quickly."

Minge thinks they did, simply by their willingness to help. Perhaps their kindness was all it took to release the woman's frenzied spirit so she could be reunited with her children.

The young men have gone back often and sat, watching. But nobody has seen the ghostly woman since.

APPARITION AND OLD LACE

Vivian Harris, who used to own a 110-year old farmhouse off Ankeney Rd. in Beavercreek told me, "We kind of fell in love with the house. We did a lot of research on it. There were signatures of former inhabitants scratched on the windows. Fifty years ago, the kitchen still had dirt floors. People told us they could remember pigs running through the kitchen. We really tried to keep it the way it was—livable, but still very primitive. People used to say about the house, 'It just engulfs you when you come in.' That was the greatest compliment they could have paid it.

"You know how old houses are. We kept hearing noises. We thought we had mice. We caught a few, and we had a cat, who always acted like he was trying to catch things, but didn't." "One night my husband said, 'What is that cat doing?' Well, the cat was right there by my pillow. Not long after, I heard the sounds again.

"This is silly, I thought. Matt must be up playing. But I checked and sure enough he was sound asleep. We always made it a point to pick his toys off the floor at night. Every morning those toys were rearranged, lined up on the floor, as if racing. One night when we put him in bed, the floor was clean. In the morning we found his train set up."

In late summer of 1984 Vivian was having trouble sleeping.

"It was the middle of the night and this almost transparent, misty thing came down the hall and just floated into our room. It was a floating, lacy image, almost like it wanted to be human. You could see limbs, covered with flowing white cloud. I had the impression it was a woman—young or middle-aged, thin, average height.

"I was just lying on my back, this thing hovering over me and I thought, I must be dreaming. I broke out in a cold sweat, and I tried to wake my husband, but I was petrified, gagging on my words. The vision floated over me and hovered over the bed. I thought I was going to have a heart attack. Then this unbelievable calm came over me. *It's OK,* the thing seemed to say, *Don't be afraid.* I remember relaxing. It stayed for just a few seconds but it seemed like an eternity! Then it floated out the door and went toward the steps to downstairs. I woke up my husband who said sleepily, 'What's wrong with you?'

"'I just saw this—thing!'

"'Right,' he said, 'Go back to sleep.' "I said, 'Look! Look at the cat!' My cat was by me, fur standing up, like he had seen something.

"That impressed him. 'Well, maybe...' he said. But I'm not sure he totally believed me.

"It's still so vivid to me I could break out in a cold sweat!" In researching the house's history Vivian found that an adult woman and a child had died in the house—a generation apart. Vivian wished that she could know more about the apparition.

"I found myself trying to stay awake. I remember being depressed thinking, It's not ever coming back.

"I got the feeling that something was around and it finally showed itself. Maybe it was somebody who knew we had the same feeling for the house and were taking care of it."

Then she says wistfully, "We still think of the farmhouse as 'home.' We will never regret having lived there."

CONVIVIAL SPIRITS
Haunted Inns, Taverns, and Bars

Drink to me.
-Picasso's last words-

Many of Ohio's inns and taverns have a spirited history.
Most hostelry hauntings go back to a time in our history when a
lodging for the night could mean a permanent stay. None of
these ghosts are the result of too many glasses of spirits. Only
the lost check in...

THE GHOSTS OF THE BUXTON INN

After *Haunted Ohio* was published, more people asked me
about the Buxton Inn than about any other story. It must have
the best-known ghosts in the state—and the happiest, for the
Buxton Inn is a delightful place to spend a night—or Eternity.

Audrey Orr and I were sitting over lunch in the Green-
house Room as she told me about the Inn's history and ghosts.
Outside I could see a graceful gazebo, pots of colorful tulips,
and a splashing fountain. Waitresses in 1800s-style empire-
waist dresses, frilled muffin hats, and black slippers glided by.
I kept looking up through the glassed-in roof of the Greenhouse
Room during lunch, thinking that someone was watching us.
But the curtains at the guest-room windows above were still.

Mrs. Orr was elegant, charming, and quietly regal. One
could see her gracing a Governor's mansion or 10 Downing
Street. Instead her domain is this inn on a quiet street in
Granville, a town full of history. She and her husband Orville
were just two schoolteachers who loved antiques until the

fateful day in 1972 when they went for a drive and, on a whim, stopped to look at the Inn. The elderly lady who had lived there for thirty years sadly told them that the Inn would probably be torn down if she couldn't find the right buyer. The Orrs talked with her a little longer, then she said, "You sound like the kind of people I'd like to buy the Inn."

So suddenly they were innkeepers. There was much to be done before the first guests could be accomodated. The Orrs figured they had about six months worth of restoration work before them. Two years and ten layers of wallpaper later, on Friday the 13th, 1974, the Buxton Inn reopened.

In those two years the Orrs dealt with termite damage, plumbing and wiring, central heat and air conditioning. They even had the original paint analyzed (buttermilk tinted with cochineal beetles) to come up with the present authentic shade of salmon-pink.

The original building was built in 1812 by Orrin Granger. Known as "The Tavern" it served as a mail delivery depot and stagecoach stop on the Columbus-Newark line. Famous visitors have included Henry Ford and Charles Dickens. The Buxton Inn is believed to be the oldest continuously operating inn in Ohio and was listed as one of the "Top Ten Best Inns of the Year" in 1988.

Major Buxton, (Major was his given name, not a military title) operated the Inn from 1865 to 1905. A photo in the lobby shows him with a basket on his arm, in a bow tie and natty fedora, looking a bit like John D. Rockefeller.

"The Lady in Blue," known in life as Ethel (Bonnie) Bounell, was the Inn's owner from 1934 until 1960. Her favorite color was blue and she died in Room Nine. She has been seen at different ages and in various clothing, usually in her trademark blue dress.

The Orrs had heard stories about ghosts, but they didn't take them seriously until two young New Hampshire wood-workers came to work on the Inn. Normally they worked late into the night, but suddenly they started leaving at dusk. Orville asked them why. They told him they'd seen a woman in blue cross the outdoor balcony between the upper-story rooms and evaporate.

When the restoration began, Orville, on the second floor, heard the heavy front door open and shut. Footsteps came up the stairway, then went down again. The front door again opened and shut. Thoroughly unnerved, Orville shouted, "You can have it!" although he obviously changed his mind later.

"He's more sensitive," said Mrs. Orr, "although at first I was leery about being here late at night." And rightly so. When she was finishing the painting in the kitchen, "I thought there was a man to my right, watching me. Naturally I thought it was Orville. He went away without saying anything which annoyed me. I went and found him in the lobby. 'Have you been watching me?' I asked him. He hadn't so I went back into the kitchen and started painting again. It happened again. I put down my brush and I said, 'I don't know what's going on, but it's scaring me!'" At that the door quietly opened and closed. She hasn't been bothered since.[1]

Mrs. Orr could also periodically smell a pungently sweet perfume in the office across from Bonnie Bounell's sitting room. Mrs. Bounell was noted for her gardenia perfume.

In 1973 Columbus psychic Maria Braun toured the house and gave her impressions. This was before any publicity about the ghosts had leaked out and she had some remarkable insights. She too smelled the ghostly gardenia perfume and pictured a woman who was theatrical (Bounell had been an actress), loved the color blue, and was tied to the building by her love for it. She also "saw" Major Buxton walking behind Orville.

By 1975, enough strange things had happened that the Orrs asked Braun, "How do we go about getting rid of our ghosts?"

"You don't want to get rid of your spirits!" Braun said emphatically. "They lend you energy and support. Do you ever get completely tired and then have sudden spurts of energy? Where do your think that energy is coming from?"

So the ghosts rest in peace at the Buxton Inn.

Another psychic gave the Orrs strong evidence about their ghosts.

"A young man from OSU, a parapsychology student, had read an article about the ghosts and wanted to give his perceptions. He sat in the dining room and he saw Major Buxton there.

"The young man said, 'He's sitting in a corner, laughing at me because of the way I look [the young man had long hair and several earrings]. He wants me to give you a message: You were thinking of opening the basement wall to make a tunnel between the front and back basement. It'll be OK to do it.'

"We just about fell off our chairs. Only three people knew that we had considered tearing out that wall: Orville, myself, and the engineer who had told us six years before to avoid doing so—that we could lose the whole front of the house."

At first the Orrs were afraid that the ghost stories would hurt business. When word began to spread, they were even accused of pulling a publicity stunt. Now it is their policy not to initiate conversations about the ghost. The staff will answer questions with facts, not fantasy—and only if asked.

Cecil Snow who has worked at the Inn since 1976 and been Manager since 1982 said, "Periodically I'll hear footsteps in the hallways and there'll be nothing there. Or I'll go to open a door and something will pull the door shut, play tug of war with me. I can feel tension on the other side of it; it's not just a draft. Normally I just say, OK, fine, and go away for a while.

"It is not a presence that hurts, but surprises. I've heard a lady's voice call out my name. I've heard knocking on the front door and when I go to open it no one is there. Nobody is even close."

After lunch the Orr's daughter Amy took me on a tour of the building. She led me up the narrow stairs with their subdued plum carpet to the second floor. The first stop was the Yellow Room, originally part of Room Nine, Bonnie Bounell's living quarters. It is now a dining room, with damask cloths, an elegant fireplace, and yellow swag wallpaper borders. I felt a pocket of cold air in this room. "It is colder than the hall," admitted Amy. She told me that it was in the hall by the Yellow Room that a water pitcher flew off a table by itself and shattered after a visiting photographer joked about the ghosts.[2]

Amy opened a door. "You need to go out on the balcony to get to Rooms Seven and Nine," the two rooms where most of the manifestations seem to occur.

Linda, one of the staff who has worked at the Inn for fourteen months told me that she was working a party upstairs one sunny afternoon when the heavy outside door, which latches with a finger latch, blew open and hit the wall. "Then it shut very slowly and the latch latched. I looked outside to see if it was windy. It wasn't. I went hot all over."

Room Seven contained a huge bed and dresser. Amy showed me a smaller adjoining room overlooking the Greenhouse Room—little more than a bed in an alcove. I shrank back. "Something wrong here," I muttered.

"That's where the cook found the woman in his bed," Amy remarked.

During the blizzard of 1978, Orville, the head chef and the chef's assistant, Andrew* were snowed in for the night. They stayed in the notoriously haunted Room Seven, playing cards and talking. Nothing happened all night. Andrew complained about not meeting a ghost, saying, "I've always wanted to meet the Lady in Blue."

The next day Orville and the chef went downstairs to plan menus. Andrew decided to take a nap. He turned back the covers on the bed in the smaller alcove and started to crawl into bed. Only there was a woman there—and she kicked him in the hip! Andrew scrambled out of bed. When he turned around, she wasn't there. He grabbed his socks and ran outside and downstairs. Mr. Orr said he was as white as paper as he stuttered, "There's a woman upstairs in the bed!" After that he wouldn't stay in the kitchen alone.

In 1991 a group of nurses from Riverside Hospital in Columbus stayed overnight. Cecil Snow, at their request, entertained them at dinner with jovial stories about the Inn's history and ghosts. Clare*, a young nurse, was assigned Room

Seven. As she lay half-awake, thinking about the next day's seminar, she heard a rustling of papers. Suddenly she was wide awake. She realized that there was a young woman in a white dress sitting on her bed.

"Are you not sleeping well?" the woman asked her sympathetically.

"No, I'm not," replied Clare. When she realized that she had just spoken to someone, she sat up. There was no one there.

Cecil heard about the incident the next morning and asked Clare, "Would you like to see a picture of our ghost?" He showed her a picture of a young Bonnie Bounell. Clare went hysterical. "That's the woman!" she screamed, pointing at the portrait.

Room Nine felt very warm and friendly. Since Bonnie Bounell had lived there, it had blue wallpaper borders and blue trim, quilts, and carpet. Perhaps it was in this room that a lady said that something had pulled like a sheet across her face and startled her awake. She fought it off her face, but it happened again as if it was trying to smother her. She complained to Cecil Snow.

Snow said to her, "I believe you, but our spirits would never hurt anyone."

A month later two elderly women were staying in the same room. One came down on a Sunday morning and said, "Do you realize that you have a ghost cat here?"

"Why would you say that?" asked Snow.

"I was resting when something jumped on my bed and curled up on my face." She felt it purring.

The door was closed and there was no cat in the room. In fact the Inn's cat was with Snow at the time. Could it have been the ghost of "Major Buxton," a fifteen-pound cat who used to greet visitors in the 1930s?

Downstairs, the stone-walled Tavern Room with its hand-hewn beams was dark, lit only by red lights. This was where the coach drivers cooked their meals over the open fireplace and slept on straw pallets on the floor. This is where a radio station recorded mysterious footsteps on a tape recorder left running all night. Where a television crew from Cincinnati filmed "person-shaped lights." Where late one night after closing, Cecil Snow clearly heard "people downstairs laughing and having a good time." He smiled at the revelry, then thought, "Wait a minute, it's *closed*."

I stepped to the right of the stairs by the tables and fireplace. Nothing. To the left of the stairs, I got a shock, the familiar psychic blow in the face. "Oh, no," I said involuntarily, drawing back. I stared at a spot to the right of the bar by a glass door. Something invisible stood there staring right back at me.

The Wine Cellar on the other side of the basement is a cheerful, well-lit room lined with framed clippings and articles about the Inn. A strapping bartender scoffed at the ghost stories. As he was on the stairs to the Wine Cellar, he felt someone come up behind him and hug him tightly enough to take his breath away.

Amy led me past a pine cupboard full of cat figures and a guest-sized umbrella rack. Beyond, the glassed-in passage with its uneven flagstones held a different time. Somehow I would not have been surprised to see coaches clattering up to the door in the brick courtyard outside. The deep alcove windows at the front of the main dining room looked out at the street through distorted glass—an antique world-view. It was a calm room with its rose satin curtains and pierced tin chandeliers. "In the main dining room after everyone's gone, things move on the tables," Linda told me. "Napkins are moved off plates—that sort of thing. You put them back—they move again."

A lady bartender saw Major Buxton in a dark suit sitting by the fireplace in the dining room. She walked into the kitchen and asked Mrs. Orr, "Has anyone taken care of the gentlemen by the fireplace?" "I haven't seated anyone," Mrs. Orr replied, puzzled. She looked into the dining room and said, "Gina, there isn't anyone there." And there wasn't.

I prowled around the Inn for several hours. I still had the feeling that someone was watching me. As I got in my car, the white-painted double-decker porches seemed like a jauntily tipped hat. I searched for ghosts in the windows, but none appeared. I drove past the Inn's oval sign painted with a smiling grey cat. And I realized that the spirits were not so much watching me, as watching over their favorite place on Earth—the Buxton Inn.

HAUNTED PUNDERSON

This chapter is based on over five years of research by a very intrepid ghost hunter, Mr. Robert L. Van Der Velde of Mentor. I am indebted to Mr. Van Der Velde for his willingness to share this material.

Punderson State Park, about thirty-five miles east of Cleveland, is a pleasant place to camp, picnic, golf, boat, or swim with its lakes and 1,000 acres of rolling woodland. But one of Punderson's lakes is haunted by the ghost of a teenager who drowned in 1977. In 1978 a group of Gypsies saw a young black woman covered with seaweed emerge from the dark waters of Punderson Lake. She walked along the shore for a few yards, then disappeared back into the water. The Gypsies packed up and never came back.

I visited Punderson Manor in late autumn when it was closed for the season. A gloomy grey sky and dead leaves rattling in the drive gave the building all the melancholy charm of an English Tudor country inn. Apparently it has all the ghosts as well.

In 1982 the Manor House was extensively remodeled, which brightened up the interior, but didn't seem to make any difference to the spirits who roam the "Tower" or "Old Section" of the Manor. Formerly the Manor House was closed during the winter and a custodian lived there to keep an eye on things. During the long winters' nights, some of these custodians discovered that they were not really alone. One young man was startled by his room lights flashing on and off and a loud knocking at his door. When he flung open the door, the hallway was empty, yet he heard footsteps pass a few feet in front of him and walk the length of the corridor.

Two of the rangers at Punderson also had a haunting experience in a hallway. As they were making their rounds, they felt an intense coldness in the second floor hall. Then they heard a woman laughing loudly behind them. The laughter swept *through* the men, engulfing them, then stopped. At that the hall became warm again.

A former employee was sleeping in one of the rooms when something woke her. At the foot of her bed stood a bearded man in shabby old clothes. Thinking that one of her co-workers was playing a joke, she kicked at the man. Her foot went right through him. She screamed as the man walked through the wall and disappeared.

One young woman was locked in a bathroom by something that breathed heavily on the other side of the door. Whatever it was held the knob so she could not turn it. A friend had to break into the room by the fire escape to release her. When she tried the knob, it turned easily.

A hostess at the Manor House Restaurant was napping one day on a sofa in the employees lounge. She was startled awake by the sounds of invisible children laughing and running around the sofa.

A night manager named Susan* actually saw the ghost children running and dancing and laughing—silently—around the figure of a woman wearing an old-fashioned dress, blue-grey cape, and a bonnet. The woman looked at Susan as if she was startled to see her, then enveloped the children in her cloak and faded away.

Susan saw the woman on another night as she floated across the dining room, into the lobby, and up the stairs while the air turned icy cold. On still another night she saw a little girl in a pink nightgown peeking at her from the stairs, a hand over her mouth, as if stifling a giggle.

The new banquet manager, Rick*, seemed to attract ghostly activity. The staff gave him the best bedroom in the house, the so-called "Blue Room." His first night there Rick sat up late studying menus. He was so absorbed in his work that he didn't notice the breeze behind him. When his papers began to blow away, he whirled to see a large floor fan floating several feet above the floor buzzing at him like an angry helicopter. Rick sat petrified while the fan whirled just a few feet from his head. Then the cord ran out, the fan unplugged itself from the wall, and settled gently to the floor like a bird.

Rick tore out of the room and down the circular staircase to the lobby. He demanded a different room, but later returned to the Blue Room with a roommate. Even then doors burst open late at night, invisible "things" sat down on his bed, and employees heard an appalling moaning noise coming from the empty room as they were showing visitors around.

Rick, manager Patricia*, and Bob*, the desk clerk, all witnessed a terrifying apparition one evening in 1979. Patricia walked through a small dining room known as the King Arthur Room on her way to the kitchen for some coffee. She never made it. She was so horrified by what she saw that she ran back to the men in the lobby and dragged them with her to the King Arthur Room. There they saw a man hanging from a rope that vanished somewhere near the ceiling.

Too terrified to go into the room, they huddled on the steps leading from the Great Hall and watched the figure, a man dressed like a lumberjack, turn slowly on the rope, his fingers twitching. They watched for three hours, until dawn came and the man gradually faded away.

After this, evenings at the Manor House were never quiet. Night manager Susan experienced inexplicable noises: rattling chandeliers and candy machines. Most unsettling was the door to the men's room which would open as if someone were coming out, then quietly close.

The spirits continued to persecute Rick. He awoke one night drenched, as if someone had thrown a bucket of water on him. Another midsummer night he woke to find his air conditioner on full-blast and the room much colder than any air conditioner could have made it. Even the windows were covered in a thick frost.

Halloween night, 1979, the staff threw a party. A cake was served, inscribed: "To the Ghosts of Punderson" and all hell broke loose after that night. Pictures fell off the wall; objects whizzed across the lobby. If Susan didn't keep a grip on her pencil, it too would fly across the room. This continued until five or six in the morning when the front door opened, as if the ghost had finished his shift and were going home. For Susan, it was no longer a joke. When something or someone unseen pushed her down the front steps, bruising her knee, she left and never came back.

Who—or what—haunts Punderson Manor House? Sessions with a ouija board indicated that there were twelve ghosts at Punderson: two in the lobby, two in Rick's room and the rest in Rick's car. A psychic claimed she made contact with the ghost who bothered Susan at night. He looked like Teddy Roosevelt—stocky with a mustache, said the psychic, and he threatened to haunt the place until his rocking chair was returned.

Susan and Rick searched the Manor but found no rocking chair. They did uncover an old set of blueprints which showed a network of passageways and crawl spaces beneath the building. On their days off Rick and Susan explored some of these passageways. They found fifteen smashed piano benches, but still no rocking chair. Then the blueprints mysteriously vanished from Rick's room.

Karl Long, a wealthy businessman from Detroit built the lodge in 1929, but never lived there. It is rumored that Long hanged himself in the attic when he lost his fortune in the Crash, but this has not been proven. Was the hanging ghost the spirit of Karl Long? or could it have been a collective hallucination? a shadow that seemed like a body to susceptible imaginations? Several children died when a tavern on the opposite shore of the lake burned in 1885. Perhaps their spirits moved to the Manor House.

In his researches, Mr. Van Der Velde discovered that a W.B. Cleveland and his son-in-law Dr. Coopedge owned the land before selling to Karl Long. A frame house stood on the site of the Manor House for many years before Long bought the property. Cleveland, who is said to have slightly resembled Teddy Roosevelt, spent much time in this frame house. Van Der Velde also was stunned to find a valuable Windsor rocker that had belonged to Cleveland in the Geauga Historical Society's Century Village in Burton.

Mr. Van Der Velde and his wife toured the Manor House and spent a night in the former Blue Room. Most of the staff was amused by the idea of ghosts and said they'd seen nothing. In touring the remodeled areas, Van Der Velde found crawl spaces and formerly hidden doors that would explain how some of the mysterious occurrences could have been staged.

However, these features do not explain everything. The ghosts still walk. Guests and staff have reported such incidents as a coffee cup flying off a table, names called by unseen persons. And the heavy metal door that closes off the Old Section from the New, the dead from the living, still swings open.

A ROOM FOR THE NIGHT OR FOREVER

The Wickerham Inn is a solid-looking rectangular brick building with an incongruously elaborate dormer protruding out of the roof above the door, like a fancy hat on a plain woman. It is believed to be Adams County's oldest brick building.

Around 1797, Peter Wickerham, a former Revolutionary War soldier, came by flatboat from Pennsylvania to Adams County where he built a log cabin. Zanes Trace, the first official road through the Northwest Territory, ran through his property. As pioneers flocked west, the entrepreneurial Wickerham built an inn, purchasing a tavern license for $4.00 in 1801.

The Wickerham Inn became a popular stage-coach stop. One evening a new coach driver sought lodging at the Inn. Somehow the rumor got started that he was carrying a large amount of money and many eyes followed the man as he went up the stairs to his room on the second floor. Early that morning several sleepers were wakened by muffled noises coming from the driver's room, but, being prudent men, they rolled over and went back to sleep.

In the morning the driver did not come down for breakfast. While the coach passengers fretted and stamped in the cold morning air, the boy who cleaned the boots was sent to fetch the driver down. The boy came staggering down the stairs, white-faced and retching. The patrons looked at each other, then made a rush for the stairs.

A bloody horror awaited them in the driver's room. Blood stains splattered the wall in an obscene pattern. A sticky, blackening pool soaked into the pine boards of the floor as if the victim had spilled his life out onto the floor. But there was no sign of a body.

The bloody bedclothes were heaved out the window into the garden and burnt. Mr. Wickerham saw to it that the floor was scoured with sand, but the stain of the huge pool of blood remained, a reddish shadow that darkened with age. Everyone tried to forget the gruesome crime, until the boy who cleaned the boots reported seeing the outline of a headless man in one of the upstairs windows. Wickerham scoffed, but soon other people—local residents, customers disembarking from their coaches, other drivers—swore that they too saw the uncanny figure silhouetted in the upper window, staring, as much as a headless man can stare, at the people below. Over the years hundreds of people saw the figure. Some also saw a little white dog walking with him, although others said that this was just an embellishment of an old legend invented to drum up business.

In 1922 the Inn was renovated. The workmen installing central heating found that the new furnace was too tall for the low-ceilinged cellar. They decided to remove the thick limestone slabs that formed the cellar floor. As they struggled with crowbar and tackle to lift the heavy slabs, something white, spindly, and horrible caught the light of the lanterns. Under the floor the workmen found a human skeleton—complete except for the skull.

Often burying such remains will lay the ghost, but the headless ghost of Wickerham Inn still walks, seeking his head and his murderer.[4]

THE GHOST AT THE OLD GOVERNOR'S MANSION

The lovely and gracious building on E. Broad Street in Columbus served as the Governor's Mansion from 1920 to 1957. Since then it has housed a party house and a restaurant, a hairdresser, and a philanthropic organization. And throughout its history, the mansion has had many strange events connected with it. Employees of a design agency that occupied the beautifully renovated mansion said that every day about two p.m., a strong smell—something like burning hair—filled the lobby. It lingered for about twenty minutes, then faded. Sometimes it returned in the early evening. Since the mansion was newly remodeled it was natural to suspect faulty wiring, but electricians found nothing wrong.

Another time a mirror, securely bolted to a wall, fell off the wall and shattered. Examination showed that the bolts were still firmly attached to the wall. The security system showed no sign of a presence—no *human* one.

In 1979 the manager of the restaurant was startled to see a black woman in a blue dress walk by the window of her office. She rushed out into the hallway, but there was no one there. She called her boyfriend to help her search the building. She had to unlock the door to let him in, but they found nothing.

Several waiters encountered the same apparition on the staircase. One did not see the figure, but felt its presence—a maid in a nineteenth century gown with her hair in a bun. He felt a happiness radiating from the invisible figure. Another waiter actually saw the woman, who he described as tall and wearing a long gown that looked like a servant's uniform. The second time the waiter saw the apparition, she spoke to him, telling him that she had been a servant, that she was happy about what was happening with the Mansion, that it was being used instead of sitting empty.[5]

THE SILENT WOMAN

Three miles west of Lancaster on the old Cincinnati and Zanesville Pike—now US 22—stood an old tavern and former stagecoach stop. Drovers were a rough lot and nearly all coaching inns have tales of mayhem told about them. In this case, the tales had a ghost to back them up.

The tavern had been converted into a house and the homeowner found that the doors simply would not stay locked. No matter how carefully she checked the locks in the evening, they would always be open in the morning.

The upstairs porch of the tavern faced the highway. In the darkest hours of the night, a headless woman with a baby in her arms would be seen pacing slowly across this porch as if feeling her way. This went on for many years.

As if that weren't bad enough, the family heard chains rattling and in certain upstairs rooms, strange gurgling sounds like someone was being choked. Odd mounds like graves heaved themselves up from the dirt floor of the basement. What looked like blood spots materialized on the floors of the upstairs rooms where the choking noises were heard.

What kind of horrific history could account for these manifestations? Perhaps the woman was a maid at the tavern. Perhaps when she presented her lover with his child, he refused to believe it was his, or was so enraged that he beat her until she bled and then choked her and the child to death. He may have dismembered the bodies and buried them in the dirt-floored cellar.

Whatever the cause, at last the family gave up the ghost and the house was torn down. Apparently the ghost went with it since it has not been seen since.[6]

THE HAUNTED SOCIAL CLUB

One of the many haunted buildings in Waynesville is an 1890s building I'll call the Social Club. Twins Dale and Dean cleaned the Club after hours when they were in high school.

"When you were down there, you would always get this feeling you were being watched," said Dale. "I would intentionally take other people with me to see their reactions. After ten or fifteen minutes, they would start looking behind them. Around three in the morning, you'd hear footsteps upstairs, like hard-soled shoes on a hardwood floor."

The upper floors were used as a library and most of it was carpeted and soundproof. "We had no idea who the "presence" was," said Dale. "Nobody knew of any deaths there."

In the back store room, there was a metal support column. At eye-level the paint had been scraped off to the bare metal and what looked like a trickle of fresh blood ran from the scraped spot. Dale, who is now a paramedic, knows what blood looks like. "Blood dries black," he said "but this always looked fresh. You'd swear it would come off on your fingers. It's been there for years."

Once when Dale was trying to get into a storage closet, "something like a broomstick or pool cue struck the door very hard from the other side. Somebody hit it hard! There was an inch of space under the door and a light inside the room. And there was no shadow under the door. It was kind of unnerving. I packed myself up and was done for the night."

Dean had stories too: a pool cue flying across the room on its own; a radio turning itself on full blast, with the volume knob still on low; a thirsty presence who would drain glasses of water left sitting out. The grave is dry. Did this spirit mistake the water for the stronger spirits it craved?

CHAINED TO EARTH

Denmark, the first town in Williams County, was founded in 1834. It says something about the temper of the times that the town was sold in 1836 to a Judge D. Parker, who opened the town's first institution—not a school, church, or post office, but a tavern.

A traveler stopped at the tavern for a drink and made the mistake of flashing his well-filled purse. After a drink or two, he found the room warm and stepped outside for some air. He was never seen again, and the tavern keeper found a heavy logging chain missing as well. The theory most voiced at the bar was that someone murdered the traveler for his coin, wrapped him in the chain, and dropped him in the St. Joseph River.

Exactly a year later, the tavern keeper locked up for the night. As he went up to bed, he heard a sound like a chain rattling down the stairs. On the landing, he found the log chain, rusty, as if it had been lying in water.

THE GHOSTS AT OUR HOUSE

Some houses have architectural features that make them seem almost human. Our House in Gallipolis was built as a tavern in 1819 with capstones above windows like quizzically raised eyebrows, and an arched doorway molding like a cupid-bow mouth. High in one wall, an attic window winks, a half-closed eye. Our House seems a heartily solid structure—a man of substance and property like Mr. Henry Cushing, the builder of Our House, who has been seen in short green breeches walking up the back pathway around midnight. The neighbors think he's just keeping an eye on the house. Cushing also appeared to the curator and her guests in the kitchen one misty day. He looked quite upset and then vanished. After talking with the guests, the curator found that they were descendants of a family Cushing didn't like.

Volunteer Henrietta Evans wrote to me, "I've heard sounds of people walking around in the house many times. One time when I was coming in from the kitchen with some guests, we heard someone running down the stairs very fast. But there was no one there.

"Another day I heard someone come in the front door. I went to look and heard them walking very clearly across the floor of the tap room. I came in from the hall and I could hear them walking into the dining room. But again there was no one there. Any time of the day, you can hear people walking in the front hall."

Our House was an unusually elegant building for its day. The second-floor ballroom hosted a reception for General Lafayette in 1825. The inn has been meticulously restored and its period furnishings include the earliest piano in Ohio, dating from the 1700s.

Jenny Lind sang at Our House during her 1850s American tour. Several years ago, the curator and her son were downstairs when they heard chairs scraping on the floor of the ballroom—as if a large crowd were settling into their seats. Then they heard a woman singing. They rushed upstairs to the sparsely furnished ballroom but found nothing. The curator's research showed the tune to have been a song popularized by Jenny Lind.

Former curator Martha Foster used to live with a ghost she called "Grandpappy." When Foster became curator she went to the Court House to learn what she could about the tavern. To her surprise and delight, she discovered that the building had belonged to "Grandpappy" for some twenty-five years.

"As I often did when I was alone in the house, I went to the foot of the stairs to look up at the window on its landing. Beyond the window's small panes of ancient glass, branches of a sycamore (as old as the inn) formed shifting patterns of green and gold against the blue of the sky. Beautiful—so beautiful— I thought. And then I thought of Grandpappy's having owned Our House, and I wondered if Grandpappy had ever stood where I was standing, savoring as was I the beauty of the window and that of the silent, listening house.

"Even as I wondered I felt a hand on my shoulder, its pressure real as that of my own on the newel post. At once I knew who was beside me, but when I turned to look at him there was a movement across my cheek as if a hand had brushed it and withdrawn. The presence and the moment were gone."

THE CHOIR INVISIBLE
Haunting music

Only music can speak of death.
-Andre Malraux-

We've all heard it: the ghost of a melody, borne on a summer's breeze. Must be a radio playing next door, we think, or a party going on somewhere. Kind of an old-fashioned tune, though, now we come to notice it, and played so far away....

A PERSONAL NOTE

I've spent over half of my life sitting in near-darkness in old churches. No, not looking for ghosts—practicing the organ. I've been a church organist for over twenty-five years and since I don't like to waste electricity, I usually just turn on the music rack light. And sometimes, someone sits in a distant pew, listening.

He is startlingly real and solid, but whenever I try to look directly at him, he vanishes. When I turn my head back to the music, he reappears and sits there quietly while I play on. I do not feel threatened by the apparition although sometimes I jump when I first notice him. He seems so real.

It's good practice to have an audience, even a ghostly one. But I wonder who he is. Does he have any requests? Or is he simply waiting for me to find the lost chord?

THE DEVIL HIS DUE

Fiddler's Green Road in North Bend, Hamilton County, gets its name from a fiddler who made a pact with the devil: his soul for the gift of music. The fiddler thought it a fair trade. But to this day he is nameless; the Devil took the man's name along with his soul.

This fiddler could play the ladies into a loving mood or the rabbits out of their holes. His music caused pots and pans to dance a jig. And if he played at a barn raising, the beams would rise and float into their places. It was whispered that he could even draw the dead out of their graves with his weird music. But all too soon it came time to pay the piper.

The night his pact with the Devil was up, the fiddler was in a melancholy mood. He went to the small cemetery next to the grounds of Mt. St. Joseph and began to play—strange wailing chords like a damned soul crying in hell. His eerie music woke Tenskwatwa, "The Prophet," brother of the great Shawnee Chief Tecumseh. Tenskwatwa rose out of his grave, drawn toward the music.

He looked at the fiddler leaning on the cemetery fence. The fiddler looked at him—a face in the cemetery mists—and played on furiously as though he would rip the strings off his instrument. Suddenly there was an explosion and the music stopped in mid-howl. All that was left of the fiddler was a pair of smoldering boots. Then Tenskwatwa, coming back to as much reality as the dead ever experience, could not find the way back into his grave. And ever since, "The Prophet" has floated about the cemetery in a cloud of glowing green lights as he seeks his resting place, cursing the fiddler who lured him from his grave and left him to dance the dance of death.[1]

DEATH PLAYS A DUET

Normally my friend, organist Ron McCarty, keeps me in stitches with his infectious gap-toothed smile and his keen sense of humor. But when he told me about Robert, the ghostly organist, he was deadly serious.

Ron first met Robert in the summer of 1966 at the Cincinnati Conservatory of Music. They immediately became friends. As Ron said, "we seemed to have been old friends in some past life." They were both gifted musicians and went on together to the University of Cincinnati where they were inseparable. They roomed together, played duets together, and were friendly rivals to see who could best perform the same piece of music.

Robert contracted tuberculosis and died in New York, September 21, 1988, just as Ron was taking up a new organ post in Columbus. After all the funeral services were over, Ron spent a lot of time getting used to the Reiger pipe organ at his new Columbus church.

"During those practice hours, I began feeling as if someone were watching over me. I caught glimpses of light out of the corner of my eye."

In November 1988 Ron found that Robert had willed him his music library. As he sat at the organ, reading through one of Robert's early Baroque scores, "I suddenly realized that there was a presence with me. There were flashes of light in the room and the temperature changed on my right side. I knew he was sitting on the bench beside me. At first it scared me to death. But as soon as I turned my head to look, something told me, 'It's all right. It's just me.' And I knew it was Robert.

"Never had I played that piece so well. It was a great comfort for me to play; playing for one another was always Robert's and my favorite way to communicate. When I left the church that night, the 'presence' stayed behind. Although it is not as strong as it used to be, every time I play from his music, especially when I play things we studied at the same time, he comes to me. He directs phrases and registrations. He used to direct me when we were students. Now he is still directing me. Many years have passed since he died, but with Robert's 'presence' I have been able to develop my abilities to their

absolute best, something we always encouraged each other to
do."

THE SONG LINGERS ON

Pat* and Sam* were gutting the dining room of their 1857
Huron County home when they were startled by a song. Said
Pat,
"We had just stripped off all the old plaster and found the
original tongue and groove paneling underneath. It was the
middle of the afternoon and we were finishing sweeping up
when we heard a couple of voices, like two little girls singing.
It was *very* clear to us. We looked at each other. We knew that
we had heard it and we thought, 'No!'
Sam, a strapping construction worker, couldn't explain it.
And he didn't believe it.
Pat said, "I looked at him and I thought, seeing his
expression, 'Yeah, Sam, you know you heard it.' It scared the
hell out of us at the time.
"It was definitely in that room. It came from the floor as if
someone were standing there. And I thought, oh, the little girls
were playing in the kitchen, singing a little play song. We have
two little boys, so we ran upstairs to check on them. They were
sound asleep. It was the strangest thing!"
"Could it have been the neighbors' children?" I asked.
"It was the dead of winter—February or March—and the
windows were shut. That was the first thing we thought,
'Somebody's outside.' But our neighbors are older with no
children."
They didn't recognize the tune, although Pat says it was a
"happy song."
"It took us by such surprise. I wish we could have had a
tape recorder to listen to it again."
Pat said that the room above the kitchen bore scorch marks
from a fire which may have started in the kitchen. Pat's

psychically sensitive sister-in-law Alexis** was very uneasy about entering this room, which had been sealed off. She said, "I felt like a girl child had been hurt in that room." Could the singing have been her ghost reliving happier days?

Let us imagine two children singing together while someone painted or plastered the kitchen wall. Did their song somehow become embedded in the wall—recorded in the paint or plaster? And how did Pat and Sam release that musical memory from the wall where it had been trapped for nearly a century?

THE ACCORDION FROM HELL

Duff Lindsay, Field Producer for Channel 10 News, Columbus and his wife live in an 1870s house haunted by an accordion.

Said Duff, "We've heard accordion music. Nothing dramatic. Just the vaguest hint...the audio equivalent of catching something out of the corner of your eye."

He and his wife have both heard it several times, but separately.

"I've noticed it mostly when I'm going up and down the stairway," Duff said. "It's almost like someone playing the accordion on TV downstairs—that off-in-the-distance sound. I didn't say anything to my wife for a long time. Then finally it came up and she said, 'What? You've heard it too?'"

Part of their South Vienna house was originally built in 1870, with at least three later additions.

"It's a sprawling old farmhouse. We've lived here about three years. The house was rented for many years so we have no good history of the owners." And he has no idea if any of them played the accordion.

But couldn't it be the neighbors watching Lawrence Welk reruns?

**See "The Haunted Garden Party Dress" in *Haunted Ohio: Ghostly Tales from the Buckeye State.*

"We have no neighbors," said Duff. "We live in the middle of nowhere. The closest neighbor is two hundred yards away down a hill with trees in between."

What kind of music does the ghostly accordion play?

Duff couldn't say. "Once you realize you're hearing it and you tune in more closely, it goes away."

He agreed that a ghost doomed to play *Lady of Spain* for Eternity is a horrifying prospect.

"I'd prefer zydeco."

THE HEAVENLY CHORUS

Crystal*, who now lives in Columbus, told this story:

One hot summer night right after my divorce, I'd gone to bed upstairs in my Mom's old house [in Fayette County]. I was feeling like I'd just thrown seven years of my life down the drain. There was a full moon, the window was open, and the room was stifling hot.

All of a sudden I had the peculiar feeling that I was being watched. Then the room got cold. All of a sudden it was pitch black. I saw something like out of a science fiction movie. All around my bed were things in monks' clothes—long dark robes. I couldn't see their faces. They were holding hands and chanting in a monotone: "Say it. Say it."

I don't know if I spoke out loud or just in my head, but I said, "No, I *won't* say God is dead."

Then I heard the most beautiful choir. It was like a thousand-voice choir, maybe more. Although I usually can remember a tune, I can't remember this song. There were no words, it was just a blending of voices. Then I saw something like golden sunlight through sheer white gauzy curtains and suddenly I could see out the window again and the moon was shining.

MR. TAMBOURINE GHOST

In 1974 musician Bob Thompson was jamming with a man named Chuck, in an old house in Fayette County. Chuck was on sitar; Bob was playing tabla and they were taping the session. They were so wrapped up in the music that they didn't notice right away that there was a tambourine playing along. Eventually they looked over and saw the tambourine, hovering about a foot off the floor, shaking in time to the music.

"We were doing some polyrhythmic things, so it was just jingling along. Then it just dropped. We played the tape back and could hear it playing along for quite some time although neither of us had heard it. Chuck packed up his stuff, left the house, and never came back."

THE HAUNTED ORGAN OF MORNING SUN

The organ is not only the king of instruments, it is the supreme instrument of horror. The organ can sigh or moan like a lost soul. It can shriek like a fiend out of hell and growl like a demon.

Back in the 1940s, a church custodian had several encounters with the haunted organ at the Morning Sun Presbyterian church. First thing in the morning, janitor Ted Clay* had to fire up the old coal furnace. One morning, over the clattering of the grates and clinkers, he heard noises overhead. He stopped and listened.

The old reed organ was playing, a sound he didn't often hear outside of Sunday morning or Wednesday night choir practice. He shrugged. It was unusual for Miss Hudson*, the organist, to practice this early in the morning, especially before the church was warmed up, but if she wanted to freeze her fingers that was her business.

Clay finished with the furnace, fetched his tool box and a bucket, and climbed the stairs to the church. There was a radiator needed drained in the sanctuary. He didn't relish listening to *In the Garden* while he did it, but everyone has a cross to bear. Now if she'd play something by Sousa...

He backed into the church, through the heavy wooden swinging doors. The church was cold and smelled like wet wool carpets and dust. The music stopped as he came through the door, as abruptly as switching off a radio.

That was fine by him. He walked further down the aisle. "Morning, Miz Hudson" he called to the organist. There was no answer.

He peered behind the green velvet curtain that screened the choir loft. The organ was closed, its cover which slid open like the lid of a roll-top desk, was down.

Then it struck him. The front doors were still locked. If she'd come in, she would've left them unlocked. He scratched his head. How in blazes had she got in anyhow?

He drained the radiator pondering this. Then he carried the bucket of water downstairs and poured it down the drain in the floor. As the splashing ceased, he heard the organ again.

This time he ran up the little curving stairs that led up to the front of the church. The music throbbed and boomed all around him. Clay burst into the pulpit and stared over the choir pews. There was no one seated at the organ. It was closed, silent.

Like a crazy man he flung himself on the organ, rattling at the lid. It was locked. The china knobs were as cold as bone.

He stood very still. Deep below him, below the basement, far below the deepest grave every dug, came the mournful sounds of an organ, like the cry of a creature from the Abyss. And then the singing began....

THE GHOSTS OF FROGTOWN

In the old days you walked out Dayton Street until you struck mud and then you were in Frogtown. Frogtown was a legal part of Yellow Springs—but not everything that went on there was legal.

Pretty Lou Keys, who lived in Frogtown, had an eye for a good-looking man. And George Koogler, when he put on his uniform, was a good-looking man, no denying it. Among his many attractions, George possessed a rich baritone voice. Walking by Lou's place, passersby could hear him singing his favorite song, "My Pretty Quadroon" so sweetly the birds sat quiet to hear him.

Andy Huntster ran an ice cream parlor across from the old post office. He'd lost a leg to frostbite and he took plenty of razzing about ice and ice cream. He had a fair amount of money and he took Lou's casual friendliness for something more. He took it real hard when George Koogler won Lou's hand. Whenever Lou and George walked by, arm and arm, or stopped in to share a malted, ice-cold hatred pierced Andy's heart.

One morning the neighbors found George sprawled on the walk outside Lou's house. Lou was inside and she wasn't so pretty anymore. Someone had split open the lovers' skulls with a hatchet. For good measure, that someone had also put an ice pick through Lou's eyes.

Of course everyone suspected Andy, but two trials failed to produce enough hard evidence to convict him.

A few nights after his acquittal, Andy burst in on Marcus* the barber with a crazy tale. He was walking out to Frogtown and he'd run smack into Lou and George! Of course it was them—he knew what his own eyes told him! They were all cuddled up, arm in arm and George was singing that damn song about the pretty quadroon while Lou smiled up at him. And then—Lou and George walked right through him! Andy broke down completely.

Marcus gave Andy another drink to steady his nerves and sent him reeling out into the darkness. It was a foggy night and Andy had had a few drinks under his belt already, thought Marcus. Anybody'd see things on a night like this, particularly a man just acquitted of murder. Out of the fog came a rich baritone voice, muffled as if very far away—"Oh, my pretty

quadroon..." *Very* far away, shivered Marcus, and locked his
door against the dark.[2]

THE RAIN DRUM

In the extreme northwestern corner of Williams County
sits Nettle Lake. Sam Coon, an old trapper who lived on its
banks in the 1870s, was as unkempt as his name. He wore his
hair and beard long and shaggy and if he ever washed them, it
was because he'd accidentally got caught in a downpour. His
clothes and shoes were pieced together out of sacking and half-
cured animal pelts. On a hot day he smelled like road kill.

Coon was a spiritualist. He kept a big Indian drum in his
cabin and he never would say where he got it. He believed that
a quick, angry beat on the drum summoned the spirits of dead
Indian chiefs who muttered to him of treasures buried along the
banks of Nettle Lake. A slower rhythm would call down rain,
with its answering thunder. The few people who got close
enough to look whispered that the drum was made of human
skin stretched over a bone frame, and that something rustled
inside.

The marshes surrounding the lake weren't the healthiest
place to dig for treasure. One day Coon succumbed to a
quartan fever. He shook like something had him by the ankles,
worrying him, and he died raving of claws and scales.

Somehow his only surviving nephew heard of his death
and came—supposedly to pay his respects, but really to search
the cabin for the treasure the old man was supposed to have
discovered. He found nothing but the drum—with its head
burst outwards, as if something that had long lain coiled within,
had escaped. The nephew left in a hurry leaving what was left
of the drum in the cabin. Something might want it back.

On humid summer days by Nettle Lake, when the air lies
in wait for a cloudburst, you can still hear the far-away
drumming, like the growl of a distant dragon.

WHEN THE SAINTS GO MARCHING IN

Sherrie Brader*, of Fostoria, writes:

"My husband Nathan* has had an organ for over twenty years with a reputation for being haunted, for playing music by itself." The old-fashioned pump organ came originally from the Catholic school in Fostoria, and was bought by Nathan's Aunt Ella*.

Ella painted the organ white, used it for a little while, and then bought a new organ. She gave the old instrument to a friend of hers, who believed that the dead nun who used to play the organ still played it sometimes. She was so sure about this that she gave the organ to Nathan at the first opportunity.

Nathan stripped off the white paint and restored the original oak finish, proudly displaying the result in the parlor.

"In order to even get a note out of [the organ] you have to PUMP like mad. Once Nathan hooked a reverse vacuum to it, which acted like a bellows and played *When the Saints Go Marching In* on it."

That was the only time *they* ever got the organ to play. But one night, in their bedroom above the parlor, they heard what sounded like one long deep chord played on the organ, resonating through the whole house.

Sherrie said to Nathan, "Now WHAT was THAT??"

"It sure sounded like the organ," he replied and Sherrie had to agree. If the Braders have their way, the lost chord will stay lost because they *don't* want to hear it again. "We've only heard it that one time, but it was enough."

MYSTERIOUS MUSIC

Strange music can be heard anywhere—in your home, your car, or church. What distinguishes it from some atmospheric freak, say its hearers, is its extraordinary beauty.

A young woman from Columbus reported,
    In Columbus...when I was sixteen years old, I

took a nap in the living room. As I awoke I heard faint strains of music. I was thinking of turning the radio up louder when the *music increased in volume*. Then I knew it was not from this earth. It was a blend of several timbres but only a bell-like sound was identifiable...*It was indescribably beautiful*. Time was suspended. *It faded away*.

To be sure that I had not mentally distorted earthly music I looked in vain for an earthly source. The radio was turned off, the only neighbors were not home and no sound came from their house.[3]

A woman from Thompson in Geauga County said,

The evening I heard the music while driving I was returning home from a Grange meeting and I was alone. I became aware of...*a choir of voices*...both male and female. I assumed it was coming from the radio, which I thought had not been completely turned off when my son had last used the car. I never turn on the radio while driving, as it is disconcerting. The music was so extraordinary I reached over to turn the knob and make it louder and then realized the radio was not even turned on. [Then the music]...*just faded out. The voices rose and fell, yet no words could be distinguished*, as though coming from a great distance. *They were uniform at all times. I could not recall the melody after it stopped yet it was fantastically beautiful* and so comforting somehow... The words were not at all distinguishable, merely a blending of male and female voices, singing in a great choir.[4]

A man from Elyria heard voices singing, "Shall We Gather at the River?" when his stepmother died in 1954. Although his sister sat next to him, she heard nothing. "As to the music, it would be hard to describe, other than it was very angelic, and as they say, out of this world...It was a choral group...a blend of voices. It was very calm and peaceful and beyond that which is produced on this plane, beautiful as it might be to us."[5]

THE ULTIMATE SONG

Ted Peters' glimpse of the past at the University of Dayton was recorded in *Haunted Ohio*. He is now a student at Miami University and he continues to have unusual psychic experiences. He has heard mystical music—"beautiful music"—since he was young.

"It's not necessarily a full orchestra, but usually a flute or woodwind instrument. Sometimes I hear a reed pipe with a plucked, rather twangy sound like a guitar or lute, never a bowed instrument like a violin. It's primitive sounding. Elizabethan is probably the closest thing to it. I never hear singers, just a hauntingly beautiful melody.

"Different movements make me feel different emotions—never joyful, 'high' emotions, but more introspective, meditative, or thought-provoking."

Ted laughed and shook his head when I asked him if he had any metal tooth fillings that might be picking up Glasgow. He finds that the music has grown fainter with the years.

"Now when I hear it it's more elusive, more of an echo, not the strength I used to hear. I haven't heard it for quite a while," he mused. "You know, I think that the world is run by the Ultimate Song, the ultimate piece of music, like the Music of the Spheres. Every aspect of life is in that music but we only hear certain parts. Or perhaps we're just one instrument out of an entire orchestra...."

THINGS THAT GO BUMP
IN THE NIGHT
The elusive poltergeist

A footstep, a low throbbing in the walls
A noise of falling weights that never fell
Weird whispers, bells that rang without a hand
Door-handles turn'd when none was at the door,
And bolted doors that open'd of themselves...
-Alfred, Lord Tennyson-

It starts with something going bump in the night, a sharp rap, or a sly scratching at the door. It grows stronger, creates sounds like plates and pianos smashing. Next cups, bottles, and Bibles whiz across the room.

Almost anything can happen next—crockery smashed on the wall; flying stones, hot to the touch; explosive raps that shake the house; objects that levitate, materialize, and de-materialize—like the birdshot that fell in slow motion from the ceiling of a hardware store in Lebanon.

Then mysterious pools of water appear. And after them, tiny fires in closed drawers or lighted matches falling from nowhere. Finally come the apparitions and voices—taunting and accusing, hideously blasphemous or profane. Nothing, not garlic, exorcism, or prayer has any effect. Yet, within six months, the worst is usually over, leaving the poltergeist's victims with nightmares and a tendency to jump at sudden noises. Typically, towards the end of a poltergeist infestation, a child will be discovered throwing things. The authorities then announce that the whole episode was caused by the child, even though it has been proven that the child had nothing to do with earlier phenomena. And yet, the child probably *is* responsible, but not in the way we normally understand.

The word poltergeist means "noisy ghost" in German. Some authorities consider them to be the riff-raff of the spirit world. They are noisy, undisciplined, violent, and very common. They have been described as low spirits who dwell between heaven and earth, just waiting for their chance to pounce on a vulnerable human.

Yet poltergeists are not spirits, evil or otherwise, despite their malign tricks. Poltergeists are random energy produced by a human being, usually a troubled child or frustrated adult who is somehow setting free the anger and violence that lies deep in her unconscious mind.

Dr. Nandor Fodor in *The Haunted Mind* makes an admirable case for poltergeists as a projection of the unconscious mind—like the result of a split personality. Poltergeist children have been filmed throwing stones, but when confronted, they can't remember throwing them since they were in a disassociated state. This is a temporary state of amnesia in which a person commits certain acts or takes on a different personality for short periods of time with no conscious memory of the switch. Abused children often develop multiple personalities to escape their torment. And a high percentage of poltergeist children are sexual or physical abuse victims. Sexuality—either blossoming, confused, or abnormal—may also be at the root of this split.

The typical poltergeist child is completely unable to express his or her hostility in any socially acceptable way. There is often some kind of emotional disturbance or at the very least, dysfunctional family conditions. Poltergeists are quite literally home-wreckers.

How do you tell the difference between a ghost and a poltergeist? Nandor Fodor says, "[a ghost] is said to haunt a house; the [poltergeist] is said to haunt a man."[1] Poltergeist phenomena follow a person from place to place. Poltergeists rarely produce apparitions or a spirit with "personality." The situation is further complicated by the fact that persons in poltergeist-producing states are vulnerable to invasion by genuine spirits.

So what can you do about a poltergeist? Although most poltergeists wear themselves out after two to six months, family therapy is the only effective treatment. If the unreleased tensions are not given some sort of outlet or if there is no resolution of conflict and frustration, the outbreaks will continue, perhaps in some deadlier form. In the notorious Tennessee Bell Witch case, the "poltergeist" poisoned a father who had molested his daughter.

A word of warning: exorcism is *never* effective in true poltergeist cases. Poltergeists hate authority figures. In fact, demonstrations of adult authority usually enrage the poltergeist, leading it to more violent disturbances.

THE ASHTABULA POLTERGEIST

From Austinburg, Ashtabula County, comes the story of the Ashtabula Poltergeist who was attracted to a young widow with a magnetic personality.

During the fall of 1850, Mrs. Helen Howell's* husband died on shipboard on his way to San Francisco, far from his wife and their two children. The following summer, as Helen was visiting a family named Cowles in Austinburg, rappings began to follow her—a very annoying development, since Helen did not believe in spiritualism.

Helen went to Marlborough [Stark County] to attend lectures on anatomy, intending to become a doctor. While she was studying surgery the bones in the dissecting room often moved around the room. In particular, skulls moved by themselves, swiveling to look at Helen no matter where she was in the room.

"At night were heard the most appalling noises, and sounds as of objects thrown in all directions, and striking at various points on the wall, table, chairs, bed, etc. This annoyance was so constant as to deprive [Helen and her roommate]

of sleep, and it kept them in a state of terrible fear and apprehension."

Worn out by the antics of a spirit calling itself "Ann
Merrick," Helen left Marlborough and went to Canton. The
spirit followed her and she returned to Austinburg on 11
October 1851.

The following Monday, Helen went upstairs with a candle
and a pitcher of water for one of her children. The hall stair-
carpet had been taken up, and the carpet-rods [metal rods
fastened at the base of risers to hold the carpet smooth] were
lying at the top of the stairs. "When Helen was about half-way
up...the rods suddenly started from their place, knocking the
water and light from her hands..."

No doubt wondering what was to come next, Helen
retreated to her room, which she shared with two other women.
The bedroom had a door opening onto a storage room where
there were about fifty muskets with bayonets and some
cartridge-boxes and belts, hung up on the wall. The lights were
put out and the three women were talking in the dark when the
carpet rods again clattered to the floor. Then there was a
tremendous crash that wakened the house. Helen rushed into
the next room.

"Piled indiscriminately on the floor were cartridge-boxes
and belts, the carpet-rods, candlesticks, combs, brushes, clothes
and almost every movable object in the room. One of the
muskets, with the bayonet was found thrown completely under
Helen's bed, having passed in its way thither twenty-five feet,
or nearly the whole extent of the two rooms. The rammer was
drawn from the musket and was found amongst the central pile.
The muskets had not been used for some years, and were much
rusted, so that the rammer could not have been drawn without
immense force."

A few days later a seance was held where the spirit of
"Ann" rapped and tipped over heavy furniture, including the
seance table with Mr. Cowles sitting on it. Then the furniture
danced in time to Cowle's violin. "Ann" revealed that she had
been born in Ireland, died in a Cincinnati Hospital, and her

body had been brought to Marlborough for dissection. "The strong medium power of Helen and the magnetic force still attached to [Ann's] own mortal remains, served, it would seem, as associative links whereby she was enabled to play her ghostly pranks amongst the horrors of the dissecting room."

On Thursday, Oct. 16, Helen's father, Ira Simms*, arrived, determined "to put an end to the whole proceeding." Simms bedded down in one room, while Helen and another lady had twin beds in the adjoining room. When the knockings started, the other lady leaped into Helen's bed for protection, but was hit—she thought—by Helen.

"What are you striking me for?" she exclaimed.

"I have not touched you," replied Helen, but the other woman was hit again and again and pushed back when she tried to get into bed. She retreated to Mr. Simms's room, pelted by clothes and stockings.

Mr. Simms had his own problems. A huge trunk was rocking back and forth in his room, his candles kept getting blown out, and furniture followed him down the stairs. Suddenly everything was silent.

"Then the silence was broken by strains of the most exquisite harmony. It seemed like instrumental music, yet there was no instrument in the house, or within forty rods of it. But there, in Helen's room, apparently close to them, music was heard by all in the house, sweeter than its auditors had ever before listened to. Some familiar airs were performed, but the most touching and delicious melodies were strange to all who listened to that mysterious music." It was "Ann's" final performance.

Helen went back to Marlborough to resume her medical studies, still determined to not become a medium. She spent a day dissecting a female subject.

"That night Helen and her room-mate and fellow-student were alarmed by the most frightful sounds. Trembling with apprehension of they knew not what, they covered their heads with the bed clothes; but when at last they uncovered them, there, standing by their bedside, they beheld the spectre of the corpse that they had been dissecting, all reeking and ghastly, as they had left it on the table, save that one of the arms was folded across the breast, a change which was actually found to have taken place when the remains were examined."

Helen begged her brother to stay the night in her room and find out what haunted her.

"He approached the bed, and saw by moonlight, a human skull, dancing up and down over their heads.

"He watched the motion of the skull for a considerable time, and then attempted to remove it; but it was only by the exertion of a good deal of strength and agility that he succeeded."

[signed] L.M. Austin, witnesses: L.M. Cowles, Rachel Cowles, S.H. Snow, Rhoda Snow, Ann J. Snow, Sarah H. Austin, Martha H. Cowles. February 4, 1853

And here the story ends, with the mysterious dancing skull seized by Helen's brother, but unaccounted for thereafter. Judging by this account, the young widow generated all types of classic poltergeist phenomena. But why? The first factor may have been sexual frustration, natural in a young widow. Second, at this time it was quite unusual for a woman to study medicine so Helen may have also been feeling societal pressures. The "spirit" of Ann Merrick may have reflected Helen's ambivalence about her career choice and possibly her frustration and anger at having to earn a living.[2]

THE PORNOGRAPHIC POLTERGEIST

The Reverend Paul Sweeny* of Columbus reminds me of traditional pictures of the Apostle Paul, with his high forehead and neatly trimmed beard. He serves a church in the Ohio State University area and as we were talking one day he mentioned that he'd once lived with a poltergeist.

In the fall of 1976 Sweeny was living in a typical half-double house in the OSU area. He had decided to become a minister, but hadn't yet begun his studies at the seminary. As

Sweeny put it, "I'd graduated from Ohio State and was living in sin with Shirley*, my future wife."

They'd lived there for about five months when "stuff started happening." Sweeny worked for Ohio State University and when he came home he noticed "strangish things."

"For instance, I'd come home from work and canned goods had been moved from the pantry at the back of the house, through the kitchen and dining room, and put on the mantle of the living room. The kitchen was quite small, but things still came up missing—like the oven thermometer and can openers. We assumed that I threw them away or brushed them off into the trash. Something would also turn the water on in the kitchen and flip up drawer pulls. The critter also had a nasty habit that if we came back after dark, the lights would be on—and we hadn't left them on."

Sweeny's pet dog also sensed something amiss.

"We had a dog named Creeper*—a typical yapping dog. Three nights in a row, he stood on the end of our bed and glared at the middle of the room. He bristled and growled. We couldn't see or hear anything, but the dog was clearly upset."

"Occasionally we ourselves would feel a little presence— like we had company. Then we'd look at each other and say at the same time, 'Fred's here.'"

"Fred's" pranks were sophomoric, about what you might expect from a college student.

"When this was really clicking, our neighbors said to us one day, 'You really had the stereo pumped up this afternoon.' We looked at each other. 'Did you come home for lunch?' Shirley asked me. But both of us had been working."

The poltergeist also had questionable taste in television.

"When we first got cable TV there was one movie on the adult channel—it was called *The Fisherman's Daughter*—that we got charged for ten times in a week and a half." Sweeny shook his head. "I don't even watch the adult channel and if I was going to, I certainly wouldn't watch the same movie over and over." But cruder behavior was yet to come.

"The most traumatic bit for Shirley was when she was standing at the sink washing dishes and she felt a very friendly little pat on the butt. She turned to give me a hug—and I wasn't there.

"She called me and I answered from upstairs. Then she called me again and I met her at the foot of the stairs. She was shaking. At that point we were sure we had a poltergeist.

"We talked about moving out, but figured if it was going to be nasty, it would have done it already. All we did was to kind of grump at it. We'd say things like 'Don't be funny!' when we found the lights on. And it slowed down. It still moved stuff, but not as often.

"Occasionally we'd talk to it. It was kind of like having an extra pet." But not quite, said Sweeny.

"It *really* didn't like our dog Creeper. It played with the dog's food. Creeper's water dish would be stuffed some place where she couldn't get to it."

Ultimately it was a dog that ran the poltergeist off.

"We got a border collie named Dinky* and that seemed to be more than the little bugger could take. Dinky was crazy. She'd herd anything. She tried to herd Creeper. She tried to herd squirrels. We think she tried to herd the thing. And after that we had no more trouble."

What was behind all this? wondered Sweeny.

I asked him about his relationship with his fiancee. I had gone to school with her. She had a reputation as a troubled girl who drank too much and went out with the "wrong" kind of boy.

"I had known Shirley about a year," said Sweeny. "She had broken up with her old boy friend and was leery about taking on a 'ministerial' lifestyle. She was *quite* dubious about that. Yet we had decided to get married after we moved in together." Then he added something that made all the other parts of the puzzle fall into place. "Shirley never could handle conflict or deal with confrontation."

It was the perfect climate for a poltergeist: A young woman in turmoil about marriage and her relationships, with no skills to handle these conflicts. An immature, addictive, self-centered personality, and a turbulent childhood history—she had been a foster child. And she had no way out. Except through switching on the stereo full-blast and watching porno movies over and over. Except through disrupting a household she wasn't really sure she wanted.

POLTERGEISTS WHO LIVE IN GLASS HOUSES...

A stone-throwing poltergeist at the Adam Fye Farm near Zanesville made lengthy headlines in 1916: "Ghost" Does Damage/ First Manifested Itself by Throwing Blankets Over Cows and Turning Horses Around in Stalls; Did it in Mr. Fye's Presence/ THOUGHT 'TWAS JOKE AT FIRST/ On Adam Fye Farm/ Later "Ghost" Hurled Great Rocks Through Side of Barn/ Has Done Much Damage/ Pitchforks and Guns Fail to Scare Uncanny Thing."

The "Ghost," as it was termed, had a limited repertoire of tricks. First Mr. Fye found his cows wrapped in old sacks and a binder cover. It *was* January but Fye knew that cows don't dress themselves, no matter how cold they get. Then he found the horses tied backwards in their stalls.

The last straw came when "he was milking a cow, which it is stated positively had no covering on her of any kind when he started milking, but looking up when he was partly through, he found the cow was securely blanketed."

Next the poltergeist began to cast the first stones. Mr. Fye was standing near the barn door when a thirty-six-pound stone came crashing through the side of the building. It tore a jagged hole in the barn wall and landed too close for comfort to the startled Fyes. Mr. Fye searched the barn, jabbing the hay with pitchforks. No culprit was found.

Soon afterwards Mr. and Mrs. Fye were standing in the yard when an enormous rock came hurtling through the side of the barn and landed at Mrs. Fye's feet.

She shouted "Quit that, you old devil." The old devil didn't. Another stone came hurtling by to land her feet.

According to the paper, "The door and sides of the barn were riddled with great holes. The Fyes were kept busy nailing new boards over the splintered openings."[3]

Could this have been a peripatetic poltergeist, the same one who dropped stones on the home of Hayes Barr in nearby Blue Rock Township in 1869? The *McConnelsville Conservative* reported:

"The stoning commenced on Friday, August 27, and continued until the following Tuesday. Great numbers of small stones, some large enough to weigh 6 3/4 pounds, are lying about the yard. The home bears the marks of the stones in many places and three panes are broken out.

"During the falling of the stones, as many as a hundred persons were around the house trying to ascertain where they came from, but without success.

"Some believed they were thrown by a young girl, the daughter of Barr; but this was shown not the case by keeping her continually under guard, at which time the stones came as fast as before. (reported by Dr. W.N. Hambleton, spiritualist of McConnelsville.)"[4]

The information that would solve this poltergeist case is lacking. It seems unlikely that the young girl suspect could have physically lifted large boulders, but who knows what her psychic rage could have done?

POLTERGEIST ON TRIAL

In 1852 Dr. Abel Underhill published a pamphlet telling the odd story of a teenager tried as a poltergeist. Abby Warner was a destitute 18-year old orphan, a charity case, and an object of horror since half of her face had been eaten away by mercury. Her mediumistic gifts were first discovered by Mrs. Kellog of Massillon, a spiritualist widow, who had taken Abby in as a servant. She persuaded Abby to sit at seances where the totally uneducated girl would write correctly with both hands at the same time, on different subjects, while a third spirit simultaneously rapped out another message. While in trance, she could also answer questions *thought* at her by others.

While visiting Massillon, Dr. Underhill took Abby and some other friends to St. Timothy's Episcopal Church on Christmas eve to see the Christmas decorations. While they were there, raps began to resound loudly throughout the church in time to the singing. The minister asked that "those knockings might cease." In response came a single resounding rap, signifying "No" in the code of the seance room. The church's sexton asked for silence, but the raps continued. Abby was escorted from the church.

Anti-spiritualist members of the congregation complained to the authorities and Abby Warner was arrested under an obscure criminal statute: "If any person...shall...interrupt or molest any religious society...the person so offending shall be fined in any sum not exceeding $20."

For three days a packed courtroom heard testimony from witnesses who could say no more than they had heard raps in the church. On cross-examination, even Abby's bitterest opponents admitted that they had not seen the girl move during the raps. Two ladies hostile to her, who had shared her pew in the Church testified that she never moved, even when the raps were loudest; they did not even suspect that she made the sounds since they sounded at points far away from the girl.

In Abby's defense, Dr. Underhill cited the "modern science of Pneumatology..."—whatever that was. And the girl was reluctantly found "not guilty" by a judge who cited a lack of conclusive proof.

In the light of what we now know about split personality, Abby Warner was a textbook case. The disfigured orphan had led a grim life with possibly abusive caregivers until the discovery of her "gifts." Her writings can be explained by a split between the right and left brains, each of which claimed to be a different spirit. Persons with certain brain configurations or persons under hypnosis can duplicate the same feat. President James A. Garfield was said to be able to simultaneously write Greek with his left hand and Latin with his right.

The rappings were Abby's way of hitting back at authority figures like those who had hurt and exploited her. They were the ultimate attention-getting device—a poltergeist.[5]

THE POOL-PLAYING POLTERGEIST
OF PRICE HILL

Poltergeist or earth-bound spirit? You decide.

In a Price Hill, Cincinnati home, things not only went bump in the night, they went slam and slide during the day. For the first nine years of their life in their big old Price Hill home, Jim and Jane Jones* didn't know that they had a ghost. They just knew that things happened in the house and that "something" shared the house with them. They accepted it all, unafraid, with a low-key attitude of hospitality for all without regard for race, creed, color, sex, or vital signs.

The door slamming was the first signal that something was unusual about the house. Jim would get out of bed at night to check the windows for drafts or burglars. Everything secured, he'd hop back in bed. Only to have the doors slammed again.

The doors slammed even louder when the grandchildren visited and Jim and Jane took some toys out of the attic for them to play with. "She slams the door especially after our grandchildren have been for a visit. There are seven doors on the second floor, and sometimes she will slam every one of them with all her might," said Jane.

"She" is "Susie," a poltergeist with a difference. For one thing, although she performs all the mischievous door-slamming, picture-moving, and object-stealing activities obligatory in the species, she seems to be the spirit of a real little girl who once lived in the house.

The Jones invited a medium to visit and he told them about Susie, a seven-year old girl who died many years before. She had fought when they came to take her to the hospital where she died, then returned as a ghost to her home.

One day, in the pool room, one of the Jones' grandsons decided to tease the invisible child. He put one of the balls on the floor and then positioned a pool cue far away from it. Invisible hands moved the cue along the floor and connected with the ball.

Another time, the number one pool ball simply disappeared and no amount of searching brought it back. The Joneses were annoyed, but not surprised. The ghost had pilfered other small items. The ball had been missing for several weeks when the Jones asked the medium to ask Susie to "please return our number one pool ball." The next day there was the number one ball, racked up with the others. No one else was in the house at the time.

Like most poltergeists, most of Susie's manifestations are mischievous. She delights in taking pictures off the walls, although she does not throw them around like a less well-bred poltergeist might. They are always carefully placed on the floor, leaning up against the wall.

The ghost has been extremely respectful to Mrs. Smith*, Jane's mother, who lives with the family. "Special treatment is accorded to Mrs. Smith in the careful folding down of her bed clothes at night, when she is in bed. The bedding is neatly folded back, a section at a time and then Mrs. Smith is covered up again." Before she found about Susie, she joked about the "dirty old ghost who tried to get in bed with her."

The medium told the Jones family they could get rid of Susie any time they want to, simply by telling her to go away. So far they haven't done so. A little girl poltergeist just doesn't take up that much room.[6]

THE PSEUDO-POLTERGEIST

When we lived on North Longview St. in Beavercreek, I was an avid reader of ghost stories. I had just finished a book about poltergeists that January morning in 1986. In the afternoon a friend of ours sat talking with my husband on the sofa. I was sitting in the recliner next to them when my chair began to sway gently back and forth.

I looked over at the men. The sofa was not moving; they hadn't noticed anything. Surreptitiously I glanced over my shoulder, then looked behind the chair to see if someone had crept up and was shaking the chair. Nothing. In a panic of unbelief my hair stood up.

"This time," I thought, "I'm really losing it."

At that, the bookcases on the opposite wall began to sway. It was an earthquake, measuring 5 on the Richter scale.

FROM THE CRADLE TO THE GRAVE
Ghostly Children

...In one small grave to lie.
-Zoe Akins-

CRY BABY BRIDGE

Back in the 1920s, parts of Fairfield County were as uncivilized as the moon. Under a train trestle stood a small church where a sect met who fervently practiced their creed, "an eye for an eye; a tooth for a tooth." Since it was the depths of the Depression, they were in bad financial shape and desperate to do something to change their luck. A sacrificial lamb was needed.

One of their members had just given birth. While she slept, hard-eyed men stole in and took the child from its cradle. They tied the baby to the railroad tracks above the church and left it there—wailing.

The men found the pitiful remains in the morning— chopped to pieces by the passing trains. And ever since that night, no matter the time of year or the weather, you can hear a baby screaming as a train approaches.[1]

Cry-Baby Bridges have been reported all over Ohio. One is in Rogues' Hollow, Wayne County where, according to legend, at midnight you can hear the cries of a baby who was tossed into the creek many years ago. Still another is a bridge on Wilberforce-Clifton Road, "The Devil's Backbone," near

Wilberforce University, where tales say a University professor accidentally dropped his child to its death in the 1950s.

NIGHTMARE ON ELM STREET

It seems like a charming brick house with a vine draped over the porch and flowering trees in the front yard. But Oberlin legend has it that the Elm Street home was haunted by a wailing baby ghost.

One version of the story says that two spinster sisters lived in the house in the early 1900s. They cruelly abused their maid, who had a small child and she, in turn, would walk up and down the servants' staircase, moaning and wailing like a banshee. Sometimes she would pinch her baby to make him howl and his screams would echo eerily in the stairway.

Properly spooked, the old women would run to the neighbors in terror. Of course, by the time they returned, all was still.

One night as the maid was howling in the stairwell, she tripped and fell down the steep steps. She got up slowly and painfully, then began to scream in earnest. The child was dead.

Another story says that the maid got pregnant while working for the two sisters. They treated her so harshly that she killed herself and the baby, then came back to have her revenge from beyond the grave. Whatever the story, the sounds in the house were disturbingly realistic.

Two Oberlin creative writing professors, Rachel and Tim Clark* moved into the house in 1968. Shortly afterwards, they began to hear something that sounded like a child crying somewhere above their kitchen. Said Rachel,

"I would be sitting in the kitchen writing letters and suddenly hear this terrible wailing of a baby just crying and crying, but quite muted." With two young children of her own in the house, Clark would run upstairs to check on them. By the time she reached the top of the stairs, the crying would cease.

This happened five or six times in two years and Rachel always told herself that it was the wind in the chimney.

"But it *wasn't* the sound of the wind in the chimney," she said, puzzled. "It was the sound of sobbing and crying, identical to the way my children cry when they have a fever."

The Clarks did brick up a stove pipe hole in their chimney. Yet the noises continued briefly and then were heard no more.[2]

THE SPIRIT BABY

Anne Denton Cridge was the sister of William Denton, distinguished geologist and one of the first scientists to test the theory of psychometry, the idea that all things give off vibrations that can be sensed, as he related in his book, *The Soul of Things*. He described Anne as an excellent sensitive and experimented with handing her objects wrapped in brown paper. She would then describe her impressions of the objects and their origins. When handed a piece of lava from Kilauea, she described "an ocean of fire pouring over a precipice and boiling as it pours."

Ann Braude recounts the story of Anne's spirit baby:

In 1857, Anne Denton Cridge lost her first child within months of his birth. "My darling is gone! the fond great hope of my life!...How bitter the separation!" mourned the twenty-three year-old socialist and woman's rights advocate. She poured out her grief in the pages of the *Vanguard*, the newspaper she published with her husband in Dayton, Ohio. Three obituaries recounted the brief life and lamented death of little Denton Cridge. According to the longest tribute, authored by the grieving mother, the conditions that separated Cridge from her baby, however bitter, were short lived. During Denton's final moments, she saw the spirits of her own dead parents above his couch, "waiting to bear his sweet spirit away." She watched her baby's spirit withdraw from his body and assume a spiritual body, with the help of his grandparents. Since then, Cridge told her readers, she held her child in her arms every day. He weighed nothing and within a week had recovered from the illness that took his life.[3]

NO REST FOR THE WICKED

There was an old house on a hill near Baileys Mills in Guernsey County. It was haunted of course—the doors opened and shut by themselves, the fireplace was stained with blood—and every midnight a baby cried.

A couple who hated each other had lived in the house. But they didn't hate each other all the time and pretty soon a baby came along. The girl who was hired to care for the baby felt sorry for the missus. When the mister was drunk, he was a demon.

The baby was fussy and colicky, right from the start. There were many nights the girl paced the floor in front of the fireplace, trying to hush its tortured screams.

That Christmas midnight the baby howled and nothing the nursemaid could do would quiet it down. The father had been dead drunk on Christmas cheer upstairs, but now he came staggering into the room.

Before she could stop him he snatched the child and hurled it into the blazing fireplace. The nursemaid tried desperately to grab hold of the child's shawl and drag it out of the fire. The man just laughed and blocked the fireplace with his massive body. Then when the wailing had ceased, he took up the poker and casually stirred up the charred logs until you couldn't tell baby from ash.

That night the man slept like the dead with no child's howling to disturb his rest. But every midnight thereafter, no matter how he covered his head with the bedclothes, no matter how drunk he got, he was always awakened by the unearthly screams of a baby drifting up the chimney.[4]

THE GHOSTS OF GORE ORPHANAGE

Gore Orphanage: the very name sounds like a 1960s horror movie staring Vincent Price as a demented headmaster. Unfortunately for sensation-seekers, the name—and the legend—are not as lurid as they sound.

A gore is a wedge-shaped piece of land, usually inserted to correct a surveyor's error. This particular gore made up one of the four Erie County farms totaling 543 acres east of the Vermilion River. In 1903 a Lutheran minister and his wife, Mr. and Mrs. J. A. Sprunger of Berne, Indiana built The Orphanage of Hope and Light in this lovely spot overlooking the valley.

At one time 120 children lived at the charitable foundation, with separate buildings for boys and girls. Former residents said that the orphanage was always run properly and there was no hint of any kind of wrongdoing. In 1912 Mr. Sprunger died and management of the orphanage was turned over to the Friends' Church of Cleveland. In 1916 the assets of the foundation were foreclosed and the tract of land was sold to a man from Columbus. With that, the Light and Hope Orphanage was extinguished.

The orphanage's print shop burned in 1910. One of the girls' dormitories burned between 1912 and 1930. The fact is that no orphans were in the buildings at the time and no one died. No trace of the buildings exists today.

But legends persist. The tales say that sixty children perished in the blaze, locked in by an evil administrator who took all the money he could, then torched the building.

Witnesses, many of them students from Firelands College, say that there are sixty neglected tombstones near the river that glow like coals. They say that they've seen the fingerprints of a little child appear on the windows of cars parked too near the site of the orphanage. That smoke smelling of burning flesh still drifts across the field. That the screams of the murdered children can be heard, reliving their final agony.

Some also say that the evil administrator still hangs about the area and if he meets you on the road at night, he may mistake you for an orphan and treat you as he did the others. And if you visit the site on the morning of a fresh snowfall you will find small bloody footprints in the snow.

Confusing the issue is a legend about another local house: Rosedale or "Swift's Folly" as his jealous neighbors called it. This magnificent Greek Revival mansion was built in 1841 by Joseph Swift, who grew rich farming the fertile bottom lands, known locally as "Egypt." With fourteen rooms, six carved fireplaces, servants' quarters, and rose garden, Rosedale was one of the showplaces of the area, rising out of the wilderness like a Greek temple. But in 1865, impoverished by imprudent railroad speculations and defaulted loans, Swift reluctantly sold the house and moved to Michigan where he died in 1878.

Later in the century the Nicholas Wilbur family occupied the house. They were spiritualists, which gave rise to many weird stories about the house. In 1893 all four of their children died of diptheria and, it was whispered, were sealed into a fireplace in the house. The Wilburs held seances where their dead children supposedly returned. Eventually the house was abandoned to the weather and what nature began, vandals completed. In 1923, a movement to save and restore the house was begun, but an intruder burned the house to the ground. No sign of the house can be seen today; a modern home crowns the hill where it once stood.[5]

Yet even that house may be infested with whatever haunts the area. It is said that the bricks from the fireplace where the children were buried were built into the house. One woman who lived there said that she could hear screams that sounded as if they were in the bricks. Does the evil that one man did live on after him at Gore Orphanage?

BABY FARM

This story was told to me by a woman now living in Kettering. She asked that the town not be identified for reasons that will be obvious.

"In the late 1880s my grandmother, when first married, lived in a small village in Ross County. The house where she was living had a staircase closed off with a door at the top. Every night she'd hear a noise—exactly at 9:00—like chains going down that stairway, then out the back door, and ending behind the outhouse.

"One time when my grandfather was traveling, she and her twin nephews decided they would see what was going on. The three of them opened the door leading into the closed stairway. They saw something like a ball of fire, which traveled down the stairs and vanished out behind the outhouse.

"Grandmother was so upset by seeing this, when Grandfather got home, she told him all about it. It turned out he had heard the weird noise too. My grandfather and some other men dug up the area behind the outdoor toilet. They found bones— the bones of many little babies. And each baby had a hatpin stuck in its skull.

"There had been a single woman who lived in the house by herself. She was very heavyset, and she had those babies and didn't know what to do with them. But what Grandmother wondered was, why chains? This was the noise that they were hearing. She couldn't understand it. But once they dug up the bodies, and reburied them properly, they never heard the sound again."

THE RAG DOLL STORY

At the Ohio Hills Folk Festival at Quaker City, they sell rag dolls with this story:

Years ago, long before the last of the one-room country schools was gone, the new teacher at one of these schools was startled to see a strange little girl in the schoolroom after class had been dismissed. The little girl wore clothing old-fashioned even then, and more puzzling, she was soaking wet.

She had in her hand an old school book, also wet, and she said, "Please, teacher, will you show me my lesson? And will you help me find my rag doll?"

The teacher was too astonished to reply and the child vanished.

The schoolmarm boarded with a family nearby and that night she told of the strange visit. The Landlady nodded her head."It's happened before to other teachers. That's why our school can't keep a regular one. Many years ago when I was small, a little girl nearby was on her way to school. It was spring, the creek she always crossed on a footbridge was flooded, and the little girl fell in and was drowned. They found the body and her school book, but her rag doll was never seen again."

The teacher spent the remainder of the evening making an old-fashioned rag doll and the next day, after school, the wet little girl again appeared. This time the teacher showed her the lesson in the school book and gave her the rag doll. The strange little girl again vanished.

"I can show you her grave," the landlady offered that evening. They went to a tiny graveyard nearby and found the small grave.

Lying on it, the teacher saw, was the rag doll she had made—SOAKING WET. From that day on, the little girl was never again seen.[6]

THE GHOSTLY DWARF

Ethel* and Harry* were newly-weds. Harry had sunk his savings into their first house—out on Route 37 between Junction City and the Fairfield County line. It was an old house, built on an even older foundation, but with some paint and some curtains it suited them fine. Until the dwarf showed up.

The first time, they were sitting at dinner. Harry had just taken a second helping of mashed potatoes when a dwarf about three feet high with a long white beard went streaking through the kitchen and vanished into the stove. The mashed potatoes grew cold as they stared, first at the stove, then at each other.

A week later the dwarf dashed through the parlor while Harry was reading the paper and Ethel was darning a sock. She ran the needle through her finger and didn't even feel it. After that they saw the dwarf any time, day or night, as he darted through the tiny rooms of what had once been their dream house.

It got worse. The dwarf began to jump into bed with the couple. Ethel awoke with a start to find his wizened baby face a few inches from hers. His eyes were malicious specks of coal. She spent the rest of the night shivering by the fire while Harry patted her hand.

The next night the dwarf burrowed under the sheets between them. They felt him—as cold as a corpse before he scrambled out of bed, leaving behind long white hairs that clung to them like spiderwebs.

When Harry saw the thing out in the barnyard he ran for his shotgun. The shots didn't even slow the creature up. But in spite of the terror the dwarf brought, Harry and Ethel vowed they wouldn't give up their house, not for any spook.

One day Harry decided to enlarge the house's original cellar, which was just a dug-out fruit cellar lined with loose stonework, and make it into a proper basement. He and the hired man pulled the stones out of the wall and dug into the reddish, sandy soil. The hired man struck something smooth and cream-colored—like an old billiard ball. Together he and Harry brushed the sand away from a tiny, grinning skull, then dug out an entire skeleton, baby-size, from the cellar wall.

Ethel washed the pathetic little bones, wrapped them in a blanket, and laid them to rest in a grave under the apple tree. And after that day, the dwarf never appeared again.[7]

THERE WAS A LITTLE GIRL...

Cleveland ghosthunter Robert Van Der Velde writes,

There is a haunted house in Lakewood just west of Cleveland. The story was told to me by a General Electric photographer who lived two or three doors away. The house was owned by a young couple who had no children. The wife's hobby was sewing, and she spent many hours at it alone, for her husband's job required his being out of town much of the time. One night she was alone in the living room, watching TV and sewing. When she ran out of thread she went upstairs to what she called the sewing room to get some more. When she turned on the light she saw a little girl standing in the middle of the room staring at her. Terrified, she ran back downstairs.

She soon came to the conclusion that she had hallucinated, that her imagination was getting the better of her. She decided not to mention it to her husband when he returned.

But one night when he was home he came running down the stairs, scared half to death. He had seen the girl in the upstairs hallway.

They told all of this to their neighbor, the GE photographer, explaining they were selling the house and not telling the new owners about the ghost.

I asked the photographer to wait several months until he got to know the new neighbors fairly well, then ask them if anything unusual happened in the house.

They were amazed by his question. On various occasions they had seen a small girl standing on the stairs. As long as they sat quietly observing her she would remain on the stairs, but if they got up for a better look she would disappear. Since the steps hid her feet they could not see all of her, but she was

apparently dressed in a floor-length gown such as
those worn around the turn of the century, when most
of the houses in the neighborhood were built.

LOTTIE'S GHOST

[In October of 1929] Mrs. Deane* was spending a weekend at the home of her daughter's nurse in Cleveland. The
nurse, Mrs. Mills*, was a widow with a young son whom Mrs.
Deane had met. Other than these facts, Mrs. Deane knew little
of Mrs. Mills' family.

On the first evening of her visit, Mrs. Deane was undress-
ing for bed when, in her own words,

> I heard a sound at the bedroom door as if the knob
> were being turned, and on opening it saw a good-
> looking young girl, normally dressed, standing there. I
> said, "Hello, who are you?" to which she replied, "I'm
> Lottie and this is my room," but when I said, "Won't
> you come in?" she just smiled and entirely disap-
> peared.
>
> Strangely, I did not feel at all nervous and slept
> quite soundly that night. In the morning I said to Mrs.
> Mills, "Who's Lottie?"
>
> She replied, "Lottie was my pet name for my
> daughter Charlotte who died a few years ago, but how
> did you know about her?"
>
> So I told her of the visit to my bedroom the night
> before and she showed me a photograph of Charlotte,
> who looked just as I had 'seen' her.[8]

LITTLE GIRL RED

A son of Mr. Carey's brother, seven years old,
Alexander by name, was playing one day, in the year
1858, in an upper room [in Cincinnati], when all at
once, he noticed a little girl, seemingly about four

years old, with a bright red dress. Though he had
never seen her before, he approached her, hoping to
find a playmate, when she suddenly vanished before
his eyes, or, as the child afterward expressed it, she
"went right out." Though a bold fearless boy, he was
very much frightened by this sudden disappearance....
It was afterward recollected that, during little Lucy's
last illness, they had been preparing for her a red dress,
which greatly pleased the child's fancy. She was very
anxious that it should be completed.

One day she had said to a sister, "You will finish
my dress, even if I am ill: will you not?" to which her
sister had replied, "Certainly, my dear, we shall finish
it, of course." "Oh, not of coarse," said the child:
"finish it off fine." This expression, at which they
laughed at the time, served to perpetuate in the family
the remembrance of the anxiety constantly evinced by
the little sufferer about her new red dress, which,
however, she never lived to wear.

It need hardly be added that little Alexander had
never heard of his Aunt Lucy, dying as she did in
infancy twenty-five years before....[9]

THE LOST BOY

June 3, 1978 was Jim Flanagan's last day as counselor at a
rural high school outside of Lancaster. He returned to the
school about 6 p.m. to finish up some work before he left for
good. The school was deserted. Jim worked for an hour in his
cramped office, then decided to stretch his legs.

He walked to the gym and started jogging around the floor.
He had been jogging about two minutes when he looked up on
the stage and saw a boy standing there.

Jim stared. He was only about fifty feet away from the
boy—directly opposite him. Jim waved and called to the boy
several times as he ran around the gym, getting closer and
closer to the stage. He could see the boy clearly in the

remaining daylight: he was about fifteen years old and wore an old-fashioned pair of jeans and no shirt. His haircut, Jim recalls, was "out of date." Jim knew every kid in school. He didn't know this one.

"He was standing on the side by the stage curtain smiling at me. I increased my speed and jumped on the stage." The boy immediately walked behind the curtain. Jim followed, grabbing at the curtain. Nothing. He searched the curtain, the stage and found the door at the back of the stage locked.

By this time the room was starting to grow dim. Jim turned on all the gym and stage lights. He looked upstairs and down. Nothing. Then he called the assistant principal and the sheriff's deputy. Together they searched the school from top to bottom for about an hour. There was no sign of forcible entry on any of the doors. Everything was locked up tight.

Then Frank* the janitor joined them in their search. Jim remarked that he hadn't heard any footsteps and he assumed the boy was barefoot. Frank looked scared. Usually jovial and outgoing, he suddenly clammed up and never left Jim's side during the rest of the search.

"Did you ever see anything while working late at night?" Jim asked him.

"No!" said Frank, but Jim got the impression the man was leaving something unsaid.

When Jim talked to the janitor's son later, he found that Frank never wanted to go back to the school late at night because he felt someone was watching him.

"I still think about that night and that boy. I remember he looked 'old fashioned' and different, but I never felt scared at any time. I still felt I had seen a real kid."

The other searchers were not so sure. The sheriff still shakes his head over the incident whenever he sees Jim. And somewhere in Fairfield County stands a school haunted by a lost boy.

TIME WARPS
Glimpses through time?

They shall be one, though their number be legion,
And with One Consciousness they shall revive
Into the bliss of the radiant region
All of the past that was ever alive
-Col. Coates Kinney-

Nothing is ever lost. Things may disappear, be destroyed, or go down into the grave, but they have only changed their form: the corruptible nature putting on the incorruptible.

Even though a building burns to the ground, its atoms still exist, floating around somewhere just as invisible radio and TV signals fill the air. Perhaps there are unusually sensitive people who can mentally reassemble these atoms and see a place as it once was. In his later years, Thomas Edison was intrigued by the idea of a radio so powerful it could pick up the sounds of the past. He believed that every sound, every word ever spoken would continue to vibrate—somewhere.

Or maybe, as quantum physics has it, there is no time. Everything that was, and is, and shall be is all here, now, but at different "frequencies." If you had the right radio dial, you could tune yourself to the past or the future. The burned building would continue to exist somewhere along the dial. Perhaps some people have an ability to tune into the past. Or there may be places where the fabric of time wears thin, places where present and past meet.

THE GHOSTS OF EDEN

A dazzlingly white wrought iron gazebo sheltered a statue of a graceful Greek maiden in the yard of Xenia's Eden Hall.

"That's the highest house I've ever seen," my daughter said, awed at the three-story Greek Revival mansion.

We climbed the steps to the front porch. I yanked on the old-fashioned bell and waited, studying the etched glass surrounding the massive door. Smiling, Mrs. Evelyn Cozatt opened the door and ushered us into the hall.

I gasped. We stood under a blazing crystal chandelier, surrounded by burgundy and grey scenic wallpapers and richly finished wood. A twisting staircase seemed to fly up into the upper reaches of the house. I turned and gasped again at the fiery ruby Bohemian glass, etched in a floral pattern that had looked like plain glass from outside.

The house was a time-capsule. Satin draperies swept from carved and gilded cornices. I stared at thirteen-foot ceilings, lush oriental rugs, hundreds of paintings, ("Around seven hundred and fifty," Mrs. Cozatt told me.), and a dizzying array of vases, embroideries, and bric-a-brac. She pointed out a black chair with petit-point embroidery that had belonged to Henry Ward Beecher.

Through a pair of tall doors, old silver and crystal gleamed softly in the dining room. Time lay frozen in that room. There was a stillness, an antique light. The long prisms on the sideboard lamps tinkled softly as we walked by.

The house, which served as the model for Sally Rausch's house in *And Ladies of the Club*..., was built in 1840 by Abram Hivling, whose freed slaves made the bricks. The Hivling family lived in the house until 1881 when the house was sold to Hivling's niece and her husband, Mr. and Mrs. John Allen for their daughter Mary, Mrs. Coates Kinney.

Colonel Coates Kinney was a lawyer, journalist (he owned the *Xenia Torchlight*), government paymaster during the Civil War, and a distinguished literary man. His most famous works were the poem, "Ode to Ohio" and "Rain on the Roof." He knew everyone worth knowing. Visitors to the house included McKinley before he was elected President, Donn Piatt, of literary and Piatt Castles fame, and Secretary of State John Hay. Many brilliant parties were held at the house.

The last of the three Kinney daughters, Clara Shields, died in 1972, aged 99. Mr. and Mrs. Paul Cozatt then bought the house and restored it, dubbing it Eden Hall, after a remark by Mrs. Shields who said that it was always good to get back to her "own piece of Eden."

Mrs. Cozatt conducted us through every one of Eden Hall's thirty-two rooms: A pantry full of majolica pottery, a hall full of Currier and Ives prints, a kitchen full of stained glass panels and cats. The basement was painted a pale green. A secret room used when the house was on the Underground Railroad is now sealed off, marked only by an arc of bricks.

Mrs. Cozatt gestured to a coffin-shaped stone trough. "I call it the sarcophagus," she said. "They filled it with water, and they kept their butter and milk cool in it, like in a spring house." Behind the house was a tiny building that looked like a summerhouse. When I asked Mrs. Cozatt about it, she laughed. "It's actually my walk-in, period doghouse" built with materials salvaged after the Xenia tornado from a house next to Xenia's City Hall.

I stood in the doorway of the Fern Room—papered in a fern pattern, furnished with white Victorian wicker furniture, mossy green carpet, and multiple ferns rioting in Victorian plant stands. From there, looking through the Music Room, I could see the huge double parlor at the front of the house.

It was a sunny day outside; light shone through the sheer curtains. I blinked, certain that at any moment a woman in a long dress of the 1840s would glide across the parlor past that window, silhouetted against the light.

The front parlor, its walls a green pale, was furnished with exquisite gilded chairs and settees upholstered in gold Aubusson tapestry. Mrs. Cozatt told us that the furniture had belonged to the Jergens Lotion family. Overhead twinkled an elaborate crystal chandelier with a huge crystal ball pendant.

When we admired the chandelier, she said that it had been purchased in dirt-encrusted fragments and took her and her husband five months to reassemble.

Then she gestured at a cabinet incongruously propping open the door into the front hall. "We've had trouble with this door banging," she said.

I told her about my impression of the woman walking in front of the window—headed for that door.

Then Mrs. Cozatt led us up the steep stairs to the third floor, our toes clanging against brass carpet rods holding the carpet in place. We stood, breathless, on the landing while Mrs. Cozatt turned on the lights. "There!" she said, opening the door to an enchanting room full of toys. It was on this third floor that she first experienced the ghosts.

"Until we got this house I never really believed in ghosts," said Mrs. Cozatt, "although I liked to read about them. I never really gave a thought to coming in contact with one."

When the Cozatts bought Eden Hall, "it was just a huge empty barn with a bed and a hot plate...The roof was just a sieve. There were more pots than I'd ever seen up in the attic collecting leaks."

Mrs. Cozatt taught school in Dayton. Whenever she came to Xenia, she'd bring a load of household items over in the trunk of her car and store them on the unfinished third floor.

"I was working on something in the kitchen at one o'clock in the morning when I found I needed something from the third floor. I went upstairs to get it and opened the door. And I was immediately encased in this awful, awful cold. It scared me because it was so unexpected, but I'd read about things like that. I decided there wasn't any use being upset about it so I went on into the attic. Then it seemed like it got colder, like it was following along behind me. I decided I better get out of there and went back downstairs. The cold followed me downstairs.

"It followed me *everywhere* inside the house for two weeks, except into the servants' quarters. I must tell you I did not appreciate it one bit. I was there in an empty thirty-two-room house and lights would come on. Doors would bang shut and there'd be other noises that you really couldn't identify. It evidently did not like me."

After two weeks, the cold went away. "One [of the Kinney daughters] did not get along with the rest of the family. She lived on the third floor. I've always assumed that she was causing the cold. I heard she was rather hard to get along with—not very nice. I don't know if her reputation was deserved, although she would do anything to embarrass her family, like dressing oddly. She was the daughter who married the music teacher in *And Ladies of the Club*." It was her son whose two daughters inherited the house.

Even after the cold went away, strange things happened to Mrs. Cozatt.

"Everything was very dirty in the house. One night I decided to coat the brick walls of the unfinished third floor—to hold the dust in. I was up there late one night when things started falling over. That was quite..." She paused. "I didn't particularly like that either. It kept on and on. I finally got fed up and said, 'Hey you! I have to get up early in the morning to go to work! Will you please stop that so I can finish my job?' The noise stopped. Then I found little footprints in the dust—six inches long, like a child's. I saved them for a long time. After that, odd things still kept on happening—like the doors would bang off and on for about six weeks.

"With all of the things going on I was having a problem sleeping. I was in one of the bedrooms upstairs when suddenly I heard music and talking. That was rather peculiar so I got up and didn't see anything or anybody. Yet it kept on and on. There were waltzes and old-fashioned dance melodies played by flutes, violins, harpsichord, and harp."

Mrs. Cozatt listened a while and thought about what was going on upstairs. "And I thought, 'No, thank you.' I got up and went *down*stairs. I couldn't sleep; I was feeling rather jittery. So I got out paint and brushes and painted the spindles under the stair rail. I spent the rest of the night painting, and got them done too."

And while she worked, the invisible residents were playing.

"'They' really had a party. They walked right by me, right down those steps, while I was painting. I could hear their footsteps. I could hear them laughing and talking. Very jolly behavior.

"There were a lot of parties in this house. I'd heard it said that people used to dance on the third floor, even though there's the huge double parlor downstairs. But they were going upstairs, and downstairs and laughing and having a nice time. It stopped at four in the morning," she added matter-of-factly.

Eden Hall is a place where the past and the present meet in a seamless join. And for some long-dead partygoers, the party still goes on.

GHOSTS AT GLENDOWER?

One day in the summer of 1988, Patty Ramsey, a volunteer tour guide at Glendower State Memorial in Lebanon, a restored 1850s Greek Revival house, heard voices at the front door.

"It sounded like three or four men and women—young adults—talking to each other as they walked up to the front door. I couldn't pick out any distinct voices; I really wasn't paying attention."

Patty got up and started to turn the large skeleton key which is kept chained to the original brass lock. As she did, she peered out of one of the sidelights and was startled to see that no one was there. Puzzled, she walked down the hall to the back door and looked out at the parking lot. There were no visitors' cars in the lot.

Not quite believing what had just happened, Patty went back to the front door, opened it, and stepped out onto the porch. She could see the caretaker cutting the grass on the lower front lawn down by Route 42.

"I knew it couldn't have been him because the lawn mower had never stopped. I was just taken aback. They sounded so real. I thought the visitors had walked around the house. But the voices were right there at the door. I couldn't figure out how someone could have gotten away that quick."

One chilly, rainy summer afternoon in 1991, Patty was sitting on a sofa by the fireplace in the library, crocheting. Suddenly she heard a noise "as if a log had fallen in the fireplace and was popping sparks." Startled, she looked at the fireplace. There was no fire there, only a decorative aspen log in the grate. Yet she could distinctly hear a phantom fire hissing and crackling in the fireplace.

Both incidents seem more like glimpses of the past than actual ghosts. Perhaps in a place so correctly restored and lovingly cared for, the lines between the present and the past become blurred.

BEYOND THE VEIL

When Gin Phillippi of Xenia found a bride in her bedroom the night of September 20th, 1990, her reaction was curiosity rather than fear:

"In the middle of the night something woke me. I jumped up in bed and looked across the room. Someone was standing there, oblivious to me. There was nothing frightening about it, but I just stared.

"It was a bride wearing a white eyelet dress and a short veil that flowed back over her shoulders. She carried a small, but beautiful bouquet of red roses surrounded with babies' breath. She had fair hair—light brown or blonde. Her face was not entirely clear even though it wasn't pitch dark in the bedroom because of the hall light. I couldn't see the bottom of the dress because the bed was in the way.

"She just stood there looking away from me towards the south. And then she turned towards me, but she didn't focus on me, didn't look at me. She was just thinking. She turned back as she had been, so I had a side view and then she was gone. I lay awake and thought about it. I wondered who she was and I regretted not speaking.

"She appeared on my husband's side of the bed," Gin said, "He's a light sleeper and yet he slept right through it. He listened very carefully to my story and made very few comments. He keeps looking for her, hoping she'll return!" she laughs.

"My daughter was quite interested. She asked me many questions as if to give me a chance to tell the story so I wouldn't forget anything. She could not believe that I didn't question the bride and find out who she was, and from whence she cometh. It was a neat experience. I'm just sorry I didn't talk to her."

Gin is going to research the history of the house. It was built at the turn of the century and she thinks she can track down the previous owners.

"I think it would be interesting to see if any of them were married on September 20th. That would be almost as much of a surprise as seeing the ghost."

Gin is adamant that the bride was not a dream. "I know I was awake at the time. My son said 'When you dreamed this...' and I interrupted him and said, 'No, it was *not* a dream.' I dream with my eyes closed. I *know* she was there. I just don't know why."

Great joy, as well as great sorrow, can leave its impression on the psychic atmosphere. The pensive bride, dreaming of the future, probably never dreamed that her reverie would haunt a woman a century later.

THE GHOSTLY SUICIDE

One Friday in early spring, 1965, Mary and her friend Teresa* drove into Coshocton. A storm came up, and as they reached the Chestnut Street bridge, the rain was coming down in sheets. Through the rain Mary saw a man walking towards the curb. She braked, thinking he was about to step in front of her, but he merely stooped as if picking something up from the gutter, then went back to the railing of the bridge and disappeared. Somehow she knew he had jumped into the river.

"That man just jumped off the bridge!" Mary exclaimed to her passenger.

"What man? I didn't see anyone." answered Teresa, looking frantically along the bridge. Mary stopped the car, got out, and leaned over the railing searching the muddy brown waters for some sign of the man.

Soaked to the skin, Mary drove to the police station to report what she had seen, while Teresa insisted that she hadn't seen any man. Mary had imagined it. She was making a fool of herself. What would the police say at such a wild story?

Mary said the police listened to her story. She doesn't know if they believed her or checked it out. There was never anything in the newspapers about the incident. No suicides, nothing. But Mary knows she saw the man jump. The only question in her mind is, did he jump into the past or the future.[2]

RE-LIVING THE DYING

In April 1965, Helen was returning from Akron, when she noticed an old Amish man walking along a fence row beside the road. He was old and his knees seemed to buckle under him as he stumbled along. As she pulled up beside him, he fell to the ground.

Her first thought was that he was ill and needed help, but she knew she couldn't lift him alone, so she pulled into the drive of the closest farmhouse to ask for help. Unfortunately, no one was home.

Helen turned the car around and stopped opposite the old man. She called out to him, asking if he were sick. He partially raised himself on one elbow and stared at her, but did not answer. Helen was certain he'd had a stroke and couldn't speak. Traffic was coming up behind her so she drove on to the next farmhouse. No one was home there either.

Helen didn't know what to do. For five minutes she stared across the lanes of traffic. At least twenty cars and trucks passed the old man as he tried to raise himself. Not a single car stopped, slowed down or even showed signs that the drivers had seen him, even though he was lying right beside the road. Helplessly, she drove on, baffled that no one else had stopped.

Helen drove the same route many times after that and she always wondered about the old man. Finally she stopped at the first farmhouse and told the people there of her experience, asking them if they knew how the old man was. They listened to her story seriously, but every now and then the man nodded knowingly, as though he knew exactly what was coming next. When Helen finished her story, the man paused, then said, "You saw a ghost."

And he told Helen how the old man had been taken sick and had tried to get help from the neighbors. He had died exactly as Helen had seen him—in April, 1897.[3]

TIME LIKE AN EVER-ROLLING STREAM....

Who was John O. Wattles? I talked to Clermont County historian Rick Crawford; John Walker, a Dayton expert on Utopian communities; and searched the Ohio State Historical Society records, but only found a 23-page pamphlet on marriage and free love. All that we know about the man is that he founded a "spiritualist" community and may have built a mysterious underground structure in Utopia.

The Clermont County community of Utopia was founded by the followers of Frenchman Charles Fourier. Fourier believed that he alone knew God's plan for a harmonious universe and that the world would go through 35,000 years of harmony during which all people would be organized into "phalanxes" for cooperative living. He also believed that the oceans would turn into lemonade.

As Fourier envisioned it, a phalanx would cover about three square miles, most of it farmland. Each phalanx had its own living quarters, library, workshops, dining hall, kitchens, nurseries, schools, storage, and stables.

The Clermont Phalanx was located on the Ohio River about thirty miles from Cincinnati. The land was fertile; the location ideal for commercial ventures. More than a dozen families banded together in 1844, paying $25.00 yearly dues for each share. A large wooden house with a room for each family and a common dining hall was built on the banks of the Ohio River.

As the community grew, a new two-story, thirty-room brick house was built on higher ground. This expense strained the resources of the community and although the original members continued to work hard, newer recruits became dissatisfied. In 1846 the property was sold and the community disbanded.

The tract of land containing the Phalanx buildings became the property of John O. Wattles and his spiritualist community of about one hundred souls. They tore down the two-story brick building and rebuilt it next to the wooden building on the banks of the Ohio River. The rebuilding was hastily and carelessly done; people were waiting to move in. By December 1847, people who had been living in temporary buildings moved to the shelter of the brick house. Rain and snow began to fall. By December 12th, the Ohio was overflowing.

People continued to seek shelter in the house, even though they had to be rowed there in boats. By the evening of December 13 there were at least thirty-four people in the brick house, most of them young people looking forward to an evening of dancing. About eight o'clock in the evening the walls of the house collapsed. All but a few of the revelers were crushed or swept away to drown in the dark waters of the Ohio.

Dredging operations in 1975 brought up bricks from the house. During exceptionally low water, the foundations of the house can be seen, about one hundred yards offshore.

Wattles himself lived in a separate building which still stands, brought to historian Crawford's attention by auto salesman Bill Mues. It is a plain brick structure with a rusty tin roof, standing under spreading oak trees by Route 52, the front yard pleasantly overgrown with wild flowers and meadow grasses. On the day we visited Utopia, Rick Crawford, Rosi Mackey, Jon Chapman, and I stood in the long grass studying the house. A suncatcher in an upstairs window looked like a ghostly face. Behind the house, in the barn, a tan dog barked wildly.

"That dog isn't afraid of anything," said Rick "except of approaching the house. He won't go near it."

There were two front doors. One led to a separate parlor where spiritualist meetings were held. The upstairs room on the southwest corner, the one with the suncatcher, may have been Wattle's office. Possibly he conducted religious ceremonies in the room.

As she was standing in this room Deborah, who occupies the house with her husband Leon, saw several people walking up the old dirt path from where the boat landing had been. They were wearing clothes of a bygone age and they were soaking wet. They were talking, almost moaning, she said. One lady in a full-length blue dress and blue bonnet wept. They crossed the road, which was suddenly not the paved Route 52, but a dirt road of the 1800s. Then they came into the house, climbed the stairs, and came into her room, talking silently all the while. They did not seem to notice Deborah and then they faded out.

Leon gave Rick and his friends a tour of the house. While he was talking to them, the bare white light bulb in the ceiling began to pulsate, but only while they were in the room. Next a "strange blue ball of light" flew out of Leon's bedroom, which is the room next to Wattles' former office.

Leon said that he had noticed "a very bright robin's egg blue light which filled up his bedroom...coming and disappearing. There was a musty smell in the room during that time, but a warm feeling."

The room [where Deborah had her sighting] did not seem threatening to Leon, Rick, and his friends until "the family cat came into the room. Leon had just said that the cat rarely entered the house and *never* came into his bedroom....Everyone but Andy Dickerson, Paul Dunaway, and myself had left the room, not feeling very threatened or creepy about it until the cat approached the open door of the closet.

"It had been walking all about when suddenly it stopped dead in its tracks before the opening. It raised its back; its hair straightened immediately. It did not move for a few seconds and then advanced another step, stopped in the same fashion again and then darted out of the room....

"The cat gets agitated in the upstairs room (Wattles' meeting room), but nowhere else in the house," said Deborah. "We love this place. If it's haunted, it's a good haunted."

Far stranger than the Wattles House is a huge underground building recently discovered in Utopia near the Brown County line. The entrances to the underground structure are surrounded by rusty chain link fences covered with dead vines. The owner of the property was not available to unlock the gates the day we visited so I leaned into the fence trying to see to the bottom of one of the deep stone-lined shafts. Half-way down, the sun revealed moss and a slug gleaming on the wall. An enormous ladder stretched down into the depths of the other shaft.

"There were steps," Rick told me. "Inside you can see where there were other things. At one time there was an enormous metal door; you can see where the supports were on the wall."

Rick has explored and measured the house. He said, "The packed dirt floor is twenty-two feet underground, the stone walls support a ceiling which is eighteen feet above the floor, the length of the building is forty-four feet and the width is twenty-two feet. It has an arched ceiling and it's the size of a small gymnasium. It was built out of stones carried from the banks of the Ohio River. We don't know what it was used for. The room may have been a storage area or a sanctuary for the spiritualists.

"It has four fireplaces at ground level. About eight feet above each fireplace is another opening in the wall. Their purpose is unknown. There's no sign of any floor. There's an enormous entrance on the east side facing the rising sun." He pointed out the arched opening with ferns growing in it. "The sun shining through the archway at dawn makes a sunburst effect on the wall."

The structure seemed unimaginably old. The only things I've seen that even remotely resemble it are Celtic monuments in Europe. A chill damp air seemed to rise from the shaft as from a tomb.

And like the grave, the uncanny structure seems destined to keep its secrets in silence.

LITTLE GIRL BLUE

This story was collected and written by Betty Miller for her "Small Town Sampler" column in the October 24, 1990 *Ada Herald*. Thanks to Betty for allowing me to quote parts of it here. Betty says she's just dying to see the ghosts—which is probably what she'll have to do if they remain as elusive as they have in the past.

Mr. and Mrs. Fisher* bought a building in Ada, [began Betty's informant].

> For several years the couple lived in a second
> floor apartment while they remodeled the third floor, a
> former lodge hall where meetings and entertainments
> were held from 1905 until sometime in the 1940s.
> When the work was finished they moved into the third
> floor apartment with its now spacious and comfortable
> rooms. Soon the woman began to sense they were not
> the only inhabitants of their new home.
> One evening as the couple came up the wide stairs
> leading to the apartment entrance, the woman thought
> she saw what seemed to be the lower section of a
> figure "wearing a black cape or long skirt" standing
> beside the door. She dismissed the experience by
> recalling, "The first time it happens, you just think, oh
> well...maybe it was your own shadow or something."
> But the figure and the cape appeared by the door
> "again and again." That winter in a small room off the

living room she saw the same black caped apparition. Later another figure appeared wearing white. The ghostly appearances didn't frighten the woman and became familiar sights. As she told me, "I couldn't tell you how many times I've seen them in seven years."

The next episode involved a rocking chair. Returning from a shopping trip...she unlocked the door of the third floor apartment. After placing her packages on the kitchen table she went into the living room. The chair was rocking as she entered and then suddenly stopped, "just like somebody put their hand on it to stop it."

[In 1988] two smaller figures, still only partially visible, appeared near the doorway of the little room. The woman describes them as "about the size of teenagers." Last winter as she passed the room, she saw the lower half of a child, perhaps five years old, "spinning and twirling around in a circle" as children do. She couldn't see the top half of the tiny figure, but the skirt appeared to be one of those old-fashioned dresses with a dropped waist that children once wore. The remarkable thing was that the dress was blue, the first color the woman had seen....

One afternoon after waking from a nap in the small room, [Mrs. Fisher's mother] reported she had seen the figure in the black cape. Unlike her daughter who saw only the lower half of the figures, the mother had seen the full figure.... she said she could not make out features since the face was covered.

[Mr. Fisher] has never seen their visitors, but he wonders [if one of them is] the woman in the old picture he found in the building. She is wearing a dark dress accented with a white lace collar, a dress reminiscent of a style before World War I, and she has "a tired, worried face." He also wonders about the door to the little room that he finds open in the

morning when he and his wife are sure they closed it
the night before.

Added Betty Miller, "In September as I walked down the
long hall to the stairs leading to the third floor apartment to
hear the story again, I thought about the people who had once
lived in the building—Robinson, Lucinda, Grace and the
others. I hoped the figure in the black cape would be standing
outside the door. When I sat in a chair facing the little room,
'their room,' I wanted to see the little girl twirling in her blue
skirt. I took pictures with my camera, hoping when the
pictures were developed a blur in the photos would indicate
something was there I could not see with my eyes. The
photographs showed nothing."

The woman who lives in the third floor apartment now
sees the ghosts, if that is what they are, on a regular basis.
Once she saw them fighting, although there was no sound. The
picture of the worried-looking woman that her husband found
has disappeared. The woman notes that the ghosts are seen less
in summer—a curious fact, since the family of the grocer who
lived upstairs, had a summer place at a nearby lake. There had
been a fire in the building—they found traces of it when they
remodeled—but they don't know if anyone died in the fire.

The ghosts seem oblivious of the living in the apartment.
They go about their daily rounds: standing, twirling, even
quarreling, seemingly unaware of the current tenants. Could it
be a time warp? A video tape of the mundane events of the
past recorded in the bricks and mortar of the building? Perhaps, to the little girl in blue and her family, the Fishers are the
real ghosts.[4]

TIME WARP WITH TURNIPS

The house is a three-story Italianate Victorian, built
between 1835 and 1840, somewhere east of Findlay. By the
time Michael Manning bought the house in 1976, it had been

well-lived in by a number of owners, including one family with eleven children, and was badly in need of restoration.

Kay married Michael in 1983; and they began to restore the house on their honeymoon. None of the five bedrooms were fit to sleep in, so they used the front parlor for a bedroom.

The first strange thing happened as the couple was getting ready for bed around 1 a.m. Just as they got into bed, the gingerbread clock on the organ in the parlor started to chime, while the cuckoo clock in the living room started to cuckoo. The couple froze. Neither clock had run for weeks and in fact the gingerbread clock read 1:10 (the correct time) while the cuckoo clock read 3:15. After twelve chimes and twelve cuckoos, both clocks lapsed back into silence. When Michael checked, both clocks were again dead.

Restoration continued and they moved into their bedroom upstairs. After a few nights of uninterrupted sleep, one evening they heard footsteps pacing back and forth right by the bed. They had heard footsteps before, in the room above the living room and in the attic—heavy men's footsteps, but these "were soft and light, like those of a woman." They lay there frozen for what seemed forever. "It seemed [the footsteps] would go to the window, hesitate, then walk back, then to the window again. When this finally stopped we looked at the clock." Once again it was 1:10 a.m.

Another night they heard a sound like water splashing in the hallway, like it was being poured from one container to another. "Having no water source upstairs, nor any rain for quite some time, we tried to fool ourselves into thinking that maybe some water had laid up in the attic and just now came through the ceiling...of course we found no water anywhere upstairs...Later on when we were visiting with one of the former owners' grandchildren, we found out that at one time there was a receptacle upstairs, which caught rainwater and it was then used to wash up at night. So perhaps we had just heard another of our friendly spirits, going about their nightly routine."

The house has many odd scents which come and go mysteriously. "some scents...seem to come and go like a breeze through the kitchen which leaves a "musty" trail behind it—a scent similar to clothes stored in an old trunk.

"Then there was the time we came through our back door which opens into our laundry room, and were greeted by a very strong smell of turnips or radishes...The smell was so strong it burnt our eyes and noses. We walked all around the room and tried to locate the source..." They searched everywhere, only to find that the smell had completely disappeared.

"Later on in we found out that what was now our laundry room, was at one time a 'scullery.' There had been a long dry sink in the middle of the room and they used it for doing up dishes and scrubbing vegetables and other chores relating to the family meals."

Kay experienced a "presence" standing beside the stove. At first she thought it was her husband so she whirled around. There was nothing there. She ran up the stairs, the presence right behind her all the way to the top where it vanished. She says that her hair stood up with a feeling like static electricity.

"I did not consciously or physically see anything, yet when reviewing the experience over and over in my mind, I see a lady in black standing there. She is taller than average, with her hair pulled loosely back in a knot or bun, she has a black fitted dress...and is looking right at me, her arms hanging straight down with her hands clasped in front of her."

Her husband also experienced a presence.

One winter afternoon, "we were just about to get into the car when a small wind...wafted around the snowdrifts and a voice that sounded like an elderly lady called out my husbands name. At first I thought it was my imagination going wild." She got into the car. Michael walked around the back of a small stone outbuilding then got into the car with a puzzled look on his face.

"I asked him if he heard something and he said he heard his name being called. I told him I had heard it too. He thought there was someone behind the stone house, possibly somebody hurt, but no one was back there."

Kay sometimes wonders if there is another dimension parallel to their own where the spirits co-exist and go about their routines as they did in life. The sound of running water in the upstairs hall and the smell of vegetables in the former pantry suggest a time warp. But most of the other events suggest that the Mannings are sharing their house with spirits. They don't mind.

"When we are not working on the house, everything seems to be quiet. They usually start in as soon as we start working and some of the things that happen seem almost as if they are 'playing games' with us.

"We only have two more rooms to restore. We think we will put it off for awhile, since they are the worst rooms in the house to restore because of rain damage. Everyone needs a rest, even spirits...."

7

BUCKEYE BIGFOOTS
And other uncanny animals

And I saw...a pale horse,
and its rider's name was Death.
Revelation 6: 8-

Uncanny animals fall into three categories: true ghost animals ("The Ghostly Dog of Spate House"), anomalous animals ("The Loveland Frog") and *tulpas* ("Bigfoot in Greene County?").

Anomalous animals are not merely pink elephants seen by drunkards. They can be as concrete as the three-foot crocodile captured in Huffman Pond near Xenia July 6, 1935.** They can be as nebulous as the Bigfoot seen walking *through* a barbed wire fence at Point Isabel in Clermont County in the 1960s. They can be as inexplicable as the kangaroos sighted near Monroe in 1968, or, more recently, as the monstrous "South Bay Besse" who scared water-skiers out of the water at Port Clinton early in the fall of 1990. They are seen in broad daylight, by reputable observers. Yet, clearly, they don't belong here.

"Escaped from the circus" is one popular official explanation. I wonder if these creatures are *tulpas*, a Tibetan word for a physical materialization of thought. Some people believe that the Loch Ness Monster and Bigfoot are *tulpas*. They can be seen and sometimes photographed. They leave tracks and droppings. But when cornered, they melt away—perhaps into another dimension. Could Ohio be the gateway to a ghostly wildlife preserve? Maybe somewhere there is a hatch that the Keeper opens so that the animals may go and feed....

**If any of my readers have any details of this case, I would like to hear from them. Even the Greene County Engineers have never heard of Huffman Pond.

THE CROSSWICK MONSTER

Warren County's Waynesville area with its antique shops would seem an unlikely place for a monster, yet in the 1880s something straight out of prehistory appeared at Crosswick, a small village about a mile north of Waynesville.

As young Ed and Joe Lynch, ages eleven and thirteen, were fishing in a creek near Crosswick, they were attacked by a huge snake-like creature. Dropping their poles, the two boys fled, only to have the thing rear up on a pair of legs that seemed to grow suddenly from its lower body. It grabbed Ed with a pair of arms that were "extruded" from its body. Joe screamed for help.

Rev. Jacob Horn, George Pendleton, and Allen Jordan were working nearby and heard the boys' screams. They saw the reptilian monster with Ed in its clutches, heading for a huge sycamore tree with a hole in its trunk. As they charged the creature, it dropped Ed and crawled inside the tree. Ed, described as being "almost dead with fright," was taken home and Dr. L.C. Lukens from Waynesville was called to treat him.

The Crosswick Monster was described as "reptilian, 30 to 40 feet long and about 16 inches in diameter with scaled legs and body; the head, about the same thickness as the body, was split by a large mouth, deep red within, from which protruded fangs and a forked tongue. From all accounts, the creature propelled itself with its tail, leaning far forward with the long tail thrust out behind as a counterweight to the body. It was certainly bipedal."

That afternoon a crowd of sixty men armed with clubs, axes, guns, and dogs surrounded the tree and began cutting it open. The hideous thing inside slithered out, reared up on its hind legs and fled at a speed said to be comparable to a galloping horse. Most of the sixty men fled too.

But a few brave souls followed the creature until it disappeared into a hole near the Little Miami. No one was quite courageous enough to follow it into its lair so they blew up the entrance, sealing the monster inside.

But when they cleared away the rocks and dirt the monster was gone. Perhaps the creature escaped out another hole into the Little Miami for it was later sighted in Shaker Swamp, three miles west of Lebanon and also by some young lovers parked at Caesar's Creek. Perhaps this walking nightmare still stalks the wetlands around the area.[1]

THE LOVELAND FROG

If the Crosswick Monster seems too bizarre, then consider the case of the Loveland Frog. On February 3, 1972, Patrolman Ray Shockey of the Loveland Police Department was on routine patrol by the Little Miami River about 1:15 a.m. when he saw something odd in his headlights. It was a three- to five-foot leathery-skinned creature with a lizard or frog face, resembling a miniature Creature from the Black Lagoon. The thing stared at Shockey for a few seconds, then leaped over the guard rail and disappeared into the Little Miami. Patrolman Shockey duly filed a report about the strange creature. One wonders what his fellow officers thought.

But on February 10, Patrolman Mark Mathews saw the same animal on the same road. It started to hop towards him. Reacting instinctively as no doubt any of us would do when menaced by a giant frog, the officer pulled his gun and fired four shots at the beast. The thing leaped convulsively and fell into the river.

There have been reports of a large frog living in the river dating from the 1950s and in 1985 two boys said they saw a German Shepherd-sized frog by the river.[2] The creature sounds like an iguana, which while never growing more than a few inches long in North American, can grow as large as six and a half feet in Central and South America. Whether that species could survive an Ohio winter is another question. It has also been suggested that the creature was a Nile monitor lizard which lives near water and can climb trees. A teenager shot and killed a six-foot Nile monitor in a pond in Findlay in February, 1984.[3]

MEET THE DEVIL

The tree stood at the top of a hill somewhere near Route 65 in Wayne County, its hulking profile like a crouching animal, ready to pounce. One of its branches hung so low over the entire road that the men who passed that way on horseback and in wagons had to bend double or swing off the road to avoid it. Anything rather than touch that tree.

It wasn't just the hard-drinking drovers who were afraid of the tree. Even the sober had seen the headless horse waiting under its branches. The ghost horse was huge—eighteen hands high—with a ragged cavity gaping where its head should have been.

One winter's night when the tree's ice-laden branch hung low, a nervous rider had urged on his horse as its hooves clattered and slipped on the icy road. Running full speed, it had collided with the branch. When the rider awoke, he found himself staring into the frozen eyes of the horse's head.

Micky Walsh, son of Big Mike Walsh, Rogues Hollow saloon-keeper, was driving his mule team through the Hollow late one night. He was a big man like his father and not afraid of the Devil.

On most trips the mules would trot right up the hill and down the other side. But this night, a raw, moonless autumn night, they spooked and danced in their harness. And as they came to the oak tree, they stopped and stood shivering.

Micky yanked on the reins, "Giddap," he yelled. He was hungry and tired and he wanted to get home. He took out the whip and cracked it above their heads. The mules quivered, but did not move.

Then he looked up into the tree and saw what looked like the Devil himself sitting on the overhanging branch.

"Guess I just sat there and didn't move for quite a spell," he said. "I was sort of numb, just like the mules. Don't know how long I was sitting there. The mules didn't move and I didn't move. You think I'm fooling? It was the devil himself.

His eyes were gleaming like balls of fire. When I woke from a trance, the mules were standing still as before."

There was no way in hell Walsh was going to try driving his team under that branch, even if they were willing. So he turned them around and headed back down the hill and went home by the Clinton road.

Several weeks later he was in Clinton, telling some friends about meeting the Devil. They listened with interest and after a few more drinks said they'd like to meet him, too. So Micky drove them over the same road and up the same hill to the tree.

"We saw the Headless Horse under the Oak. When we got closer we saw the Devil with those bright red eyes mounted on the Headless Horse. Our team stopped short.

"Then in an instant the Headless Horse was gone in a cloud of dust. We just stood there as the hoof beats sort of faded away. I was glad that my buddies were with me and saw the same thing as I did. It kept me from thinking that I had been seeing things. The Devil was there that night riding the Headless Horse."

The tree is gone now, blown down in a hellish storm that howled out of nowhere. They say nobody would touch it, to drag it off the road, but the next day the tree was gone. But the stories of the headless horse remain. He has found another tree with an overhanging branch to haunt, waiting for it to knock the head off a rider so he can have some company.[4]

THE GHOSTLY DOG OF SPATE HOUSE

At Moscow, a sleepy little town on the Ohio River, Clermont County historian Rick Crawford pointed out the cobblestones of the old steamboat landing to Rosi Mackey, Jon Chapman, and I. Gamblers and high rollers, marquises and kings had landed here to visit Spate House.

It was a sunny day; the house stood in the shadow of its many trees. The brick around the boarded-up front door was crumbling; the front steps were covered with ivy. A butter-scotch cat prowled through overgrown bushes in the yard.

Rick showed us the row of houses overlooking the river built by riverboat captains and told us the story of a house that had been a stop on the Underground Railroad. I recalled what I knew about the history of Spate House from an article Rick had written.

The two-story brick mansion was built between 1796-98. It hosted Louis Philippe, the exiled King of France, who played cards here in the winter of 1815-1816 while, as "schoolmaster John Smith," he awaited a message recalling him to the throne of France. The house was also honored by the presence of the Marquis de Lafayette during his 1825 farewell visit to the United States.

Many less illustrious visitors also came to Spate House. Moscow's situation on the Ohio River brought travelers in search of hospitality and recreation. And those recreations— the card games that took place on the Spate House's second floor—were notorious for their questionable dealings.

Sometime in the late 1820s, one man brought his little dog and his card-sharping skills to the game. Another man brought a pistol. When the first man was caught cheating, the second resolved the disagreement by shooting him.

The house owner shook his head. His clientele had always managed to settle their arguments more quietly. This sort of thing was bad for business. He waited until dark and then he had two of his men take the body out secretly and bury it on the hillside north of the village. They also spread the story that the man with the dog had lost heavily at cards and had stalked off in anger.

Then they remembered the dog. They found the tiny red-haired animal whining and cowering under the card table. His coat was stiff with his master's blood. When they dragged him out, he must have smelled the man's scent on their hands for he started howling and barking like a hell-hound. They offered him sausages, they soothed him with, "Good dog, there's a good fellow," and finally they beat him. But he only howled louder.

In desperation the men who had buried his master bundled him into a grain sack and tied it shut while he bit and clawed through the cloth. Then they carried the squirming bag down to the Ohio River and threw it in. The dog howled until the bag grew waterlogged enough to sink.

Since then the house has been haunted. Doors creak open and shut mysteriously. People are heard moving around upstairs. The piano plays by itself. The clock restarts and resets itself.

At Halloween, 1978, Rick Crawford, his friends Lynn Maloney, Mike McMullen, and two others decided to brave the ghosts of Spate House overnight. There was no one living in the house at the time; they told no one they were going.

"We had the attitude, 'Boy, this will be fun!' Rick recalled. "It was your typical old house. There were cracks in the wall and every time the wind would blow there would be a whhooooo sound."

What was not typical were the strange cold spots that followed them around the house.

"The cold spots *were* rather bizarre. You'd be walking along, the temperature would be normal and all of a sudden it would be cold enough that you'd want to put on sweater. So you'd move to another spot. A minute or so later, it would be cold again. It was the last thing we expected. We expected to hear sounds upstairs or in the central hallway, where most of the manifestations have occurred. But nothing on the first floor."

Rick said he's known a "couple dozen people who say they've heard the dog." He emphasized, "These are not cranks. People who don't know each other have told me stories that matched up. Before I wrote my articles there were no written accounts of the Spate House hauntings, so the stories were not cribbed from anywhere else."

One woman alone in the house suddenly heard the barking of a dog upstairs. She heard the barking move down the stairs, through the front parlor where she sat, and out the front door. Then it died away at the bank of the Ohio River.[5]

As we were driving back to Xenia, Rosi asked me, "What was the story of Spate House?" We'd been so busy I had never mentioned the details of the ghost story. I told her about the gambler's murder and the woman hearing a dog barking in the empty house.

Then Rosi said, "Like that little red dog sniffing around the retaining wall as we drove away?"

"What dog? There wasn't any dog there," I said.

"Oh, come on, it was right there by the wall," she said. "It looked like a very close-cropped red-haired poodle. I remember thinking that I'd never seen a poodle that color before."

And I hadn't mentioned the color of the dog at all....

STUMPY, THE MAN-FACED DOG

In the early 1800s something strange haunted the Allen Glen area of Norwich, Muskingum County.

"Coming home from church one Sunday evening with her brothers and the neighbor's children, my grandmother felt something tugging at her dress. Her brother John often teased her in this way and she cried out, 'John, let me be,' and was surprised when John answered her from several yards ahead of her.

Peering intently she saw a dog, or what looked like a dog, move ahead, pass the others and disappear. Comparing notes they agreed it looked like a dog except it had a man's head."

The creature also frightened the cows at "Aunt Allen's" farm.

"Alone in the house and busied with some task Aunt Allen's hired girl happened to look out and saw the cows coming from the pasture to the barn or milking shed. Now cows coming into the barn in mid-afternoon is an unusual occurrence, so unusual that the girl went out to see "what ailed the critters. Driving the cows was a large dog, a dog with a man's head! Naturally one presumes the girl did not linger long to make observations, but she got a good look at it and also recalled that it looked at her with fixed gaze before their paths diverged.

"On another occasion a doctor, driving in from visiting patients and dozing in his buggy, suddenly became aware that he was not alone! Seated beside him was a large dog—a dog with the head of a man!...gazing at him fixedly [the dog] leaped...from the buggy seat and disappeared in the night. He heard a loud thump as it landed in the field."[6]

THE GHOST-WHITE WOLF

On a Hamilton County back road, late one night, Michael Berger saw something that to this day he cannot explain.

It was a very dark night, without a moon. I was watching carefully for deer as I drove, since it was common for small herds to feed in the corn fields, a sight I loved.

I had just stopped at a stop sign, had slowly begun to pull ahead, when I saw a white wolf sitting off to the right of the road. I was wide awake, as I was used to late hours, and I'd had nothing to drink. I am quite familiar with dogs of all breeds , as well as with wolves, and what I saw was *not* a dog.

It took a few seconds for the sight to register. I had just driven by it when I slammed on the brakes and froze. I couldn't move, turn around, restart the car, or anything. I just sat there shivering and looking at it.

It was large, sitting on its haunches, the top of its head was about 4.5 feet off the ground. It had the mane of a timber wolf, and its tail was curled about its feet where it sat. It turned its head to watch me drive past. And it was white—the kind of glowing soft-white that things turn when there is a full moon.

After about 10-15 seconds, the frozen feeling passed, and without turning around, I sped away.

I have since talked with the owner of the property and he assures me that he knows of no such animal in the vicinity. I drive by the spot often and each time I get a chilled feeling, a shadow of what I felt that night.

DEATH OF A PRINCE

Do all dogs truly go to Heaven? Louis Bromfield, whose dog Prince returned after his death to Malabar Farm, might have wondered.

After returning with Baby [another dog] through the storm from the high farm, I went to bed early and took a sleeping pill so that I wouldn't wake up and lie awake thinking about Prince. The place on the foot of the bed where he had always slept on an old green rug was empty for the first time since he had come there as a puppy.

Presently I fell asleep but twice during the night I was wakened, despite the sleeping pill, once by the feeling of something stirring and pressing against my leg. The feeling was so real and so intense that I thought one of the other dogs had taken Prince's place. But when I sat up and reached down, there was nothing there.

After a long time I fell asleep again only to be wakened this time by the sound of scratching on the screen door. It was exactly the sound made by Prince when, in wet weather, the door stuck and he was forced to crook his paw against the grille covering the lower part of the door and give it an extra tug. I listened for a moment and then concluded one of the other dogs had gone out and, without Prince to open the door for him, could not return. I put on the light and went to the door. The storm was over and the moon was shining high over the ravine. Outside the door there was nothing.

The two experiences were not imagined nor were
they the result of drowsiness for each time I lay awake
for a long time afterward. I do not know the explanation—save perhaps that no creature, in some ways
even a human one, had ever been so close to me as
Prince.[7]

MYSTERY CAT IN OTTAWA COUNTY

Despite their connection with witches, unearthly cats are
relatively rare. A beautiful white and grey ghost-cat has been
seen by a number of people at a Victorian mansion used as a
party house in Dayton. Phantom cats have been heard wailing
in the walls at Dayton's Sinclair Community College. (See
"Old School Spirits" in *Haunted Ohio*.) More common are
tales of mysterious big cats.

Black panthers have been reported all over the world
although the color is in fact very rare in panthers. And it
simply doesn't exist in Ohio, say the experts.

But *something* was prowling Ottawa County near Port
Clinton. Something panther-size that crept through the fields,
wailing like a cat. The creature was first seen in 1989 by
residents of Erie and Carroll townships, about twenty-five
miles east of Toledo. The animal is described as eighteen
inches high, three feet long, weighing about sixty-five pounds,
and having a long tail and a ferocious wail.

"There is something definitely out there," Sheriff John
Crosser said, who had seen the photos taken by Sheriff's Sgt.
William Windnagel in Erie Township. Several of the pictures
showed what seemed to be a large cat with a long tail. The
Sheriff's Department received reports about the animal, but,
oddly, no complaints of livestock being killed or of the animal
threatening people. An assistant county dog warden reported
watching the animal from her truck for about thirty minutes as
it wandered in a field. She said she didn't know what the
animal was, but it was certainly not a house cat or dog.[8]

Carroll and Erie Townships front on the Ottawa National Wildlife Refuge, a marshy area along Lake Erie. It is not impossible that some unusual animal could have taken refuge in the Refuge. But what does it eat?

During the spring of 1977 in Richland Township and later at Lafayette, Allen County, sheep farmers were terrified and baffled by an epidemic of sheep mauling. One man had fifty-seven sheep badly mauled in two days. Another lost nearly twenty sheep to a creature that ripped apart the gates to the sheep pen, leaving behind claw and fang marks in the wood. By mid-May 140 sheep and a number of dogs and birds had been killed by the thing. Yet while the animals were found literally torn apart, none of their flesh was eaten.[9]

Some say that these ghost-panthers are "psychic vampires," that they feed on terror. If so, then none of us, so long as we are afraid, are safe.

THE MULE WITH THE KEG OF SPIRITS

Pleasant Valley in Hocking Township is haunted by the ghost of a man riding a ghostly-white mule with a keg tied behind the saddle. The ghost rides along the road and disappears into a swamp near the old schoolhouse.

The ghost is believed to be an aged eccentric who lived on the far side of the swamp. Some evenings he rode his mule to the distillery in the valley where he spent several hours drinking and spinning tales. Then he'd strap a keg of rum behind him on the mule and ride home.

One day somebody missed the old man. The searchers followed the mule tracks into the quagmire. They could see the torn grass the man had clutched on his way down, the slashing hoofmarks where the mule had tried to find footing, and at the very edge of the quivering morass, desperate fingermarks in the mud.

Bubbles burst on the surface leaving a stink like a corpse, but searchers could find no trace of the body, probe as they might with long poles. When a sheriff's deputy nearly followed the old man to his muddy grave, they called off the search for the bodies, hoping they would surface eventually.

But they never did. On foggy nights near that swamp you can hear the mule's frantic braying and the old man's drunken cursing. Other nights you can see the old reprobate riding his luminous mule, bobbing like a will-o-the-wisp, and hear him sing, *Show me the Way to Go Home*.[10]

THE JERSEY ANGEL

Back in the 1870s an Englishman named Joseph S. Saberton bought the land which is now John Bryan Park. He never really fit in with the people of Yellow Springs, partly because he was a foreigner, and partly because he had outlandish ideas about raising cattle. He sailed back from the Isle of Jersey with the first Jersey herd ever seen in Ohio. The dainty animals with their beautiful silky coats and their long eyelashes seemed like pets, especially since Saberton had given them all frivolous names like "Flora," "Buttercup," "Betsy."

"Johnny Bull's heifers," scoffed the locals, dubbing Saberton "The Jersey Angel," but the small animals quickly out-produced the local breed of shorthorns.

Then suddenly Saberton contracted "black erysipelas," a streptoccocal infection, and died, asking to be buried in his cow pasture, near his beloved animals. He had no one to take over his herd so a sale was held to sell off the stock. Farmers came from miles around to laugh at the "midget cows," but some canny souls who had heard about the herd's milk production, quietly bought the Jerseys at a bargain price.

Saberton was buried in his pasture, but he must have been lonely for the pasture stood empty. Finally his brother came from Chicago and moved Saberton's body to a grave out west.

John Applegate and his brother Bert rented the farm. One night, two years to a day from the time Saberton's body was exhumed, the Applegates were standing on the back porch, smoking silently in the moonlight. Suddenly they heard a horseman ride by, whistling for his dog and calling his cattle.

They recognized Joseph Saberton's voice at once: "Come, Betsy, come Buttercup, go get 'em, Shep!" But they saw no one and the ghostly rider and his herd swept by

When folks laughed at his story, John Applegate walked into town and offered to swear to it before a notary. His brother Bert swore he'd heard the same thing. *They* at least believed that "The Jersey Angel" had returned—to drive his beloved cows to the greener fields of Heaven.[11]

THE RUSHCREEK MONSTER

One summer night some Lancaster men took off for coon hunting with their dogs panting out the back of the pickup truck. When they got to Rush Creek, behind Berne Union High School, they parked the truck and let down the tailgate. The dogs took off down the trail; the men followed. They could hear the dogs yelping ahead, then suddenly hunters and dogs were all mixed up as the dogs ran over the men, scrambling back to the truck as if the devil himself were after them.

The men couldn't even keep up with the dogs, they were moving so fast. By the time they got back to the truck, the dogs were cowering in the back, crying pitifully. The men couldn't coax them out of there for nothing—not blows nor biscuits. Disgusted, the hunters drove back to Lancaster.

To their surprise, the men had to coax and then drag the whimpering dogs out of the back. And under the streetlight, the men saw the giant scrape marks down the side of their truck, like something with a huge clawed hand had deeply raked the metal.[12]

THE CROOKED SERPENT

Few historians share the belief of a well-known nine-teenth-century Baptist minister who argued that Adams County's Serpent Mound was built by the Creator Himself to commemorate the site of the Fall. The small mound between the jaws represents the forbidden fruit, about to be devoured by the old serpent. In support of his claim, the minister cited Job 26:13: "His hand hath formed the crooked serpent."

But could Serpent Mound have had a living model? There are recurring stories of immense serpents in the fields around Rogues Hollow. In 1905 George Matson was driving his team of oxen in a field on the William McCloud farm. As he drove them along a track in a field of grass, they stopped and refused to go any further, lowering their heads and shaking them.

He urged the animals on, then goaded them, but they just stood there refusing to budge. Then he saw why. Beyond the team the head of an immense snake reared out of the grass, swaying, and looking at them. It seemed to Matson that the body of the snake was at least six inches in diameter with a much bigger head. He wheeled the team around and drove away, refusing to return to the field after that.

In 1918 one Anthony Paridon said he saw a path about two feet wide in an oats field like something huge had slithered through it. On May 1, 1944, William Hummel, who was home on leave from the Marines told some friends in Doylestown that he'd just seen a huge snake. They laughed at him, but he finally talked them into coming with him to the field behind the Clyde Myers home.

There they found what some described as a "huge python." It was very big. Fortunately it was dead. Around the body the tall grass was bent and broken for thirty feet where the snake had thrashed and turned in its death agonies.

The creature measured thirteen feet, six inches in length and six inches in diameter. It was displayed at a service station in Barberton, where it was supposedly photographed for the local daily papers.[13]

The reference librarian at the Barberton Library checked microfilms of their newspapers from the 1940s, but could find no trace of the old serpent. A hoax? A May Fool's joke? Or another *tulpa* case where the photographs vanished as mysteriously as the creature?

THE PENINSULA PYTHON

An equally elusive snake terrified residents along the Cuyahoga River in Summit County in 1944. On June 8, Clarence Mitchell saw an eighteen-foot snake slithering across his corn field. It left a track "the width of an automobile tire." Other farmers found similar tracks and on June 12, a woman called the fire department when the giant snake climbed over the fence to her hen house and swallowed a chicken.

The Cleveland and Columbus Zoos offered rewards for the capture of the creature—alive. A posse was formed. On June 25th, the residents of Kelly Hill hunted through the hills in search of the Peninsula Python, as it had been dubbed by the wire services, but found nothing.

On June 27th, the python slithered out of a willow tree, terrifying Mrs. Pauline Hopko and her milk cows, who broke their tethers and fled. Two days later Mrs. Ralph Griffin saw the snake reared up, man-high, in her back yard. The same day it came crashing out of a tree by the Cuyahoga River, startling a housewife who was taking out the garbage. The posse found broken branches and a trail leading to the river. Professional searchers were called in. The snake was sighted a few more times, but then disappeared, never to be seen again, dead or alive.[14]

BUCKEYE BIGFOOTS

Bigfoot has been around a long time—since Cro-Magnon times, some people believe. Nearly every North American Indian tribe had legends about hairy wildmen. We usually think of Bigfoots or "Abominable Snowmen" as haunting the remote mountains of Washington State or Tibet. Yet these hairy humanoids have been spotted throughout Ohio including Clermont, Coshocton, Franklin, Lorain, Muskingum, Richland, Stark, and Vinton Counties. Space will not permit a complete listing, but we can mention a few recent cases.

At Coshocton, a woman sleeping with her baby awoke early January 2, 1988 to see a large black, hair-covered creature with luminous red eyes staring through the bedroom window seven and a half feet off the ground.[15]

One Saturday night in August, 1972, eight residents of the Brookside Park area, just west of the Cleveland Zoo, reported seeing a "monster animal" more than seven feet tall. Officials of the zoo denied that it was one of theirs; both of the zoo's two gorillas were in their cages at the time.

The creature was described as black-haired and bigger than one observer who was six feet, three hundred and sixty pounds. It was described as standing up straighter than a gorilla. Bushes behind a fence north of the zoo were found matted down as if a large creature had pushed through. An identical creature was spotted in mid-August, 1973, at Lorain, about twenty-six miles west of the sighting above.[16]

Also in 1973, Albert Hartman of Mansfield saw an eight-foot high "shaggy-haired stinking beast with reddish glowing eyes" by his barn at 2 a.m. He fired at it. Two men cornered it and it chased them back to their cars. The thing was also seen at Oberlin and Massillon.[17]

Craig Young of Harmony Hills Stables in Columbiana County went out on a trail ride on a March afternoon with a friend. When they got to a frozen creek crossing, they saw what they thought was "a guy in a black parka fishing." When the thing looked up, it had "a flat face like a monkey, all wrinkled looking." It stuck something under its arm and ran up the hill like a man with very long arms. It stayed up on its legs too long to be a bear. The men couldn't get their horses over the creek to follow it.

Craig came home and said to his wife Nanette, "Boy if I told you what I saw, you'd commit me." Nanette and four other riders had a terrifying encounter on one of the bridle trails with what may or may not have been a Bigfoot.

"Late August, early September in 1991 we had gone out on a two-hour trail ride, when suddenly it became very dark. The horses stopped dead. We heard something, we didn't know what, coming through the woods. Whatever it was was breathing heavy; you could see the trees parting as the thing pushed them aside. We didn't hear any footsteps, like the thing was floating.

"I couldn't imagine anything that would frighten the horses so bad as to freeze them. We urged them on and finally we kicked them. They wouldn't move. Real soon that thing was going to be on top of us. It was as high as the horses' heads—past six foot. It was definitely hair-raising. Whatever it was, it was not touching the ground. I thought we were dead. Finally one of the girls screamed and that unfroze the horses. We rode so hard out of there, I thought sure one of the horses would go down. When we got back to the barn we slammed the door shut. We were lying against door; nobody said a word. I could hear my heart. And I thought, What could that have been?"

When they went back the next day, branches and shrubs were broken where the creature had come crashing through the forest.

BIGFOOT IN GREENE COUNTY?

I live in Greene County—home of rolling farmland and down-home people—not where you would expect to find a seven-foot monster. Yet one Greene County woman is certain that such a creature haunts her property.

Even though Tori Art* of Xenia was convinced I could explain the strange things happening at her house, she took a lot of coaxing to tell her story. Repeatedly she said, "I'm reluctant to talk about it because people won't understand. You're the only one who can tell me if someone else has experienced this kind of thing." She had heard me discuss the connection between Native American sites and ghosts and wondered if the Indian burials in the area might cause what she experienced. "I want to know what it is!" she insisted.

In the late summer of 1986, she and her husband and children were living in a new two-story house they had built on

ten acres near Faulkner Rd. which Tori says is "pretty isolated."

Tori and her three-year old son were asleep in the front
bedroom next to the porch. The shades were pulled down, but
it was hot, so the screened windows were open.

Suddenly she was wakened by "a growling and a chuckling with a demonic laugh at the end." She froze, terrified.
"My mind just wouldn't work. All I could think was, 'What in
the heck is this?' No spook show you saw ever came close to
it! I felt paralyzed." She managed to touch her son. "I was
afraid it was going to reach right through the window and grab
my kid. I thought if I opened the blind, that thing's face would
be right there by the screen."

Somehow Tori roused herself and ran to the living room
where her husband had fallen asleep in front of the TV. "The
sound was very very loud—loud enough to wake me up, but
Mike's a heavy sleeper," she explained. She flipped on the
porch light.

"Nothing was there. It was over that quick. My son never
did wake up. I tried to explain it away, but I felt very strongly
that it was something that was not human."

Tori told her best friend Sandra* about the weird noise.
Sandra saw how frightened Tori was, but shrugged off the
incident, thinking that Tori, who had grown up in the city, had
heard some unfamiliar country noise.

In late summer of 1989 Sandra and Tori were walking up
to the house from the barn when they both heard the very same
noise—the growling, chuckling sound—down in the woods.

Sandra turned around very slowly, her hair standing on
end.

"What in the world was that?" she asked.

"That's it! That was it!" Tori exclaimed. Then Tori asked
Sandra a very interesting question, "If you had to picture this
thing what would it look like?"

Sandra did not hesitate, "Something big and furry. Something like a bigfoot!"

Tori had been thinking the same thing. She explained to me, "When this thing made that sound again, I felt like it was big; it almost sounded like it was up in a tree. Or tall. But if it was that tall," she wonders "why couldn't I hear it when it ran away?"

That same month her son Doug* came in from feeding the dog, terrified.

"Well, Doug," she said to him "what's the matter?"

"Something's out there," he said, shaking "I'm not kidding! Something's out there! I heard it running towards me."

Tori tried to reassure him. To prove that there was nothing there, she started to go outside. The boy threw himself in front of her.

"No don't go out! Let it go!" He wouldn't let Tori go outside. That's when Tori knew he was really scared. "Doug was 13 and he was not normally a scared kid," said Tori. "He was an honor student and very truthful. He was shaking!"

Doug described the exact sound Tori and Sandra had heard—the growl and the chuckle. Tori's husband tried to convince his wife and son that it had been an animal—telling them that grey foxes and owls make strange noises, that it had to be something ordinary. But Doug stuck to his story, "No," he insisted, "it was something that ran on two feet because I could tell from the footsteps." He was so afraid that he dropped to his hands and knees, not sure if "it" had seen him. He crawled part of the way to the house then ran for it.

"Whatever it is, it hasn't hurt anybody that we know of. It must not mean any harm." Tori didn't sound entirely convinced. "Something that big would have to have been seen unless it's a phantom. [A *tulpa*?] I don't know if it's anything physical. By the sound of it you would think it is. But why was it on my porch?"

Whatever it was, its presence remains.

Said Tori, "You feel like if you turned around the 'thing' would be there. I wish I could hear it again. I think I would go and try to find out what it is. I picture that it would have these red eyes and some kind of demonic face...." She broke off sheepishly, "I'm a big talker now, but I don't know if I'd be brave enough to face it again. Sometimes I think, 'Where are you? What do you want?'

"You start to wonder if you're crazy and you want other people to hear it too. I never would have dreamed that Sandra would hear it. It was almost a relief because you know what you heard and you don't know how you can get other people to understand. The weirdest thing is the demonic laugh that comes at the end of all of it. The growl was bad enough. I wish I could tape it."

Tori admitted there is not much to go on. "How would we make anybody believe it? It all comes back to just one flat statement, 'I heard the noise.'" Then she added, "I don't know what it is. I don't have any explanation for it. But I do know it's going to be back."

8

A GASP OF GHOSTS
A creepy catch-all

The boundaries which divide Life from Death are at best shadowy and vague. Who shall say where the one ends, and where the other begins?
-Edgar Allan Poe-

A potpourri of poltergeists, a wreath of wraiths, a sheetful of spooks... Whatever you call it, these are stories that were so strange, they just didn't fit in anywhere else.

THE GHOST WHO STOPPED
THE REDS GAME

Mary James'* father-in-law hated flowers.

"Ah, you can't eat those things," he'd say good-naturedly. "You gotta plant a garden." And he did, digging up the yard next to Mary's house, just across the street from his Cincinnati home. In August of 1979, he died after a long illness.

"There were so many funeral flowers!" said Mary. "I remember thinking, 'He would have rather had onions or celery.'"

At the time Mary felt the spirit of her father-in-law near the garden. "It was like getting hit with heat. It was August, but this was like a breeze of hot wind. It wasn't scary. It just *was*."

The Monday after the funeral, Mrs. James gave Mary the remaining baskets of funeral flowers. Mary kept remembering her father-in-law's words: "You can't eat flowers." It worked on her to the point that she took the flowers and dumped them in a corner of the garden and said out loud, "Here's your flowers, you old buzzard!"

"That was the way we talked to each other," explained Mary. As soon as her husband Greg* got home from work that evening, Mary told him about dumping the flowers. About nine o'clock the same night, they were listening to the Reds game on the radio until the game came back on the TV. "A garbled voice drowned out the sounds, as if the TV and radio were dead."

The voice was neither human nor normal. It was not male or female. In an emotionless monotone it said, "I appreciated the flowers."

"There was no inflection, it was almost singsong. We couldn't figure out what had caused it. I know what CB skip sounds like—this *wasn't* CB skip. And we had never had any interference on any of our equipment before." "My husband and I lay there in bed and didn't speak for twenty minutes. Then Greg said, 'I'll bet Pop did appreciate the flowers.'"

The next Saturday, Mary said to her husband, "Greg, he's not there any more." The spirit was no longer in the garden.

"Then, slowly, Greg told me what happened on Friday. He and his father had worked together in an electrical business. When Greg went on a run for parts, he was startled to feel his father in the truck with him.

He told Mary, "I could smell Pop in the truck even with the windows open. When I came out from the parts house, he wasn't there anymore."

Greg had the feeling that his father was saying, "I couldn't get through to you [son] so I got through to Mary with the flowers."

ALPHA AND OMEGA

Mark and Kim McMillan's quaint Cape Cod house is a 1929 Sears kit home, shipped in pieces to its site in Alpha, the oldest settlement in Greene County. "There's quite a bit of history to this area," mused Kim and, in fact, the McMillans believe that they have a few pieces of history living with them.

Mark and his first wife Vicki moved into the house on a dark and stormy night in 1980. It was the perfect beginning to a nightmare. It began with things disappearing for weeks and months at a time.

"Things constantly disappeared around the house," said Vicki "Then they would reappear in places that they had absolutely no business being. Kitchen things would end up in the bathroom. My clothes would disappear; we lost the vacuum cleaner attachments. At times it really didn't make sense."

In addition, a luminous silver ball would roll around on the ceiling, shoot across the room and disappear. There were the "black veils" that "danced around like a scarf on a string. You couldn't look at them straight, only out of the corner of your eye." And ghostly figures of men and a woman.

One night Mark and Vicki had just gone to bed when Vicki asked Mark if he had turned down the furnace. He got up, turned it down, then went into the living room where he smoked about half a cigarette before he heard Vicki talking in the bedroom.

When he walked in, Vicki asked him where he'd been. Something had come into the room and sat down on the end of the bed with its back to her, the bed sinking down under its weight. She thought it was Mark.

"She spoke to me," said Mark "and I just walked out of the room. Then I immediately came back and she couldn't understand why."

A couple of months later, at the same time of night, Vicki went into the bathroom. Mark was half asleep in bed, when "the bed moved. It jumped! We had a night light on, and I could see the indentation on the bed where somebody was sitting. Then I heard a scream from the other end of the house."

When Mark ran to the bathroom, he found Vicki in hysterics.

"She was standing on the holding tank, backwards, facing the wall, yelling, 'Get it out of here!' She saw somebody standing in the bathroom right in front of her."

"He was medium height and build; middle aged," said Vicki. "He was dressed in the clothes of the early 1900s. I remember a dark coat. He had longish hair and a full beard. The figure was very plain, not transparent, but not really solid either. I saw it more than once. The first time, I was a little startled but I always had a feeling that I wasn't alone in the house. At first it bothered me, but I got used to it.

"The 'thing' sitting down on our bed happened quite a bit. That was what scared me the worst because you could see and feel that something was sitting there, but you couldn't see it. It was," she paused. *"different."*

Mark said, "I believe in our ghosts. My father passed away in 1973. He was a believer in things with no explanation. He was always curious. He always said that if he ever died, he'd come back."

Mark thinks that the silver ball is his father and "I think the [ghost] lady might have come with the house."

The lady used to own the house. In the late 1940s she fell down the back steps and broke her back. Half-paralyzed, the eighty-year old woman crawled into the front bedroom where she died.

"The only time she really appeared was at the original back steps where you enter our new kitchen," said Kim "Someone else built over the steps. We notice things in that kitchen and hall."

Things like a steel noodle pot left in the center of the kitchen floor or cabinet doors opening and closing by themselves—no mean feat since they have snap locks which require some pressure to open. One evening Kim got fed up with it all and yelled from the living room, "OK! If you're going to open the cabinet door, the least you can do is to close it when you're done!" The cabinet quietly closed itself.

Kim said that she has smelled perfume and felt a "cold presence" while standing in front of the kitchen sink, washing dishes. She could also see the outline of a large, elderly woman behind her, reflected in the kitchen window. And whatever stood behind her, it touched her. Vicki too saw a reflection of the man who in the bathroom, "just staring at me." She turned quickly, but he was not there.

When the McMillan's water main broke, the reconstruction job involved tearing down walls and rebuilding flooring.

Mark said, "I was tearing up the floor in the hall by myself about ten at night and I'd just gotten down to the original flooring. Out of the corner of my eye, I caught something in back of me."

When Mark turned, he saw "a torso from about mid stomach up. It was an older, heavy-set lady." The figure wore a ruffled white top, like something "an older person would have worn in the 1930s. She had kind of short hair, pulled back and a very hollow-cheeked face," Mark recalled "and she told me 'No!' very firmly.

"I put down my tools and got out of the hallway real quick. It was the first time I'd seen something that clear or had something speak to me." His natural reaction was to gulp and to run the other way. Then, recovering his composure, he turned back to confront her, but she was already gone.

Things disappear in the house but they also materialize. The McMillan's daughter Amy was in the house by herself one afternoon, taking a shower. She had just gotten a new Doberman puppy and had locked the dog in the bathroom with her. When she got out of the shower, she saw the dog playing with something on the floor. She shooed him away and picked it up. It was a beaded skullcap from a bridal veil made of very old, yellowed lace on a wire frame. And it didn't belong to anybody in the house.

"Where that came from, we have no idea," said Mark. "The dog didn't have it when he went into the bathroom."

Such oddities are called "apports": things that come from nowhere, like the impossible photo Mark's friend Jeff* found inside a wall.

Early in 1991, as part of the reconstruction, Mark and Jeff were tearing down the wall between the kitchen and the bath.

"The wall was sealed on top—it's plaster and lathing. Everything was out of the room and we were using hammers to break the wall down. Jeff* pulled this picture, an old Polaroid snapshot out of the wall."

When Mark's mother visited, Kim and Mark talked about some of the strange things happening in the house.

"For example, take this picture," said Mark, showing his mother the photo.

"Where did you get this?" asked Mark's mother, her voice trembling.

"We found it inside the wall."

"That can't be! This is the apartment your Dad and I had before you were born—the Van Buren Apartments in Kettering! Get a magnifying glass and look at the picture."

Mark's mother had only glanced at the photo yet she described it all, down to the figurines on the table—invisible without a magnifier.

Mark's friend Jeff,* who found the photo, loudly refused to believe in the ghost. He got locked in the bathroom. Kim explained that this was impossible. All of the doors have old-fashioned deadbolt locks with skeleton keys. "You can't close the door if the door is locked," said Kim. "It has to be first closed, then locked. Jeff couldn't get out of the bathroom!"

Kim and Mark have learned to live with their ghosts. Sometimes it scares her, says Kim, but she adds, "I don't want to say they're friendly, I just know they're not going to harm anything."

PENNIES FROM HEAVEN—
OR SOMEWHERE ELSE

Frank E. Evans of Clayton reports:

"I moved into Apartment 41 on November 1, 1990. The apartment is a standard one-bedroom Cardinal type, with two sets of apartments back to back.

"When I do something new, I take pictures to send to my sister in California. I had a little 110 camera. I took a picture of the inside and left a couple of exposures for the outside. I left the camera on the room divider and thought, I'll finish it up tomorrow.

"I watched a little TV, then got into bed and stretched out. The mattress moved like an ocean wave. It started at the foot end, went from right to left, like a giant rat was under it. It felt like it was going up about four inches. I thought, What the devil is going on here? Are there rats in here? I raised up the mattress and didn't see a thing. I got in bed, and couldn't sleep, got up for a while and went back to bed. About 3:15 a.m. I heard two women arguing but I couldn't make out what they were saying. It got louder and louder. I looked out the front window. The light in front of the apartment was shining, but there were no lights in the other apartments. When I went into the living room, the arguing sounded like it was in the utility room. I told it I wished the devil it would shut up. It did. I went back to bed a little later.

"The next morning I sat on the edge of my bed, putting on my socks. And I heard my name called four times: Fra—nk. It was some lady. I sat there with my mouth open."

Next he went out into the living room where he had left the camera on the divider.

"The camera was gone and I haven't seen it since. Years ago a woman told me that if you take pictures, the spirits don't like it, it makes them angry. I guess I must've made them mad. I told the manager I wanted to move. And I moved to apartment 71."

Then Evans began to find mysterious pennies.

"I found a penny right in the center of the table, another one right in the center of a chair, another new penny heads up, right in the center of the davenport. They were always in the center of things.

"I always look in a cup before I pour anything in it. I looked, went to pour my coffee, and there was a penny in that cup, looking up at me.

"Right now I have collected forty-four pennies and one dime—fifty-four cents. I had a choice of moving to apartment 71 or 54. 54 backed up on 41. Was my camera in 54? Maybe I was supposed to move there."

"Have 'they' given you anything else besides pennies?" I asked him.

"A headache!" he exclaimed, describing mysteriously burned-out car batteries and disappearing plates.

"I keep saying to 'them,' 'If you have something to say to me, tell me.' I think they laugh at me—holding their hands over their mouths. I get a feeling there's more than one. Yes, I do. I get real cold, like cold air coming down over you. And then someone [invisible] walks by. It's kind of weird. You feel like there's someone right there; like they're going to grab you."

I suggested that these particular spirits have it in for him.
Said Evans, "I think I'll leave when my lease comes up."

THE HAUNTED SWIMMING POOL OF STIVERS MIDDLE SCHOOL

That grey February day at Stivers Middle School of Dayton I felt like I'd stepped into a time warp. The building was brick with tall windows, like every other school built in the early 1900s. Inside, broad steps led up to a landing with stained glass windows. The woodwork was dark; the walls dingy. It was as if the light was absorbed by the walls, making it perpetually twilight inside the echoing halls.

The principal greeted me jovially, "Oh, you're the ghost lady!"

I pretended amazement, "You can see me?"

Another teacher smiled at me and said to the principal, "Who are you talking to, man?"

Chuckling, they directed me to a classroom in the basement. I was nervous but I couldn't say why. Was it the lack of light, flashbacks to my own unpleasant school days—or something in the atmosphere?

Teacher Jenifer Burns, a petite brunette woman, greeted me. She seemed enthusiastic and kind, with just the right amount of toughness to keep her group of sixty seventh and eighth graders in line. I was struck by how often she complimented her kids, by how they hugged her or just draped an arm over her shoulder affectionately.

"I used to have a room on the second floor," she told me. "I was very happy when I got this room. When I first saw it I thought, 'It's the nicest room in the building!' Then I realized nobody else wanted it. And I couldn't figure out why."

To me, it was obvious: It had something to do with the sinister square iron trapdoor set in the tan linoleum at the far side of the room. Or it might have had something to do with the coldness of the room and the breeze that swept into my face out of nowhere.

"It's always cold in here and there's always a breeze," Jenifer said, pointing to a cardboard horse that moved gently back and forth above my head. "Sometimes it gets so cold, the kids want their coats."

"It's coming from that duct back there," I said, pointing to a grating high in the wall.

Jenifer shook her head almost apologetically. "Nope. That's been sealed off and the janitor swears that nothing can get through there.

"The whole bottom floor of the school used to be an athletic complex. Sometime in the 1930s the area was divided into classrooms. Stairways that led to locker rooms are now stairways to nowhere. The swimming pool was simply built over."

The workmen laid plywood and then linoleum over the sixteen by thirty foot swimming pool. Today it is a language arts classroom bright with posters, students' illustrations, and mobiles.

Jenifer told me that "something" shifts her things around on her desk and moves them around the room. She opened the closet to show me where lights go on and off. Several times when the class was working, the TV came on suddenly, mysteriously. The TVs can be switched on at the main office, but Jenifer checked and no one had turned them on.

Jenifer asked two of the boys to lift the metal trapdoor, which I kept thinking of as a porthole. The first thing I saw was a ladder going straight down into darkness. First I felt dizzy, looking down into the black hole. And then came the mind-prickling, sickening sense that I get in the presence of the unseen.

Jenifer lowered a bare light bulb fixture into the hole and switched it on. The boys were eager to climb down to have a look, but Jenifer shooed them away. Reluctantly I stooped, craning my neck backwards to see below. It was a complete olympic-sized swimming pool, never filled in, just covered over. Its walls were made of dirty white tiles streaked with blood-red rust stains. What I could see of the floor was covered with bits of plaster and debris.

They would have to kill me before I would climb down that ladder, I thought. And I turned away as soon as I politely could. Whatever was down there was very nasty.

During the 1920s the pool was reserved for students during school hours, but teachers could swim after hours. A teacher named Mrs. Tyler* always swam on Friday. One Monday she was found floating in the pool, fully dressed, one hand clutching a broken pointer, the other holding a locket that had been torn from her neck. One of the waterlogged photos in the locket was of Mrs. Tyler's parents; the other was of a man—from the neck down. His head had been torn off.

One of the strange features of the case was that Mrs. Tyler had a senior student who always helped her. He was a quiet boy, but a good student who never missed a day of class. The Monday that they found her body, he didn't come to school. In fact he was never seen again.

"It gets cold in here when we talk about it," said one of the students, shivering.

Another raised her hand, "This year we put on *Waiting for Godot,* only we changed it to the "Ghost of Stivers" instead of Godot. After the cast party, we were waiting around for our rides home about eleven at night. We heard footsteps and rustling around inside this room. And the door was locked."

Another student who had also stayed late for a rehearsal was walking on the third floor when she kept hearing doors open and shut and then the sound of a lock. Then she heard footsteps—"high-heeled footsteps" she says—walk between the doors. When the student went to the second floor, she heard the same sounds. When she got down to the first floor, they were there too. "And I never heard it take the steps."

In 1991 just after school, NaQuan, Crystal, and Rayshawn were headed for Jazz Band practice. They were standing on the stage when they heard someone in the auditorium calling, "Rayshawn!" They looked down into the auditorium and saw "it" standing in a side aisle: a lady in white with long hair. NaQuan described her as "bright, glowing." As they watched she slowly faded away.

In August of 1989 Assistant Principal Jolene Wallace was working in a back office about 6:00 p.m.

"I was the only person in my end of the building and the doors were locked. As I was back there typing, I could hear what I thought was the principal opening and shutting the file cabinets. I called to him. He never answered me. I could still hear the drawers moving and I called to him again. No answer. I went out to look and there was no one there. 'Oh,' I thought 'he just went out as I was coming in.' So I went back and typed again and I heard the files again.

"'I thought you were gone,' I said, walking out of my office. There was nobody. Nobody anywhere. And no noise. So then I really started listening. I could hear those drawers open and close, open and close. I thought, 'Whatever it is that is out there, is going to have to *stay* out there.' I need this job. I want this job. I'm not going to be run out.' And I ignored the noises."

"Then I heard my name called. A teacher and her daughter came into my office.

"'I'm so glad you came,' I told them. And I explained about the noises.

"'Oh, it's just your imagination,' said the teacher and she teased me.

"The daughter didn't say anything. Naturally the file drawer noises had stopped. We chatted some; then I heard it.

"I said, 'Mrs. F.*, did you hear that file cabinet?'

"'No, I didn't hear a thing. It's just your imagination!' she said.

"I looked at her daughter. That child's eyes were about the size of half dollars.

"'Did *you* hear it?' I asked her.

"'Yes, m'am, I did.'

"Then they left and went to the front of the office complex. The noise never again happened up front where they were. But there were some file cabinets around the corner from where I was, and the noise moved back there. I went and looked and looked and looked. I was so nervous! Normally I'm not a nervous person; my thing is to go and look for an explanation. But that has stayed with me."

Just as the ghost of Stivers has stayed at the site of her death. If you listen closely, perhaps you can hear the ghostly lapping of water beneath the floor.

I WALK THROUGH A GHOST

The house was a small nondescript bungalow in Beavercreek. Usually I prefer to visit a haunted house without any information about the ghost, but Tammy had already told me that she had seen the former owner's ghost in the kitchen. Tammy's husband, Gary, showed me where he had removed the breakfast bar and turned the former living room into a smaller dining room and bedroom.

While he was telling me about the renovations, I paced around the kitchen. I didn't feel a thing. Uneasily I thought, "There's absolutely *nothing* here. I'm going to have to tell these nice people they're crazy..." I looked around for a place to write some notes.

"Sit down," said Tammy, ushering me into the tiny sky-blue dining room adjoining the kitchen. As I crossed into the dining room, something went wrong. I was surrounded by what felt like a buzzing current of electricity. I began having trouble breathing and concentrating. Bewildered, I turned around. I blinked to clear my vision and sat down abruptly at the dining room table. It was becoming increasingly difficult to think. I looked up at Tammy, still standing in the kitchen.

"I don't know what it is," I said, "but I just walked into it."

Tammy screamed, "That's where I saw him!"

"Here?" I panted. "You said you saw him in the kitchen."

"No, it was right there," she said, pointing to a spot just to my right. "He walked from the kitchen into the dining room and through this wall."

"I think I'll find somewhere else to sit," I said. Shaken, I moved to the breakfast bar along the wall in the kitchen. Gary brought me a Pepsi and I tried to recover my breath while I took notes. Tammy and Gary were gleeful about this independent confirmation of their own experiences. Their words tumbled out, interrupting each other in their eagerness to tell their story, to verify that they weren't crazy.

Rudy* built the house in 1957. Tammy and Gary moved there in April 1990, but didn't notice anything—"or admit it to ourselves," said Tammy, until the end of their first summer in the house.

The first strange thing was the lights. Tammy would leave the bathroom light on, then find it off. Then the same thing would happen with the kitchen *and* the bathroom light.

"And the switch would actually be flicked," said Gary, adding that he'd installed brand new switches when they moved in.

Then the family experienced a mysterious odor like "overripe cantaloupe," which nobody could account for because the only fruit in the house was apples. The odor was so strong and pungent even the dog sniffed at it. Then it went away.

Next Tammy heard a jingling sound coming from her daughter's empty bedroom—"like a guy putting his hands in his pockets, jingling his keys and change."

She got up and looked down the hall. It was pitch black in her daughter's room. Uneasily Tammy sat back down, then heard the jingling sound again. As she peered down the hall, suddenly the lights went on in the dark bedroom. Tammy was terrified but she made herself walk down the hall to that room to make sure nobody was there. She turned off the lamp and jiggled the wires. The lamp stayed dark.

Not satisfied with rattling his change, the ghost rattled his chains as well, making noises like a chain being dragged along the siding or like their dog's chain collar. He also made noises like running footsteps.

But he didn't put in an appearance until December, 1991. It came at 9:45 p.m. on a Tuesday night. The children were in bed. Tammy was watching *Coach* in the recliner in the family room while Gary laid on the floor. Christmas lights outlined the door into the kitchen, but the rest of the house was dark.

Shivering at the memory, Tammy said, "I don't know why, but I looked towards the kitchen. I saw a person walk through this chair." She patted it. "He was encircled with white smoke like steam coming off a road. I could see that it was a man by the build even though I couldn't see the face. It was almost like he'd been there for a while, just waiting for me to look at him. Then he moved. I couldn't see any feet. He hung about a foot off the floor. He just glided through the chair into the wall and a mist came up."

Tammy stared, frozen, then exclaimed, "I just saw Rudy in our kitchen."

Gary was skeptical. He watched Tammy pace the floor, nervous and shaking, and "he knew I wouldn't act that way for no reason. I couldn't even hold anything, I was so shaky!"

Gary suggested Tammy might have seen car headlights shining into the dining room. They waited for cars to pass, but when they did, the lights shone into a far corner of the room.

"That's not what I saw," said Tammy firmly. She believes that she saw the ghost of Rudy who died of a heart attack in the kitchen.

Gary shook his head. He isn't sure what he believes about their ghost. Only two things have happened that he couldn't explain: A floor fan moved itself around in their bedroom while they slept. And their small kitchen clock, although its batteries were dead, has restarted and reset itself to the correct time.

"I'm eighty percent convinced," Gary said, and smiled. "Until something sails across the room, I can't believe in it one hundred percent."

If the presence *is* Rudy, Gary wonders what he wants. "I sit out in the family room nights watching for him. I even say to him, 'Goddammit, Rudy, if you want to talk to me, I'll listen. Tell us what you want. I'm listening.' He never speaks."

THE GHOST BLIMP

Before her retirement in the early 1980s, thousands of people saw the *America*, the flagship of the Goodyear blimp fleet hovering at football games. But few of them realized that she was built around the remains of an earlier Navy airship, the L-8, built in Akron, also known as "The Ghost Blimp."

On August 16, 1942, the L-8 lifted off from Treasure Island, San Francisco on a routine training mission. She carried her pilot, Lt. j.g. Ernest D. "Bill" Cody," and Ensign Charles E. Adams, maintenance officer. Both men were considered to be among the most experienced blimp operators in the Navy.

Aviation Machinist's Mate Riley Hill, 18, had begun the flight that morning, but, just minutes before take-off, Cody ordered him to leave the aircraft, giving no explanation. Hill jumped out onto the runway, closed the door behind him, and watched the L-8 take off. When he last saw her, she was flying smoothly at about 700 feet. At 7:42 a.m. Treasure Island got its last radio transmission from the L-8. Lt. Cody reported, "Am investigating suspicious oil slick—stand by." And then silence.

Four hours later Walter Herdtle of San Francisco was driving home when he saw the airship limp by, her bag partially deflated. He also noticed an officer with a white officer's cap looking out of the gondola window "like he wanted to see what was underneath the gondola."

Police and fire units sounded their sirens to clear the way for the blimp which drifted through the streets of Daly City like a huge blind whale. Mrs. Ethel Appleton was in her home on Bellevue Avenue when "she heard what sounded like "heavy chains dragging across the roof." Then the room darkened and she smelled gasoline fumes. "When Mrs. Appleton looked out the window she saw the entire sky filled with a big airship that had perched...on her roof. The blimp made a short hop and pushed its way through a power line, sending huge crackling sparks into the air." Mrs. Appleton's neighbor William Morris looked out of his window "just in time to see his 1928 Dodge disappear beneath the envelope of the airship." The L-8 was down.

Frantic fireman chopped holes in the envelope, mistakenly trying to prevent a Hindenburg-type explosion. The rumor spread that they were looking for men trapped inside. One of the firemen climbed inside the gondola. The door was latched open and "the safety bar, normally used to block the open doorway was not in place."

A pilot's cap lay on the instrument panel. The ignition switches were turned on, the gasoline valves were open and there appeared to be plenty of gasoline in the fuel tanks. Yet the engines were stopped—as though they had stalled. Three parachutes, one life jacket and a rubber life raft..were still inside....[there was] nothing amiss in the interior of the airship, nothing broken or spilled, nothing out of place. There was neither blood nor bullet holes nor the smell of gunpowder from the airship's machine gun. Everything was exactly as it should have been with the exception of the crew."

Cody and Adams had vanished. No life vests, clothing or bodies ever surfaced, although two of the three life vests and two float lights were missing. A year after the incident, Cody and Adams were declared dead.

The Navy salvage crew found "no shell holes in the gondola or the envelope, no evidence of structural failure, no stress from the weather, no evidence of loss of control, and no evidence of any emergency situation aboard the blimp. There seemed to be no logical reason for the engines to have stalled." The radio was on and working; the exterior loud speaker on the L-8 had been switched to the "standby" position as if the crew had been speaking with someone outside.

Had a Japanese submarine shanghaied the crew? (L-8 was part of Airship Patrol Squadron 32, which was detailed to warn of impending Japanese attacks on the west coast.) Were they captured by a UFO? One theory suggested that the men had a score to settle over Cody's wife and had fallen to their deaths over the ocean although Mrs. Cody insisted that she had barely known Adams.

The Ghost Ship was brought back to Ohio by Goodyear. They test flew her and found nothing amiss. They renamed her *America* and she was the star of many football games until she was retired to a hanger just outside Akron where her ghostly grey gondola sits, shorn of her envelope, her wings clipped. If you have extra keen sight, perhaps you can see the ectoplasmic envelope hovering above her, feel her plotting, waiting for the chance to break free again and soar off to join her pilots somewhere beyond the clouds.[1]

A *REAL* JAYCEE HAUNTED HOUSE

This is the story that something or someone didn't want told. Twice it erased itself from my computer—hard disc and backup. When I sent a draft of the story to Tom*, who told me the tale, I joked that he should xerox it before he sent it back because of the trouble I'd had. Tom travels a lot and after correcting the story, handed it to a hotel desk clerk to mail. It disappeared in the postal system somewhere between here and Missouri.

In real life Tom is a salesman for a plastics company. After dark, he used to design and build haunted houses for the Dayton-area Jaycees. He has even won the coveted "Mr. Haunted House" award for his work.

Said Tom, "This particular haunted house was up by Hara Arena. We rented it from the Rattigan family from 1982 to 1988 when the house mysteriously burned down. Somehow a rumor got started that Great-grandpa Rattigan didn't believe in banks and kept all of his money in an upstairs room. One night a robber broke in. When Rattigan woke up, the robber panicked, grabbed an ax, and chopped off the old man's head. The head and the fortune are still in the house with old man Rattigan guarding both. As usual, the story kept expanding until it was unbelievable. But there were still strange things that went on at the house.

"Barry Hobart, 'Dr. Creep' of the old Dayton TV show, *Shock Theatre* came out to the house in his Creepermobile a couple of times. He claimed that he could 'feel some unwanted force, angry that we were there.'

"Everybody always lost things in the house. I was working there one night, went away for half an hour, and my hammer disappeared. I thought that I must have carried it upstairs, but it was lost for good. I lost four or five hammers in six years at that house.

"There was a twenty-foot deep well in the basement, just a hole in the cement floor. In 1982 we put a cobwebby papier-mache skeleton in the well, positioning him so he looked like he was trying to climb out. We put a strobe with a slow beat over the well and it really looked like the skeleton was moving!

"We forgot about taking the skeleton out of the well until January 1983. When we finally remembered, we turned on the house lights and walked through the house. None of the strobe lights, which we use when the house is in operation, were on. Parts of the house were pitch black.

"In the basement we climbed down into the well. The skeleton was falling apart from the humidity. We were laughing at how dumb we were to have left it in the well so long. Then we looked up and saw that the black light above us was on. We couldn't figure it out. We'd only turned on the house lights, which are ordinary light bulbs on a different circuit from the running lights—the strobes and black lights.

"'You must've turned it on by accident,' I told my friend.

"We went upstairs and found *all* of the strobe lights on and *all* of the house lights off. The switches were inside an electrical box that was upstairs by the staircase. Not an easy thing to find."

They groped their way to the electrical panel and found that the running light switches had been flipped.

"We searched the whole house, but nobody was there. The front door was shut and we had left it open. When we returned to the basement, the house lights were still on above the well, but nowhere else in the house. We never did figure that out.

"In 1987 two of the guys were kind of fooling around, nailing a cross to a wall. One of the men swore that on his backswing (with the hammer *behind* him) the hammer head broke, or was ripped off the handle, flew forward, and hit him square in the chest. They freaked out and ran out the door, leaving all the lights on. At the next meeting we gave them an award for the biggest lie. Most of the guys didn't really think they were making it up, but it was fun to have something to tease them about.

"After the season the guys were always going to spend the night in the house. But nobody could ever stay a whole night there. They always found an excuse to leave. Then a year or two later they'd say, 'Weren't you scared at the house that time? I was!'

"It always surprised me that it was so cold in the house all the time. It could be seventy degrees outside and you'd have to wear a long-sleeve shirt to be comfortable. "One August night in 1986 I had to go over to the house to collect my Dad's sawhorses. My friend Dan's* wife, Sylvia* was psychic.

She'd heard the stories about the house and wanted to visit. The minute we opened the house, it was cold. Just stepping across the threshold was like walking into a walk-in freezer. Sylvia immediately thought that there was something wrong.

"My Dad's sawhorses were in the basement so we went downstairs. I grabbed the sawhorses. Then we heard three or four footsteps above our head and a big thump like a door slamming. Sylvia started to freak out.

"'We contacted him, he doesn't want us here!' she cried."

Then it got even colder.

"*Too* cold, *too* fast," said Tom. "Outside it was eighty-five degrees with lots of humidity—a typical August night. Inside the house I had goosebumps and we could see our breath.

"'Let's get the hell out of here!' I said."

He fumbled with the locks to the back door and they all fled into the warm night. Then Tom discovered that he'd left the sawhorses in the basement.

"Dan refused to go with me, so I went back in, got the sawhorses, and came back out. Then I remembered that the only way to lock that back door was from the inside. I had no flashlight, no lights. 'Dan, go with me,' I said. 'Noway,' he said."

Tom couldn't leave the house open, so he braced himself and went back into the house one more time. He locked the back door. Then he turned and faced the darkness.

"I grabbed a two-by-four, thinking 'there's a bum in here!'"

Tom groped his way up the steps, spooking at every noise.

"I was really shaking. I had never felt it that cold!" As he reached the first floor the chill eased off so he couldn't see his breath any more. The darkness seemed to reach out for him, but he made it to the front door. It was shut. He hadn't shut it. He got the door open and stumbled out into the hot summer night. Humidity had never felt so good.

"I still thought it was our overactive imaginations, or some kind of coincidence, or some cold blast out of the well. The only thing that makes me think differently is all the things over the years taken cumulatively.

"People were totally terrified in this house! I've built scarier houses, but we had to build an addition on the maze and they were lined up a quarter mile down the street. We were turning people away! We've never had this happen before or after.

"I always stood at the exit and listened to people's reactions to see if they would mention something that I didn't put into the house. I never heard anything. I kept thinking maybe Old Man Rattigan would pop out of a corner—it'd be the perfect cover for a ghost—he'd have a little fun and people would think 'what an awesome effect!'"

THE INVISIBLE TOUCH

At the Beavercreek house I fought several curled-up cats for a spot on the sofa, while Ellen, an engaging woman with fluffy blond hair, told me her story. As she talked, a rag throw rug in the kitchen began to slither across the floor. My heart jumped. Then I leaned to the right and saw the cat doing an excellent imitation of telekinetic movement with the rug.

Ellen's tiny two-bedroom cottage was crammed with antiques: country cupboards stacked with quilts, oak china cabinets and writing desks. Bits of lace, sunbonnets, vintage baby clothes, and everywhere rabbits—china, pottery, metal, stenciled, and painted. The air was scented with simmering potpourri. Ellen shares this friendly house with her twenty-four year old son, four cats, one dog, and a ghost who impressed me as an immature fifteen-year old boy who liked playing tricks. She moved into the house in February of 1991 in the aftermath of a traumatic divorce. From the start there were strange noises in the night.

"For a long time, I thought it was the cats. But one night when I was in bed, something in the basement went 'BAM BAM!' I said to myself, 'What is going on with these cats?

They're going nuts!' I sat up in bed and counted cats—all four of them were there in the bedroom with me.

"I heard, 'BAM BAM!' in the basement again—like somebody beating on the furnace with a pipe. '*That* was not the cats!' I told myself.

I suggested that furnace noises are sometimes startling in a new house.

Ellen smiled, "The furnace was dead when I moved in. We used the Buck stove for heat and didn't fix it until this year. This spirit enjoys *big* bangs. But the ghost comes and goes. Nothing's happened in quite a while." Something bumped in the basement. "The furnace!" we said in unison.

One night Ellen was sitting with her son's fiancee on the couch. Suddenly from the kitchen came the sound of plates smashing rhythmically on the floor: break, fall, break, fall....

"Kendra went left into the dining room. I went right into the kitchen. There was nothing there, but it sounded like a whole cupboard had gone. I looked at her and said, 'Kendra, you know I'm getting sick and tired of this.'

Kendra looked sheepish. "Mom, there's something I should have told you. This house is haunted." Kendra told Ellen that her sister Mary, who had lived in the house for ten years heard a *ton* of noises. She always felt something was watching her.

"Once she was crouched over, changing her child on the bathroom floor when something tapped her on the shoulder three times—attention-getting taps. Ellen has also had a tap on the shoulder, and a more familiar caress.

"I was unfolding the blankets at the end of my bed and I was laughing and playing with the cat when something stroked my left hip. I stood straight up. My goodness, was this my little spook? I thought. It was like the cat and I were having so much fun, it just had to get in on it.

"Another time when I was in bed and my arm was above the covers, something rubbed my left arm very lightly. I dove under the quilt! Then I said to myself, This is stupid, I'm not going to let this bother me. All the same, it was kind of a difficult night to go to sleep."

The most terrifying touch came early in the morning in February of 1992.

"I was sound asleep and something woke me up. I was lying there very quietly on my stomach with my fist balled up in front of my face when I realized that my sheet was slowly moving back and forth. Three times the sheets and two antique quilts crawled over my body. One of the cats would have had to have been on each corner to make it happen.

"Just as I was beginning to think I ought to scream, a hand suddenly grabbed my hand and kind of pulled on it and wiggled it back and forth for about ten seconds, like it was trying to wake me up or get my attention. I thought I would come unglued!

"I knew what it was and I moaned like I was disturbed and I rolled over. There was not a cat in my bedroom—and there's always a cat in my room—and no spook that I could see. And I haven't slept well since.

"The following Thursday my cousins called and I told them about the ghost. When I got off the phone, I knew it was standing there, listening. I felt kind of silly, but I just said to the air in the kitchen, 'Please don't scare me again. I didn't like it and I don't want you to scare me again.'"

But the noises continued, like the slow footsteps that paced through the kitchen and dining room at five in the morning. "It was walking around like it was bored or thinking—not quick or purposeful. This went on for about ten minutes."

She now talks back to her ghost. One day as she was in the basement ironing, she heard a sound "like a slab of something hitting the cement, a wall falling down or a pool table taking the plunge!" She set the iron down firmly and said, "All right, we know *that* wasn't the cats, *don't* we?"

The cats also figured in an unusual photograph. In January of 1992, Ellen shot several pictures of her cats to finish up a roll. One of them shows an "extra" that looks like a pink ribbon in a spiral. It is not a real ribbon: it is transparent and runs over and under the cats' whiskers.

The photo was taken with a thirty-five millimeter camera, using an automatic flash. It was developed at the Kettering Meijer store. None of the other photographs on the roll have anything strange about them.

"It looks like a haunted ribbon," said Ellen.

It does indeed. On part of it, there are holes that form a weird face with slanted eyes and a pouty mouth. Ellen tried to print more copies from the negative. None of them showed the ribbon. I was only able to get more copies by getting a new negative made from the original.

"Do you ever think of moving?" I asked her.

"Let's just say I'm considering it. I stay very alert all the time."

She also goes around the house singing *Amazing Grace*.

"Listen," she has told the spirit. "if you're in this house, you're going to find out that I'm good, religious person and we're going to have some fun."

"At first I was scared to death. Then I realized that it was a silly ghost [as opposed to a hostile one.] I keep a good attitude. Of course, a few hymns don't hurt either." She laughs. "Maybe my voice will scare it away."

9

DEATH ROW
Haunted jails and
law-enforcement ghosts

Each in his narrow cell for ever laid....
-Thomas Gray-

Think of a prison, its walls echoing with curses, prayers, or the ravings of madmen. Think of the deaths—the smoking corpse in the chair or the homemade knife in the throat. Then think of the violent deaths that the police confront every day of their careers. If madness and violent death produce ghosts, every jail, every police officer must be haunted.

DEATH AND THE MATRON

In some ways, Eula Bonham, matron at the Summit County juvenile detention home, is the ideal employee. She opens and closes windows, turns the TV, radio, and lights on and off, types her reports, and makes her rounds. But this conscientious employee receives no paycheck. She's been dead since November 27, 1955.

Employees at the facility have circled that date on the front desk calendar as if to mark their belief in the ghostly matron. Many of them have personally experienced inexplicable phenomena like the deputy who had a slice of pizza levitate out of her hand, a pen fly out of her pocket, and her cigarette, smoldering in an ashtray on the table, dumped unceremoniously onto the floor. One could almost hear the matron scold, "No smoking in the building!"

Mrs. Bonham, 59, had been a matron at the detention home for sixteen years when she was brutally murdered during an escape attempt by a group of nine girls. When she entered their room, the girls jumped her from behind, tied her up with their belts and stuffed a washcloth soaked with ammonia down her throat. She suffocated instantly.

Despite her appalling death, jail employees and inmates believe that Mrs. Bonham is a friendly spirit, not one out for revenge.

"She's a good ghost," said a deputy. "I feel good she's here. She watches over us."

One inmate said, "I think she is a very nice ghost. She just wants everybody to know she's here."

And letting people know "she's here," she does, by levitating forbidden cigarettes, breezing by people in the corridors and the cellblocks, and continuing to be the most conscientious—dead—employee she knows how to be.[1]

HOME SWEET HOMICIDE

Paul McNeely had a reputation in Coshocton as a hard worker, a good father and provider, a sensitive, well-liked man. But he had a dark side: McNeely had spent time in prison for armed robbery back in the 60s and he drank too much. His wife finally walked out on him early in July, 1976. McNeely spent the day of July 19 drinking and brooding over his crumbling world.

As McNeely was weaving homeward, Officer Sanford Stanley Jr. stopped him and gave him a warning. It was the final humiliation. McNeely had never liked Stan. Now, smarting from his losses, McNeely went home and got a shotgun, a rifle, and a revolver. Then he walked into the City of Coshocton Police Department, where he shot Sanford Stanley Jr. once through the heart with the shotgun and once with the revolver. Stan staggered out the front door as McNeely fired twice more. He collapsed in front of the police station and died shortly afterward at Coshocton County Memorial Hospital.

McNeely only got as far as the alley beside the police station. There he was arrested on the charge of aggravated murder of a police officer while on duty—a charge which could mean death in the chair.

Seventy police cruisers accompanied Stan's funeral procession to the cemetery. The day they buried him was sunny—until taps sounded over his grave. Suddenly dark thunderclouds boiled up out of nowhere and lightning split the sky. His friends figured it was Stan's way of saying he really hated to go.

Stan knew Becky Stockum from seeing her on the job at the hospital. He was also a good friend of her sister Chavonne's boss. The patrolman was a kind of father-figure to the two girls. Stan would sometimes call Becky at work and tell her to "get the brat"—meaning Chavonne who was less than half his age—and both of them would join him at the L&K Restaurant after they got off work.

"We were younger, but we were also brats. He was a cop and so big—I just felt safe with him around. He'd give us his stern cop-look if Chavonne and I were riding Main Street later than he thought we should be. He always watched out for us. He checked up on people we ran around with and made me promise I wouldn't speed any more."

When Becky's husband Buck told her that Paul McNeely's house was for sale, she was instantly repulsed by the idea of buying *anything* that belonged to the murderer of her friend. How could she do something that would benefit her friend's killer? she asked her husband. Buck countered that the *house* didn't have anything to do with what had happened. Becky gave in.

The moment she saw it, she fell in love with the "little doll house" as she called it. It did seem like a doll house with only four rooms, white paint and black shutters. McNeely, who was an expert bricklayer, had recently redecorated the house in her favorite colors. It seemed like an omen.

Buck and Becky bought the house and moved in at the end of October— just as McNeely was being tried for Stan's murder—the first time. The trial ended in a mistrial. And suddenly things began happening in the house.

One December night Becky and a friend who also worked the 3 to 11 p.m. shift were relaxing in the living room. Sitting on the living room floor, they heard footsteps creaking hollowly across the wooden front porch. They waited. Nobody knocked and they didn't hear anyone walking away. They looked at each other. Finally they got their nerve up to switch off the living room light and look out the window. There were no footprints in the smooth snow that had drifted over the porch.

Another morning when Becky was in bed, she heard the back door open and footsteps on the kitchen floor. She assumed it was her husband and called out to him. No answer—and no more footsteps. She was baffled. It all seemed so real. Then she heard a clicking noise—a familiar sound, but one she couldn't quite place.

Becky called her sister Chavonne to tell her about the incident. She was trying to describe the noise, when she heard it again. It was her sister at the other end of the line, flicking her lighter open and shut, open and shut.

Then Becky remembered. "Chavonne and I had given Stan a lighter engraved 'To our favorite pig—[signed] The Brats' He had a habit of flicking the lighter open and shut as he talked."

Becky says, "I never saw anything in the house. I only heard things I couldn't explain." She decided any ghost who felt so "friendly" must be Stan and she took to talking to him, feeling that he was a protective spirit—as he was in life. Was Stan haunting his killer's house because he was worried that McNeely might try to return?

In April, 1977 McNeely was tried again and sentenced to death on July 19, 1977, exactly one year after the murder. The day of McNeely's sentencing, all of the noises in Becky's

house stopped. Officer Sanford Stanley Jr. had seen justice
done and could rest.

DEATH ROW

The first man to be hanged for murder in Greene County
was a fellow named Ramsbottom who cut his wife's throat in
the kitchen of their Fairfield home. The night before the
hanging, some last-minute visitors gave him a plug of his
favorite Cavendish chewing tobacco. When a pompous thrill-
seeker in his best white Sunday shirt marched in and demanded
to see Ramsbottom, the murderer just chewed thoughtfully and
then let fly. The tobacco hit the man in the eye and ran all over
his nice shirt. Ramsbottom was still laughing when he
mounted the scaffold with a plug of Cavendish in his pocket.

Thirty years later a farmer named McCaslin was accused
of shooting his neighbor near Ludlow, now Yellow Springs.
Looking for evidence, the sheriff found a wad of paper used to
ram home the charge of buckshot. It had been torn from a
McGuffey reader—perhaps the same torn McGuffey reader
that the sheriff found in McCaslin's home. On this slight
evidence, they lodged McCaslin in the same cell Ramsbottom
had occupied.

McCaslin was a nervous sort, but he had a pretty good
alibi and swore he was innocent. The deputies worked him
over a couple of times and pointed out the irony of his occupy-
ing Ramsbottom's old cell. Funny coincidence, wasn't it? But
maybe if he confessed everything, he might not have to swing...

They left it at that and left him sitting in the dark, in
Ramsbottom's old cell.

The next morning the turnkey found his blackened-faced
body hanging by a strip of bedsheet from his cell door. A
scribbled note said, "Ramsbottom, I'm coming."

Had the dead murderer returned to his old cell, laughing
and luring McCaslin to follow him with a tempting chaw of
tobacco?[2]

DEATH MAKES HIS ROUNDS

Chuck*, a night watchman at Dayton's Sinclair Community College blinked and looked again. Head of Security Chief Quimby* had just gotten off the elevator and was walking into his office. This wouldn't have been anything unusual except that the Chief had died suddenly the week before. Dazed, Chuck followed the figure, which looked as real and solid as a living man. He had to unlock the door to the Chief's office to get in; the office was empty.

For months after that the Chief continued to show up for work. After the initial shock wore off, somehow this didn't surprise his subordinates who said that Quimby had practically lived at the campus.

One evening Allan*, a night watchman, who was never one to kid around, said Chuck, saw Quimby walk right through the wall into the cafeteria. It was an alarming experience, but eventually the reason for the visitations became clear. Several watchmen reported that the Chief had come to give them a message.

Said Paul*: "Chief Quimby came. He touched me on the shoulder to tell me that he was all right and we didn't need to worry about him any more."

Quimby had taken Paul under his wing and helped him get a full-time position in security. Paul was touched that the Chief continued to look out for him even after the man's untimely death. After that appearance, the Chief apparently retired, because his ghost hasn't been seen since.

THE HAUNTED HALFWAY HOUSE

The Drury mansion in East Cleveland, a fifty-two room, half-timbered mansion built in 1912 looks like a set from a Christopher Lee movie. There is a broad center stairway with carved newel posts, towers that loom over an interior court, miles of twisting corridors with unexpected rooms opening off of them, even a tunnel that runs under Euclid Ave. to the Drury

Theater, built in 1914. Francis Drury, a Cleveland industrialist who made his fortune in cast-iron stoves, built this ostentatious house of horrors for his family. It has been a boarding house, then a home for unwed mothers. In 1972 it was leased to the Ohio Adult Parole Authority by the Florence Crittenden Foundation as a halfway house for convicts.

Hardened criminals and police alike have been terrified by the ghostly goings-on. Two special-duty police officers were assigned to guard the empty building in 1972. They spent the night back to back, clutching their shotguns. "They were scared witless," said the Superintendent of the Center.

What is so frightening about the house, other than the usual creakings and groanings of an eighty-year old structure? Doors drift open by themselves; sash windows open and close without help. Inmates and staff have sworn that they have felt people walking through the building. When the premises are searched, no one is ever found.

In 1978 a counselor actually saw a ghost. Around 3 a.m., he saw a woman standing on the main stairway. Her hair was swept up on top of her head in a knot. She wore a long brown skirt, like someone from the turn of the century. The counselor saw the same woman once more, at roughly the same time of night, outside the kitchen door.

There could be explanations for the windows and doors opening and closing by themselves: the expansion and contraction of aged wood might make the stairs creak like footsteps, might free sash weights to move by themselves. But what in the world, or out of it, can explain the figure of the woman on the stairs? Perhaps she too finds it a halfway house, a stopover on her way to wherever ghosts go.[3]

THE GATES OF HELL

If any jail is haunted, it should be the Ohio State Penitentiary in Columbus. The grey stone walls loom over their surroundings, casting shadows even on dark days. Inside the walls, prison buildings decay in silence. A pile of paint chips like a snowdrift lies against one building. Rust has eaten through a metal door. In some of the cells you can still see graffiti scrawled on the walls by convicts long dead and long forgotten. On April 21, 1930 Easter Sunday, some disgruntled inmates set several fires, thinking to escape in the confusion. The cellblocks quickly filled with choking black smoke, fed by a heavy tarpaulin covering one of the roofs. Later it was whispered that the authorities deliberately delayed unlocking cells until it was too late for many. Over three hundred convicts died. Old photos show the bodies laid under sheets in the exercise yard like rows of graves.

The penitentiary has stood empty for many years while public officials debate what to do with it. Suggestions have included a shopping mall or a tourist attraction. One retired state highway patrolman who was a guard at the Ohio State Penitentiary in 1930 reacted angrily to the last suggestion.

"I wouldn't care if they dynamited the place," he said. "It's the entrance to Hell itself. I can't tell you what is there and what is seen and unseen." Then he caught himself and said, more subdued, "It's just a bad place."

Some say that the cell blocks are still haunted by the men who died there. Some say that if you stand in the yard and listen, you can hear the distant roar of flames, the shrieks of men burning alive in their cages.

THE VAMPIRE OF THE OHIO STATE PEN

His name is listed in the records as James Brown but they called him "The Bloodsucker." His story begins in 1866 somewhere in the Indian Ocean, on the whaler *Atlantic* out of New Bedford. Brown was found in the hold of the ship cradling the body of a shipmate, lapping the fresh blood from the man's broken skull. The body of another sailor lay nearby, drained of blood—at least that was the story allegedly told by his Portuguese shipmates at his trial for murder.

Brown admitted the killing in a letter to "your Excellency. Sire. President Cleveland," but there is no mention of

vampirism. Brown was cook on the *Atlantic* and had been
ordered by Captain Frank Wing to keep close watch on the
rations. When another sailor, James Foster, demanded more
food, Brown tried to explain that he couldn't give him any
more.

> Foster said to me I will also make you obey me. I
> then said to him it will be a very cold day [in Hell,
> before I obey you]. There and then he struck me with
> a belaying pin on the back of my neck. I fell to the
> deck when I got up he struck me again. I saw the
> blood running on my shirt. I said to him what do you
> mean he struck me the third time. I then stabbed him
> with my knife. I was then put in irons and the next
> day the carpenter made a coffin and the deceased was
> buried on the island of Raudriedge for we were
> cruising along that island.

Brown pleaded for the court to wait until the ship's captain
returned. "The men who have testified against me," he said,
"speak only Portuguese. Wait, I beg you, until an English-
speaking witness arrives."

But the court refused and condemned him to death. The
sentence was commuted to life imprisonment by President
Andrew Johnson. Perhaps Captain Wing returned in time after
all.

Brown spent his first years in federal prison in Massachusetts where he was a thorn in the side of prison officials. He
had a violent temper and the strength of the deranged. He was
transferred to the government insane asylum in Washington,
after he became "melancholy."

Cured by his stay, Brown was sent back to Massachusetts,
much to the dismay of the prison's warden who wrote to the
federal authorities,

> Is it not possible that the order returning James
> Brown can be revoked or that he can be sent to some

other prison? His often expressed hatred of Massachusetts and all of its officers...makes me think that this
prison would be more likely to excite him than one
where the surroundings are new—...I do not think it
safe to put him into the Shops with other men as there
is a greater fear of Brown's treachery among the men
than the officers of the prison...the bearer of this letter
will tell you of his disposition if you should bring him
on, which I shall greatly deplore.

Despite this appeal, Brown was sent to Massachusetts.
There he killed at least one fellow prisoner; wounded several
others. The governor got him transferred to the Ohio Penitentiary in Columbus.

His Ohio Penitentiary file describes him as a "dark-
complected negro," illiterate—and "Intemperate"—meaning he
was a drinker. Just what he drank is not specified. A brother
living in British Guiana is listed as next of kin. Under "Identi-
fying Marks" there is a drawing of a tattoo on his right forearm.
It looks like a crudely drawn heart pierced by a snake.

Brown's temper did not mellow in Columbus. He was
taunted by the other inmates who hissed, "bloodsucker" at him
as he shuffled sullenly in the exercise yard. He killed three
other men, in separate incidents and became notorious for his
screaming rages which took several men to subdue. Ten days
in "the dark cell"—a cold, slime-walled coffin of stone—on
bread and water did nothing to convince him of the error of his
ways. Instead, he fell again into melancholy. Authorities sent
him back to Washington—this time forever.

According to an article in the second edition of the
Washington Evening Star, June 25, 1895, titled "A Murderous
Maniac":

To-day the fast mail train on the Baltimore and
Potomac railroad brought here a prisoner from the
Massachusetts State's prison for admission to the
government insane asylum. His name is James

Brown, a Portuguese negro, who, in 1865, killed his
captain at sea and drank his blood from the cloven
skull. He was tried and convicted in the United States
Court in Boston and sentenced to death, but in 1867
his sentence was commuted to life imprisonment.
Since that time he has committed no less than twenty-
six murderous assaults on fellow-prisoners and on
officials of the prison. Visitors who have curiously
peered into the iron room have instinctively likened
him to a tiger in a menagerie. A few days ago, much
to the relief of the warden, an order was procured for
Brown's removal to the government insane asylum at
Washington and last night United States Marshal
Banks and his deputy, Galloupe, started with him. The
prisoner was closely ironed, and in addition, his arms
were pinioned behind him. He was met at the depot
here by parties who had the necessary papers for his
admission to the insane asylum from the Interior
department and he was at once taken to his new place
of abode.

The Government Hospital for the Insane *Register of Cases*
is an enormous volume bound in brown buckram, mended with
shiny black tape. The names on the pages lie in regimented
rows, like beds in a hospital ward, neatly hemmed in by razor-
straight pink lines. Like the Book of Judgment, all the facts
about an individual's life are recorded: station in life, single,
married or widowed, number of admission, former case
number, form of disease on admission, cause, duration on
admission, color, sex, age, nativity, residence at time of
admission, degree of education, and last religion.
The register lists the old names: Augustus, Catharine,
Jacob: men and women born in Ireland or Prussia and over-
taken by madness in wartime, childbirth, plowing a hot field.
The diagnoses are repetitious, like a string of curse words from
a madman: chronic dementia, acute melancholia, senile
dementia, chronic melancholia, caused by masturbation, acute

mania, caused by sunstroke. There is also a place in the register for "Outcome." The dead outnumber the recovered by ten to one.

Our vampire was born at Georgestown, Dimmarada in South America. He was "colored," fifty-two years old. His station was, "United States Convict;" his education was "limited;" and his disease was chronic melancholia, caused by prison life. His patient number was 6340.

The National Archives file on the vampire is slim: mostly monotonously obsequious letters written to his doctor. His handwriting is not uneducated but his grammar is fractured, either by ignorance or insanity. "This statement show that I am not Crazy...I am a Citizen my money can not be yours so open these doors and let me out. I am a Citizen. I am a Citizen. I am a Citizen."

He pleads for privileges, such as permission to take tea with a charitable lady; tells tales on the other inmates; and protests mistreatment of patients by hospital workers. He was given a pair of pet ducks he dubbed Rosaliene and Susanna, and was devastated when one escaped and the other died. "I am very sorrow for my birds," he wrote.

I found it hard to reconcile the reports of him having killed a man in prison, of his supernatural strength and rage, which required four men to subdue him, with his claims of innocence, with his sly, almost childish letters to his doctor: "I am not crazy, you know that, Doctor W W Goddard. You know they tell lies about me, calling me 'bloodsucker.' I never killed a man except in self-defense, you know that, Doctor W W Goddard."

And the longer I read those documents, those protestations of innocence by a man condemned on the evidence of Portuguese-speaking witnesses, the more I wondered if the vampire was the victim of mis-translation.

"Blood-thirsty!" "bloodsucker!" were epithets one seaman might have hurled at another who had murdered a shipmate. But in translation they might have meant something much more deadly, much more attuned to the Calvinistic conscience of a

Massachusetts jury not far removed from the trials of other
supernatural beings.

Brown spent his last days in the National Insane Asylum,
feeding the birds and writing obsessive letters to his doctor. He
died in 1910, a stranger in a strange land to the end. If he
wasn't insane when he was admitted to the hospital, he became
so before he died. His last letter, scrawled on a sheet torn from
a newspaper, lay folded in a separate envelope in his file. As I
opened it, I flinched as if something had flown out of the paper.
The madness was palpable; a crazy energy sweeping off the
page into my face like a blow. I quickly put the letter away and
walked briskly out into the sunlight. There, at least, no
vampire could follow.

THE MOST HAUNTED TOWN
IN OHIO
The Ghosts of Waynesville

*It's almost like there are so many souls down there—more than
in other places—that they spill over into the land of the living.
It's far weirder than your normal place.*
-Mary Sikora-

As I looked out at the people crowded into the meeting
room at the library in Waynesville, waiting to hear me speak on
"Ohio, The Haunt of It All," I reflected that talking about
ghosts here was like bringing coals to Newcastle since most of
the audience lived in haunted houses of their own.

Waynesville is built on a prehistoric Indian site; there are
earthworks at one end of the village. Miamis and Shawnees
also lived here. The first white settlers came in 1797. Since
slavery was prohibited in this area of the Northwest Territory,
Waynesville became the largest Quaker settlement in the
United States, and later, an important stop on the Underground
Railroad. The town is honeycombed with tunnels that ran from
the banks of the Little Miami River to houses with secret rooms
that sheltered escaped slaves. With more than thirty antique
shops in town, Waynesville can fairly claim the title "Antiques
Capital of the Midwest." It also deserves the title, "Most
Haunted Town in Ohio."

THE NOT SO DEARLY DEPARTED

Waynesville's resident ghost-hunter and town historian, Dennis Dalton, estimates that there are at least three dozen haunted sites in town. He normally includes thirteen sites ("lucky thirteen!") on his "Not So Dearly Departed Tour."** Dennis, who describes himself as looking like "a chubby Ichabod Crane" in the authentic eighteenth-century garb he dons for his walking tours, says, "There's been a whole lot of living in Waynesville and life can be hard to let go of." Dennis speculates that the energy of the early pioneers lingers because their lives were filled with emotional and physical hardships. "Any deep emotional trauma—deep loving, deep giving, an incomplete period of great creativity...can be the basis of a haunting." Join Dennis now, as he takes us on a mini-tour of the invisible sights of Waynesville.

STETSON HOUSE

The most famous stop on Dennis's tour is the Stetson House where John Stetson, of hat fame, is seen peering out of an upper window. Stetson visited his sister Louisa Stetson Larrick at the house in the 1860s. Louisa died there in 1879 of tuberculosis contracted from her brother.

The house is now an antique shop where mirrors refuse to stay on the walls, former owners say. If anyone is so rash as to bring a mirror into the house, the mirror is found smashed in the middle of the room—with hanging wires intact. A former owner also found a small wooden cupboard tossed twelve feet from its nail which remained solidly in the wall.

Dennis also smelled gingerbread baking in the Stetson House—but only on Sundays and in spite of the fact that there's no longer a kitchen in the house.

A small, dark-haired woman has also been seen in the front doorway. One neighbor, who thought it was odd that the

**See the appendix for his address and phone number.

antique shop owner was wearing a long, old-fashioned dress, watched the apparition dissolve into a wall. The ghost may be Stetson's sister Louisa who was miserably unhappy in Waynesville, or Lila Benham, a schoolteacher, who lived in the house in the early 1900s.[1]

THE HANGED MAN

At one of the many antique shops on Waynesville's High Street, a former shop owner climbed the building's narrow stairway, tied a rope to the banister, slipped a noose around his neck, and jumped. The rope broke the man's neck, the fall broke the rope, and the floor broke the man's fall. Sensitive people can still hear his footsteps and the thud as his body plummets to the floor.

THE GENTLEMAN VANISHES

A young salesman—or drummer, as they used to call them—once came to town driving an elegant carriage with a pair of the finest horses. He put up in the Miami House and flashed a lot of money. The next day, the salesman disappeared and—coincidentally, you understand—the innkeeper filled in a perfectly good well.

The innkeeper was suspect right away but nobody wanted to accuse him since he was one of the richest men in town. He said the man had run off without paying and after a week, the innkeeper confiscated the man's carriage and horses.

In 1866 Charles Mumler, a spirit photographer, came to town. He took a portrait of the innkeeper. When the image was developed, it showed a ghostly white disembodied hand pointing accusingly at the man.

THE DRIVE-IN GHOST

There was a ghost named "Harvey" at the local drive-in. Three waitresses watched as a milkshake glass slid from the top of the counter to the center of the room where it fell and shattered. One waitress said the ghost locked her in the walk-in cooler in the basement. It was two hours before her boss found her and let her out, tugging on the massive door which was too heavy to blow shut by itself. Most of the staff complained of "presences" in the kitchen where they frequently heard dishes rattling. One waitress was so spooked by something that brushed by her that she refused to be in the kitchen alone. A young dishwasher heard voices from a storage area. Thinking it was a waitress, he talked to her. When she came in and he found out he had been conversing with a spook, he refused to go into the kitchen again.

THE SATTERTHWAITE HOUSE

Elizabeth Lynton Satterthwaite died in 1879 but she still lingers on to protect her old home. She occasionally plays tricks hardly in keeping with the dignity of an ancestral ghost, like the time she nearly made the family late for work because she'd hidden the alarm clock in the cookie jar.

Dennis personally felt a cold hand on his arm in the guest bedroom. Chairs rock by themselves and a soft but distinct voice asked a child warming himself by the fireplace, "So you want to get warm do you?"

THE GHOST OF CHARITY LYNCH

Charity Lynch and her husband Isaiah left Bush River, a South Carolina Quaker settlement, in 1805 to move to Waynesville. Isaiah died of diptheria and left Charity unable to finish the house where they were to have lived. Impoverished, she was forced to give her children to other families until she could get back on her feet. In 1818 she moved to Springboro where she was reunited with most of her children.

But, "Little Mary had been sent to live in Cincinnati," said Dennis. "She pined away there, wanting her mother. The people buried the child in Cincinnati's potter's field." Charity later tried unsuccessfully to find her daughter's grave. Charity spent a good part of her life grieving in the house on Maple Street overlooking the Meeting House and the Quaker Cemetery. Dennis feels that the energy she brought to her work as an evangelist along with her depression over the loss of her family may have caused her to haunt the house.

"We know Charity has talked to two people in the house. A cleaning woman was once on the back porch and heard a woman say 'pot liquor.' That was all she heard, and that's not a common word anymore."

A woman named Mary occupied the house for many years. While her husband was sick in the hospital, she was awakened "every morning at 4 a.m. for two solid weeks" by a voice calling, "Mary!"

"At first I thought it might be my husband calling for me....but he would have called me, "honey." It was a very peaceful thing—it seemed to be coming from within the room."

Mary didn't understand what the voice meant until her daughter told her about Charity's search for her daughter.

"I never felt so sure in my life that it was Charity calling for her child."

Miss May Wright, the city's first librarian, bought the house in 1917.

"People say that she held seances in the living room," remarked Dennis.

There is a walnut cupboard in the dining room. Although normally the cupboard's bottom doors are hard to open, at times they mysteriously drift open.

When Dennis was housesitting the Lynch house in 1974, he had a group of people in for a party. The after-dinner conversation turned to hauntings.

"Just about that time those doors opened. You would have thought I had wires attached everywhere!"

"I stood up and said, 'Well, May, Charity, or whoever, I'm tired of shutting your goddamned old cupboard.'

"I sat back down and I told my friends that it's not a good idea to argue with ghosts. I had no sooner said that than there was a loud rapping on the bay window and two whole shelves of colored glass came crashing to the floor. The room seemed to stand still and everybody got colder. The shelves were broken right in the center."

Examination showed that the glass had been cut, as if with a glass cutter.[2]

THE QUAKER MEETING HOUSE

The Quaker Meeting House is not on the Tour, but several people told me of their experiences there.

Mary Sikora of the *Dayton Daily News* visited the Meeting House while researching an article on the ghosts of Waynesville. As she stood in the locked building, she heard the muffled clatter of pots and pans and the sound of people moving about in the kitchen—only the Meeting House doesn't have a kitchen. Mary later learned that it formerly had one in a separate building that stood where she had heard the sounds.

"It was the most striking thing—hearing people in a kitchen that didn't exist. It was like a family gathering when I was a kid—everybody doing dishes and talking: that's what I heard.

"I'm a pretty open person," said Mary. "Hearing it was one thing, finding out that there was nothing there was another. When I realized the building was empty, I wasn't afraid; I enjoyed the experience, it made me smile. I felt a kind of kinship with these people from the past, and a feeling of awe that I could be susceptible to that.

"I'm usually very cynical, but I didn't have any doubt at all that the stories about the Meeting House were true—there was too much behind them."

One night in 1985, Rebecca Edwards and her boyfriend David drove by the Meeting House. They turned onto the road that runs beside it and Rebecca yelled, "David! Stop! Look!" In the right hand window was a light.

"I knew that nobody was in there cleaning on a Friday night at two in the morning. But we saw a figure like an old-fashioned school teacher. It was the silhouette of a petite woman, her hair pulled back. She had her back to the window. She turned around, looked out the window, then turned her back to us again. I could see her hair was in a bun."

"We drove around to the front. No matter which side of the Meeting House we went to, that figure was looking out of the window. It was really eerie when it kept following us."

The next weekend, they took witnesses.

"I went over there with David, my uncle, and his friend. David knocked on the door. *And this thing knocked back!* And you could hear organ music playing. There has never been, there is no record of—*any* organ in that building. And it was coming from behind that door, not like someone was playing the organ in their home across the street."

THE HAUNTED FIREHOUSE

"Daniel* doesn't move anything or turn on lights," said paramedic Dale Edwards, speaking about the Waynesville Firehouse ghost. "He just makes his little rounds. For a long time he had the key to the firehouse because he lived right next door. In fact, Daniel, who died in 1982, donated the land for the present firehouse.

"He was a little old man—five foot five or six—in his early 80s. He walked all stooped over, shuffling his feet. When Daniel was alive, he'd go in the side door of the firehouse and walk around the equipment. Then he'd go out the back door or upstairs into the new addition—just take a cruise around the fire house.

"Since Daniel's death there have been numerous instances when you still hear the side door open and close, hear the feet shuffling around the concrete floors, and go out the back door, or go upstairs. There is never anyone there."

Dale and another guy heard the side door open and close.

"We got on our hands and knees to see under the engine. We could hear the feet shuffling on the other side of the engine, but we never saw feet. There were no shoes, no feet, no legs, no nothing. The shuffling went out of the bay, into the kitchen, and out the back door. We got a little chilly. Other guys have heard the footsteps in the upstairs halls, going in and out of doors, but there is never anyone there.

"None of this started until Daniel passed away. He always loved the fire department. I guess he just comes in, checks things out, then leaves."

When Dale was dating his wife Becky in the fall of 1987, they were standing at the top of the stairs when they heard the door open, then the footsteps came "up the stairs, right between us, down the hall and out the door.

"The guys just accept it. People sometimes spend the night upstairs. They're always hearing things up there. We sort of attribute it to the hot water heating system, but there are only so many things you can put off on the heating system!"

THE HOMESICK HAUNT

After my talk at the Waynesville library, a couple approached me.

"Would you like to meet our ghost?" asked a tall, dark-haired woman. She introduced herself as Wren* and her husband, a sandy-haired man with a mustache as Trevor*.

"Tonight?" I asked.

They nodded. "It's not far."

Wren started to tell me about their ghosts, but I stopped her. I don't like to know.

The house was built in 1850. I stepped cautiously into the living room. There were ruffled curtains at the windows. Interesting baskets and antique clothing were hung on the walls. Yet somehow the house seemed very dark, as if no lamps could make it light. Wren, Trevor, and I talked in the living room while their fluffy little white dog pranced around us.

Wren used to be a nurse, but now stays home with their two young children. Rarely smiling, she had a kind of controlled power about her. She seemed eager to learn anything she could about their ghosts, yet distracted, almost as if she were listening for some other voice beyond mine. Trevor had a shy smile and seemed easy-going and relaxed, unafraid of whatever shares their house with them.

I strolled through the dining room and stopped at the door of a room strewn with children's toys.

"There was a suicide in that room," said Wren evenly. I swallowed and stuck my head into the room, but didn't try to step around the toys. There didn't seem to be anything wrong with the room.

The kitchen was a different story. Something struck me in the face, stopping me dead, taking my breath away. A curtain was drawn over one end of the room. I had absolutely no desire to look behind it.

"There's something wrong in the kitchen," I said. Wren and Trevor exchanged glances. It was one of the places they notice things. Just that evening Wren had left the door to the broiler open before she went to my talk at the library. Trevor found it closed when he got home. It's on a stiff spring and hard to close without force. Wren's oldest daughter also saw a woman in "turn of the century clothes" in the kitchen doorway. I did not linger in the kitchen.

Upstairs Wren showed me a hidden room at the back of the master bedroom closet. The house was said to have been on the Underground Railroad. "I don't want to look," I told her, backing away. I felt something hidden, something sealed up and decaying for a long time.

Stepping into the tiled bathroom was a relief. "This is fine," I said "this feels a lot better." Trevor said that one of his missing tools had reappeared in the bathroom.

In the next room, a small one at the top of the stairs, I walked through a curtain of cold air. When I mentioned this, Trevor and Wren burst out, "The kids hate this room!"

Said Wren, "Our daughter said she saw a pair of red eyes looking in that window." Trevor chimed in, "and the boy said he saw a man coming in this other window." The room was dark and not particularly inviting, but I didn't feel a presence there.

After the tour we stood in the dining room and talked.

"How do you get rid of ghosts?" Wren asked.

I shrugged, "I don't really do that sort of thing, but generally you address the ghost by name, if you know it, and say, 'You're dead. You don't know you're dead, but you are and you need to move on.' As I spoke, I found myself staring into the dark kitchen, hugging myself. I went on,

"Tell them, 'Look around you until you see a light. Maybe it's just a little pinpoint of light, but it will get bigger and bigger and in that light will be someone you love. They've come to take you home.'"

As I said this, three luminous globes began to play in front of my eyes. I blinked and shut my eyes, thinking it was a speck on my contacts. When I opened them, the lights were still there, set in a triangular pattern like a pawnbroker's sign. I shook my head and turned my back on the kitchen. I couldn't see them in the dining or living rooms, but when I turned around, they were hanging in the kitchen doorway. I watched the lights of passing cars to see if it was some kind of reflection. It was a totally different light—yellowish white and luminous like a very dim soft-white bulb. I turned around again and then they were gone.

We talked a bit more, standing in the dining room. Wren said, "I don't think [the suicide is] the ghost. I feel he's at peace." Trevor agreed. But after I left the house and they had driven off to pick up their children, I felt restless and sad. Without knowing why, I drove around the block several times, thinking that I would see a face looking down at me, luminously pale in the dark of the upstairs window. Inside, the golden light glowing on the woodwork made the house look warm and appealing. Yet I had an overwhelming feeling of someone standing outside looking in at the life there or of someone looking wistfully out the window at me, trying to make contact. Someone lonely.

"I wish I was still alive," I found myself thinking, as if in a trance. I longed for the warmth of a human embrace, for the scent of cooking, for lights and laughter and all of the things that the grave lacks.

As I drove back towards Xenia, I glanced at the clock. Suddenly it seemed very late. And life far away.

THE GHOSTS OF THE AIR
Ghosts at the USAF Museum

Unnumbered spirits round thee fly,
The light militia of the sky.
-Alexander Pope-

The brief mention of the hauntings at Dayton's United States Air Force Museum in *Haunted Ohio* brought a variety of responses. Skepticism from some, an anonymous phone call from a young man who angrily insisted that the stories of ghosts at the Museum were lies, all lies, and a flood of stories from other people who have experienced the ghosts of the air.

THE WOMAN WHO TALKS TO AIRPLANES

Beth* is in love with airplanes.

"I've been known to go up and kiss airplanes," she admits. "It's not professional, but I do it anyway."

Beth is very psychic. When she was a little kid, her father used to take her around to used car lots every Saturday.

"He'd say, 'Put your hands on this and tell me if it's a lemon.'" She could tell him if it was a good car to buy. If he disregarded her advice, he usually regretted it.

"It's psychometry," she says. "It's always been with me. Sometimes I hate it, but I live with it."

With these kind of skills, Beth finds the United States Air Force Museum a fascinating place.

"I've had some pretty unusual experiences. And all during daylight hours."

THE WORST PLACE

In the Nissen Hut which houses the Visitors' Center, I shook hands with Eric* and Beth who took me on a tour of the Museum. Eric was a sincere, matter-of-fact man who instantly produced facts and figures about every exhibit. Beth was equally knowledgeable, although more emotionally intense about the aircraft.

I mentioned that many people had told me that the *Lady Be Good* exhibit was the worst place in the Museum. Beth shook her head emphatically.

"That's not the worst. I think the worst is...."

I stopped her. "Maybe you better not tell me. Just let me see if I can feel it myself."

It was the weekend of the Air Show and the Museum was packed with visitors. An atmosphere less conducive to ghosts would be hard to imagine.

We walked by a figure of a red-suited pilot in a glass case. By some video wizardry a talking human face was projected eerily onto the mannequin's face and a voice track welcomed visitors to the Museum.

We skirted the crowd gathered around the mannequin and to my right I could see through a small door into the gallery. I was immediately stricken with a kind of sick terror, all the more terrifying for having no cause. As we walked through the door I was vaguely aware of an exhibit case labeled "POWs."

"Oh, God," I said "This is bad."

Eric walked beside me, watching. The air darkened and grew thick. It was an effort to push through it. I began to mutter, trying desperately to be controlled, not make a scene. I wanted out.

"I just walked into it again. This is really bad. I'm walking through it. Can we go now, please? This is *really* bad..."

Beth nodded knowingly. "This is the worst place in the Museum."

Heavy black waves of cold and fear like lines on an oscilloscope rippled around me. I forced myself to breath normally and kept walking. Then we were around the corner and the waves of terror receded.

BLACK MARIA

Our first stop was a helicopter painted to look like *Hop-along*, a Korean/Vietnam-era helicopter tucked under the wing of the enormous B-36 Convair with its 230-foot wingspan.

A caller had told me that *Hop-along* is haunted by the ghost of a former co-pilot whose blood still stains the seat.

"All the janitors see him," he said. "He's flipping switches and trying to get back home."

Beth and I felt nothing about *Hop-Along*, although I was still shaken from my earlier experience. Could my caller have meant another helicopter? Eric led us through a brightly-lit tunnel to the Modern Flight Hangar where another helicopter, *Black Maria,* was displayed. The atmosphere in the tunnel was completely different and the pressure on my head eased up. We came out of the tunnel and headed for *Black Maria.* My first sight of the sinister, flat-black ship was a shock. I didn't want to get too close. If I just stay back, I thought, I'll be all right.

Beth said that she felt "some kind of trauma" from *Black Maria.*

Eric explained that the helicopter had flown classified missions in Vietnam that no one knows much about even now.

I peered up at a window. "It feels like there's somebody in there," I said to Beth. "Do you feel that way?"

She shook her head, "I just feel this intense vibration. Nobody knows what she went through. You just feel drained around her."

We walked to the back of the ship. Eric pointed out small circular patches riveted in place.

"She has a lot of bullet holes that have been patched. I talked to a pilot who flew her. He was picking up some guys when he saw a Viet Cong sniper taking aim directly at his head. He forced himself to sit on the collective so he wouldn't take off before all the guys were loaded. Somehow the sniper's bullets completely missed him and as soon as all the men were on board, he took off."

For *Black Maria* memories of wartime trauma still linger. The inside of the ship, stretchers still strapped in, was lit by a cold fluorescent light. I felt a deep sadness, lives ending in pain. Someone *was* still there. Perhaps a co-pilot who had bled his life away, trying to bring *Black Maria* home.

THE RIDE OF THE VALKYRIE

Beth is fascinated by one particular aircraft, an XB-70 Bomber called *Valkyrie*.

"I had come to the Museum to meet the Valkyrie, the airplane of my dreams. Eric and I agreed to get together and look over the airplanes. I got there at 9:00 a.m. Eric led me straight to the Valkyrie. I was completely bowled over by her. She's the most magnificent plane you've ever seen. I get an overwhelming sense of power when I stand by Valkyrie."

I had to agree. The only word that seemed to describe the plane was "magnificent." She is a stunning white delta-wing aircraft with the long neck of a swan. Built in 1960-62, she was the first large Mach-3 bomber and, said Eric, "She's responsible for much of triple-sonic aircraft technology."

I noticed an ugly jack under the long neck, as if it were in danger of snapping off, and asked Eric about it.

"It's just a precaution. There was a problem with her nose gear. It still supported her OK." Beth said, "After I saw the Valkyrie, I felt that there was something wrong with her landing gear. Eric looked at her left main gear, but not at the nose gear. Now she's got a broken ankle and a jack under her nose. It makes me sad to look at it."

THE LAUGHING AIRPLANE

Off to one side of Valkyrie was an F-106 Delta Dart. Beth went over and nuzzled the airplane.

"My baby..." she murmured, then turned to us, smiling.

"When I first came to the Museum, Eric said to me, 'By the way, come over here. What do you think about this little airplane?'

"I didn't know anything about it. The sign with the text was in front, and I approached the plane from behind so I couldn't see it. I walked around to her flank, and put a hand on her. I got this incredible impression of giggling!

"I told Eric, 'This airplane is just laughing up her intakes.'

"Eric was astounded, 'What!?'

"'She's giggling.'

Eric walked around to the front of the plane and pointed to the text. There Beth read the airplane's incredible story.

"Delta Dart did something very strange in her life. She flew herself. She took off from a Montana Air Force Base on a training mission and for some reason—they don't know why—she went into a flat spin. The pilot fired the drag chute; it didn't help. The pilot punched out. In a matter of seconds, the plane straightened herself out. She missed every mountain for nine and a half miles which is kind of strange in Montana. She made a gentle belly landing in a snow-covered alfalfa field and freaked out a rancher who was watching. He came running up, expecting to find an injured pilot and found nobody.

"Her engine was still running! She only needed minor repairs—mostly sheet metal—and flew seventeen more years. The Delta Dart is a very special airplane! You can hear her talking to the other airplanes about the day she soloed."

CALL TO GLORY

Said Beth, "There's an F-4 Phantom cockpit on the floor of the Museum that the public can get into. Eric and I were walking around and I said, 'I want to sit in here.' There were a bunch of Boy Scouts in front of us and when the last kid got out I climbed in.

I sat in the front seat and I had a *rush*. Eric says my face turned from red to white and I started to shake. I didn't know what was happening to me. I just wanted to get out of there.

Eric helped her out anxiously, "You all right?"

"I don't know."

She was so disoriented she ran into the stairs next to the cockpit.

"Get me away from this thing!" she told Eric.

"It was a horrible feeling. They used it in the TV show called *Call to Glory*, but it wasn't that. I tried to find out where they got it and couldn't. I don't know if the Museum even had it documented. It probably slammed down on a ship's deck or had an accident. It was something pretty horrible."

Eric remembers the incident well. "Beth was shivering as she got out of the cockpit. It was something powerful, but we could never find out anything about it. Maybe the plane had a bad landing."

Beth has a theory about her beloved airplanes. "All of these planes have been built and maintained and flown by thousands of people. Some of those thousands of hands must have rubbed off. That's what keeps these airplanes alive.

"Every airplane in here is something very special. *Bockscar* is very sad. Very. I got that impression just by looking at her. *Shoo Shoo Baby* shows a lot of love. She was a well-loved airplane. She came back in pieces in a crate.

"*Goblin*, the tiny parasite fighter, [the XF-85] is a little embarrassed to be there."

GOBLIN

We walked up to *Goblin*, a misshapen little hobgoblin of an airplane—"An engine with wings and a pilot on top," Eric described it. I began to laugh. Designed to be lowered from a B-36 bomber on a trapeze, it was a very strange looking plane with odd horns and hooks.

Then I seemed to sense the plane's embarrassment and I wanted to pat it and say, "There, there, I didn't mean to make fun of you."

BOCKSCAR

Bockscar, named for her original pilot, Frederick Bock. Another pilot flew her as she dropped the atomic bomb on Nagasaki near the end of World War II.

Eric pointed up at the side of *Bockscar* where five figures—four black and one red—were painted. They were silhouettes of a plump man like Alfred Hitchcock—the Fat Man: the nickname for the Bomb.

"The chilling thing for me about this plane is those figures. The black figures represent test runs with dummy bombs. The red figure is the attack on Nagasaki."

There was one more black silhouette after the red one. Another test?

Eric nodded, "The Japanese hadn't surrendered and we were getting ready in case we needed to do it again."

Guards have seen a little Japanese boy run by *Bockscar* in the middle of the night.

Dayton's Channel 2 shot part of its 1991 *Dayton and Beyond* Halloween program outside the Museum. The night the program was aired, a young man named Mike called me. He's a sixteen-year old Explorer Scout who volunteers with the Security Police at the Museum.

Mike says he was talking with one of the food concession workers when the man suddenly asked, "Have you ever seen the little Asian boy by the *Bockscar*?"

Mike gulped and said, "No, but I know people who have."

Mike is well-acquainted with the guards and cleaning staff at the Museum. "The Museum does make strange noises," he admits, "like electric generators, and metal expanding and contracting. But there's more to it than that. I know for a fact there are ghosts down there."

STRAWBERRY BITCH

Strawberry Bitch, a B-24, has a blue-clad, red-haired pinup girl painted on her side. Her light-hearted nose art belies the fact that she flew fifty-nine missions in less than nine months during World War II. She was damaged on at least nine of those missions.

In June, 1991 at 2:30 a.m., Mike saw lights in *Strawberry Bitch*. He was standing with a guard at the World War II death camp exhibit.

"The cop was looking at [the exhibit]; I was gazing at the plane. And there was a light inside. It looked like somebody was looking for something with a flashlight. I moved around and it was not a reflection. There's no electricity in the plane."

The plane's spiky guns pointed from the ball turret. I again felt a presence, expected to see gloved hands grasping the handles. In August, 1991, Mike saw the plane's waist gunner's gun shaking. "You could hear it going 'ch ch ch ch,'" he remembered.

"In September, 1991 a custodian was sweeping behind the plane by the general's car exhibit. She felt somebody following her. When she turned around, something hit her in the head. She ran screaming out of there."

THE MAN IN THE PLANE

It was 6:00 p.m. The Museum had just closed. Lee*, a janitor, saw a guy standing on top of a plane. Since it was so near to closing, Lee figured that the man was allowed to be where he was. The Museum often hosts functions just after closing.

The man waved cheerily at Lee who was looking quizzically at him.

"Oh I just used to fly this plane," he said. Lee turned around, then turned back and the man was gone. Lee was badly frightened.

Later, Lee was flipping through a collection of pictures in the Museum bookstore when he came across a picture of that very plane. He leaned closer. The man in the picture was the same guy he'd seen standing on the plane.

THE GHOSTLY GUNNER

Naturally some things that go on in the Museum are the work of practical jokers. Mike had one prank backfire.

"One of the cops was bringing in his wife. Me and another Explorer decided to scare them. We were going to scare them in one area, then run into another area and scare them there.

"Originally I was going to grab her leg from under a table. As I was lying under there I heard somebody say, 'Hey!' real loud. I looked up and didn't see anything. Then I heard, 'HEY YOU!' and I was going to jump out at whoever it was when I saw the gunner mannequin *shift* and point his gun.

'Hey! Hey you!' the voice said again, really loud. It was not a cop or the janitor. Nobody was around so I took off!"

LADY BE GOOD

Mike said, "In front of the *Lady Be Good* exhibit—that's a particularly weird area. Everybody who's worked there at night has had experiences. The custodians and guards tell him that the entire B-24 area is the worst. Eric has heard the same thing. He said he gets "weird little feelings" when he sees the *Lady Be Good* and added "One of the janitors has a relative who can't spend much time over at the *Lady Be Good* exhibit because she feels 'something.'"

Lady Be Good is a World War II-era B-24. She went down in the Libyan desert. Searchers found six of the crew by the plane, dead. The seventh man managed to walk 179 miles without water before perishing. One legend about the plane says that there was another crewmember. Searchers followed his footprints into the desert, where they abruptly ended, as if he'd taken flight.

A wall of photos, memorabilia, and plane parts tells *Lady Be Good's* sad story. Only a few large fragments of twisted metal are on display, but the men of her crew have been seen walking the halls of the Museum.

"They don't just stay with the planes," said Mike, "they're all over the Museum."

Eric had saved the *Lady Be Good* exhibit for last on our tour. As we approached it, I wrote "Lady B Good" in my notes. And that was all I could write. I stepped over an invisible line into what I could only think of as a circle of influence. By the time we got up to the photos and the case with one of her engines, I was so sick at heart I barely gave the exhibits a glance. One look at the engine and the psychic blow struck me in the face. I groaned inwardly. There was a roaring in my ears.

"I can't stay here," I muttered. "That's enough." I began to walk away. Just a few yards and I was out of the worst of it.

AFTERWARDS

As we talked in the cafeteria after our tour, I sat, completely drained of energy and confessed to Eric and Beth that I felt like a real baby for getting so upset.

Said, Eric, "I have not personally felt the sense of death that you and other people have felt, but I respect the possibility that something is there. You can be walking around that museum, you'll hear a noise, you don't know what the hell it is. It doesn't scare me, although it can be a scary place, especially at night."

Beth agreed, even though she loves these airplanes. For her, it is a strange experience since she feels all of the emotions of long-dead pilots and crews. When I asked her more about *Black Maria,* she said, "I don't handle Vietnam-era aircraft very well. I become very traumatized; I want to get away." Then she added, "There are a lot of vibrations in the whole Museum. These planes *are* warbirds."

I thanked Eric and Beth for the tour and walked out of the Museum into the world of the living. I won't go back.

HARMFUL HAUNTS
Dangerous ghosts and houses of horror

*Hill House, not sane, stood by itself against its hills,
holding darkness within...and whatever
walked there, walked alone.*
-Shirley Jackson, *The Haunting of Hill House*-

In reality, ghosts who hurt or kill people are uncommon. Yet the exceptional ghosts in this chapter have injured their victims either physically or, worse, psychologically. The most frightening story of this kind that I've heard cannot be told. My aunt taught a girl in high school who told her that the ghost at their house had tried to kill one of her sisters. Ultimately the family had to move. When I contacted the woman, she wrote back apologetically that the incident had been so traumatic, their family had agreed *never* to speak of the matter. Fortunately such ghosts are rare. But not rare enough...

THE GHOST AT THE PALACE

"Don't let anybody tell you the Palace Theatre isn't haunted. I was *there*," Steve* warned me.

Columbus' Palace Theatre was newly renovated and Steve had been invited to a private pre-opening party.

"They had invited Harry Blackstone Jr. to come for the opening. Somebody decided to have a medium hold a seance to try and contact Thurston the Magician, Harry's father's archrival."

The seance was held in one of the lobby areas on the main floor. The party included the medium, Blackstone Jr., and at least a dozen other people. The medium pointedly invited Steve to sit at the table with her.

"I said, 'No, I'm not good at this.' Frankly I was uncomfortable. I didn't want to be close to whatever was going to go on. I wanted to sit back and watch.

"In the process of trying to contact Thurston, we got a real wrong number. The medium went into a trance and the ghost of an old man who had been murdered or had died in the theatre came through. It was quite frightening!"

The spirit found it difficult to communicate.

"He had obviously had a stroke or something. The medium physically changed. She got up from the table and limped away like someone with an impairment. Blackstone Jr. was dumbfounded. The tension was so thick you could have cut it with a knife. It was like electrical energy. It couldn't all have been a put-on—if it was, it was one of the best I've ever seen. There were no rappings or hoopla. Looking back, I think it was more real than we wanted to admit."

After the seance broke up, Steve stood around talking with the medium and some of his friends.

"She looked at me through this crowd and said, 'Why did you not sit at the table?' I shrugged off the question with some noncommittal answer.

"'That's a lie,' she said. 'Why do you say that? Because you know that it's a lie. You know you have a gift. I'll prove that you do. Go upstairs to the second balcony and walk back and forth. Then come back down and tell us what you experienced.'"

Steve went upstairs and started across the balcony.

"I got to the middle of the balcony and I was absolutely suffocating. Every ounce of my energy was drained. I couldn't breathe. You talk about dark and heavy air—it was there. It was already dark, but it got darker. All of this occurred in just one particular spot and it ended as soon as I moved out of it."

But moving out of it was a real effort for Steve. He could barely continue across the balcony.

"I was so frightened and startled by it that I decided I would go back to the lobby through one of the stair tunnels."

As Steve went into the tunnel,

"I was overwhelmed by a feeling of impending doom, dread, horror, and then some. 'This is worse,' I thought, 'at least up in the balcony I know what to expect. I can force myself through the thing on the balcony, but I cannot make myself go into this. So I went back through the balcony.

"When I came back to the group I was trying to be nonchalant. As I told the story, one of my friends blurted. 'That's almost verbatim what she said you'd say.'

"So you can tell me there are no ghosts in the Palace Theatre, but I don't believe you. I experienced it."

THE WOLF AT THE DOOR

When the Browns* moved to a house built among the Indian mounds in the north end of Xenia, three of their children, Richard*, Joe*, and Gwen*, encountered a creature straight out of a fairy tale—one with a nasty ending.

The house was a one-year old bi-level, built in 1958. It was nothing special, said Richard, except, "This house definitely had a Presence. You always felt like someone was there."

"I used to feel something standing next to me and I'd get the shivers," added Joe. Gwen agreed, "In that house I never felt alone. We always heard lots of noises. I always thought it was because of the Indian mounds."

A night of horror began when Richard thought he heard something in the kitchen in the middle of the night.

"I snuck out in the hall and looked down into the kitchen. There was a translucent, white wolf in a bib apron, standing on its hind legs at the stove cooking something that smelled like eggs."

Richard raced back into his room, and dove into bed, but the wolf followed him. He could see its shadow in the hall. "It came to the door and looked at me."

At breakfast the next morning he and his brother and sister sat in a daze. He didn't say anything until he caught Joe's eye.

"I saw something in the kitchen last night," said Joe finally. He described a "wolf in blue bib overalls cooking supper."

"So did I," said Richard

"So did I," said Gwen, telling of the same weird hairy figure standing on its hind legs in the kitchen. "I ran into Mom and Dad's room and got in bed between them. The wolf walked down the hall and stood in Mom and Dad's doorway, staring at me. I just froze! I stayed there until morning. I've never forgotten it—I can see it still. It was standing up like a person, but it was definitely a wolf, with the long nose and big ears."

After hearing their story I wondered about the Indian mounds. The wolf sounded like a totem animal. But bib overalls? a bib apron? *And* a violent temper.

Said Richard, "When Joe and I were ten or eleven years old, our parents left us alone for the first time without a babysitter. He and I were downstairs watching TV in the family room when we heard two very loud bangs above our heads."

"Richard and I just looked at each other," Joe said. "I wasn't going to go up there. Richard wasn't going to go up there. It scared the hell out of us!"

"When Mom and Dad came home they yelled at us to come upstairs. 'What have you guys been doing?' they demanded. 'Who's been jumping on the bed?' There were hammer marks on the ceiling and plaster dust and pieces of the ceiling on the bed."

The boys had a tough time explaining it.

"But it wasn't us! There wasn't anyone else in the house," said Joe.

The wolf especially disliked Richard. The door to Richard's bedroom was always open a crack so he could see the light in the hall. Something came up to the door, blotting out the light. As Richard sat on the edge of the bed, watching tensely, something smashed him in the face, knocking him out.

"It whacked me good across the eyebrows," he recalled. "My father heard a noise and found me with the blood running down my face."

Joe also remembered the night, although he slept through it. "When I woke up, Richard had a cut on his forehead. 'What have you been doing?' I asked him. He told me that he was sitting in bed when wham! something hit him. Whatever it was, it didn't like him much."

Joe also recalled, "We used to invite friends over to spend the night in the large bedroom under our parents' room. You'd hear knocking on the doors—tap tap tap. Even the closet doors would tap. A couple of our friends wouldn't ever come back. I kept my headphones or the radio on so I wouldn't have to hear it."

"My Mom thought we were all crazy," said Gwen. "She felt safe there. One day we were all outside planting flowers. I went inside to use the bathroom and on the way down the hallway, there was definitely something behind me. I ran out of the house, in fact I broke through the glass in the door. It haunts me still."

"It was *not* a fun place to live," Joe said firmly.

THE GHOST THAT ROARED

In 1960 Jeanne*, age fifteen, and her family moved into a 100-year old house in the Price Hill area of Cincinnati. After the closing, Jeanne and her Uncle Warren* visited the empty house to decide where the furniture would go, and to check the furnace and wiring. Warren was in the basement furnace room while Jeanne was on the first floor. It was dusk so Jeanne turned on the lights. Suddenly they began flickering on and off.

"Quit fooling around," Warren called from the basement.

"*You* quit fooling around," she called back, thinking he was moving the main switch. Finally they both realized that neither of them was pulling a prank. An electrician was called and found nothing wrong. It was the beginning of a nightmare.

Jeanne and her younger sister Elizabeth*, who occupied a second-floor bedroom, began to hear frightening footsteps. They were heavy, ponderous steps, like "a tall, heavy man wearing boots," sometimes accompanied by the clank of chains, "like a slave or a prisoner." The girls would hear and feel the vibrations as the steps pounded up the stairs, then the noises would stop outside their door, "scaring us out of our wits night after night. We had the feeling that something very evil was out there." The air would turn piercingly cold—a terrible cold—and the girls would "cling together and shake" until the cold dissipated or they drifted off into an exhausted sleep.

"Elizabeth and I were the targets of everything. We told everybody, but they said, 'It's just your imagination. You've been watching too many scary movies.' We wanted to leave, but our parents had just bought the house and they would have lost money if we moved so soon."

One night Jeanne and her older sister Martha* were watching TV while the rest of the house was asleep. Suddenly the knob to the front door began to turn. Jeanne and Martha were terrified, but after the knob stopped turning they checked it to make sure it was locked, knowing that burglars sometimes turn knobs to find unlocked doors. They found the outer storm door locked.

There was a third-floor room that Jeanne's father jokingly called "the morgue" because it was impossible to heat. Even with the windows propped open in summer or a heater placed in the room in winter, it would inevitably be freezing.

One day Martha went to clean the third-floor bedrooms. Her mother, Betty* called up to her, "I'll be up to help as soon as I finish cleaning down here." Almost immediately Martha heard footsteps coming slowly up the stairs. She thought it was her mother trying to scare her, although she didn't think her mother would play such a joke. Martha heard an unknown woman call out, "Yoo-hoo!"

"Mom, is that you?"

The strange voice replied, "Yes."

Martha went out to the landing for a look. No one was in sight. She hurried down the stairs to the kitchen where she was shocked to find Betty. "Were you just upstairs?" asked Martha.

"No," said Betty. "I said I'd be up as soon as I finished the kitchen."

Martha told her what had just happened and they both went upstairs to investigate but found nothing.

After living in the house for about six months Jeanne and Elizabeth wondered if they should try to contact whoever it was that was clumping up and down the stairs. "If we could only free it," Jeanne argued, "maybe it would go away and leave us alone. Wouldn't it be nice if we could just help the poor soul?"

In their bedroom Jeanne said to the ghost, "Whoever you are, whatever you are, we know you're there, and if you would like to communicate with us, knock on our headboard: once for yes, twice for no."

Huddled in the bed, they waited and then heard one knock on the headboard above their heads. The room got very cold. They shivered closer to each other, but Jeanne continued,

"Are you a spirit?"

One knock.

"Are you a man?"

One knock.

"Did you live in this house?"

One knock.

"Did you die in this house?"

One knock.

"Do you mean to harm us in any way?"

Two knocks.

"Did you die a violent death?"

One knock.

"Were you murdered?"

One knock.

Elizabeth was ready to collapse in tears. She pleaded with Jeanne to stop, saying, "We are getting too involved in things we know little about."

Jeanne stopped asking questions, but the room stayed frigid and they continued to feel the man's presence.

One evening Jeanne went up to her second-floor bedroom, intending to read. She bent to pull out a book on Buddhism from a lower shelf of the bookcase. Suddenly a "terrifying, hideous, demonic sound—a sound that was surely inhuman. A loud, horrible, bestial howl" shattered the air. "It was almost like an animal's roar, a very powerful, growly type sound like a lion. It sounded like it came from inside the bookcase."

Jeanne dropped the book and fled down the stairs in hysterics. Her family tried to calm her, but, mysteriously, they hadn't heard the sound. She still slept in the bedroom, although she never again entered the room alone. It was a long time before she could gather the courage to take another book from the bookcase.

Early one morning, Betty walked down the stairs to fix breakfast for the family. She was only three steps down when, she says, "I felt like I was pushed from behind. I felt a hard push—that's what made me fall." She fractured her wrist, dislocated her jaw, and was badly bruised. Jeanne said, "We heard a tremendous crash and awoke to find her unconscious at the bottom of the steps."

Betty had always disbelieved in anything supernatural in the house and maintained that her children had overactive imaginations. But now the family moved out of the house, "before somebody gets killed," remarked Betty's husband. "Even if we lose everything, we have to get out."

Just hearing Jeanne's stories made me shudder. Jeanne agreed, "It was really a terrible thing It stays with you forever.

"Just a few weeks ago I got a phone call and I heard the same voice that I heard in the bookcase. It wasn't a human voice, it wasn't a monster. And it said, "You know who this is."

THE LUNATIC IN THE BASEMENT

The house in Wauseon is white clapboard with a big Dutch roof like a barn, a porch swing, and a forsythia bush—a nice, ordinary house. But when the Durbins first moved into the house in 1984, Linda thought she was cracking up. For months she heard footsteps pacing the hallways at night and a rocking chair creaking back and forth by itself. When she finally broke down and told her husband Charles, he nearly collapsed with relief. He had been experiencing the same things, but had been afraid to admit it, fearing *he* was going crazy.

"We were on the brink of insanity," said Linda. "While the house was not evil, the basement was very depressing. It made me want to cry."

The Durbins researched the house's history and found that it had been built in the early 1900s on a much older foundation. When they contacted several former owners of the house, most didn't want to talk about "that house." One family finally admitted that they had heard voices and felt a sadness—and an overwhelming fear, particularly in the basement where, local legend says, a mentally defective woman was once chained by her family.

Linda said that her sixteen-year old son Sean's personality changed abruptly when he moved into a basement bedroom.

"My son was changing. He got quiet, withdrawn; we had to serve him his meals in his room. You could even see the change in his facial features. He had a hard look, a squint, he looked like he was angry. Sean kept telling us that it was so noisy down there. We didn't listen. We should have listened to him and gotten him help. But how could anyone else believe it when we didn't believe it ourselves?"

On August 18, 1991, Sean disappeared and Linda is certain that the house drove him away.

"Sean walked to church every Sunday....He always went. He was reaching out for help, but he didn't know how to get the help he needed." Fortunately Sean was found at his father's house in Toledo. He later returned home, but he has never been able to say what happened to him. "My Mom says that I block things out," said Sean. "Things go on, and I'll block them out." He mentioned seeing a "misty white figure" in the corner of the living room. "It's not scary so much as startling."

The family has also been tormented by smoke which fills the basement, then mysteriously vanishes.

"I'll fly out of that bed at four in the morning, and the burning smell will be so strong I can't stand it," said Linda. The Durbins found charred beams during their renovations. They don't like to think about a woman chained in the basement watching the flames flickering nearer and nearer.

In the basement the Durbins feel "bodies brushing up against us. On the basement landing, I walked into one," said Linda. "I was frozen solid on the inside, like it was passing through me, only my skin was warm. The same thing happened to my son."

Linda has often seen visions of a young boy. "I always see him pass from one room to another, just out of the corner of my eye. At first I thought the figure was short, like a dwarf, but then I realized I was only seeing him from the knees up. I also see him in the upstairs window as I'm coming down the street. I always think it's one of my own boys. I fall for it every time." Linda has also heard her name called: L-l-i-n-d-d-a. "It was long, dragged out. Like whoever it was was having a hard time talking. I still hear it a lot and that bothers me."

One of the former residents reported hearing that same drawn-out voice when she lived in the house as a child. She fled screaming downstairs to her mother. A local preacher came and blessed the house from top to bottom.

"My husband was against that," said Linda, "He said, 'There's no way you're going to get rid of a thing that's been here for years in fifteen minutes.'"

Linda accompanied the minister and his wife through the house. The wife was extremely reluctant to enter and Linda saw her get whiter and whiter as she toured the house. "The minister said that he felt pressure when he first came in. He went to the basement first and he said 'it' was running from him. By the time he got to the attic, he said, the pressure was unbelievable." Linda ran outside during the ritual, fearing the minister might be doing more harm than good.

"That house got so quiet it got deafening. The wind was blowing outside, but there was no sound inside. 'Does this seem weird to you?' I asked my husband. 'I'm not buying it.' he said. I called it the calm before the storm. We were just waiting for things to go haywire."

Two days later Linda phoned her husband to ask him to pick her up at work and take her to lunch.

"He sounded really funny over the phone. He was so quiet, and stalled around, and wouldn't answer me. I thought he was mad at me. When he picked me up, I asked him, 'Did you not want to pick me up for lunch?' 'No, that's not it,' he said 'it was really weird. I heard this echo-like voice on the phone. It would say something, then you'd come on and say the exact same thing in your normal voice.' We've had a lot of phone trouble here," said Linda. "We've gone through eight or nine phones. Finally I had the phone company replace all the wiring. Over and over the phone will ring and there will be static, a shhhhhh sound like wind in the wires, and faint voices far away. I can't make out what they're saying, the static covers the message. I'll hang up, then try to make a call, and the line is clear."

But since the minister's visit things have calmed down.

"It doesn't seem to be so threatening. The noises haven't stopped, though. Whatever floor you're on, you'll hear the furniture moving on the other floors."

Linda asked, "I want to know why they want to stay on earth. Did they do something so awful that they can't leave? Is it that they have some unfinished business? I don't want to force them out if they need to tell us something. We've put up with them, and they have put up with us, but we have no solid explanation for it. What bothers me the most is not knowing. That is the most frightening thing of all."[1]

JUST WILD ABOUT HARRY

Margaret Taylor* has lived with the supernatural all of her life. "Some people, I think, attract entities," she says. "I'm one of them." She can see auras, both in color and in light. And she has always felt that she was reincarnated, ever since she was a tiny child.

Margaret lived in a house of horror on Dawnview in Dayton.

"In the seventeen years since we left, no one stayed for more than a year. It was a HUD house, and stood empty for quite a while, boarded up. Someone lives in it now, but it's still sad-looking. I think it's because of the 'things.'"

"Things" started happening to the Taylors as soon as they moved into the house. They had two small daughters and they could not get repeat babysitters, "because of the noises and all." In desperation they asked Mr. Taylor's sister to babysit. She did—once. After that she wouldn't come back to the house on Dawnview. She would babysit at her own house, but not there....

Then Margaret found a cake of soap at the bottom of her coffee pot. "This was unusual because I never kept soap in the kitchen. The family always washed their hands in the bathroom. But there it was.

"Once the washing machine started by itself in the middle of the night. It was a front loader; water was going everywhere, just pouring out!"

Fed up, Margaret consulted a medium who said the ghost was "a protective person, someone who is trying to warn you about things." The Taylors even had a name for the mischievous entity.

"We called him Harry. I had a stillborn in 1946 and we thought maybe it was him."

The ghost had a particularly unpleasant way of manifesting himself. "We would get an extreme odor of urine in the house. Just in a corner somewhere. We never did know where it was coming from; it was like it was in the wood. We had a Pekinese; she would never go to those areas, but walked way around them.

"Shortly before our older daughter, Kathleen* was to be married, I thought I heard a noise. My husband is a firefighter and he was gone that night so I was wondering what was going on. I walked from my bedroom into the living room. All of a sudden I was hit as hard as could be on the back of the head and knocked down. The house was all locked up and no one was in that house but me. Again I went to a medium. She asked me, 'Who is opposed to that wedding?' *Someone* must have been very much opposed to it because the marriage was a major disaster!

"Another night I heard a terrible noise. I thought my younger daughter Holly* had knocked over her dresser upstairs. *She* thought the piano had fallen over in the living room. I went flying upstairs; she went flying downstairs. We never found out what it was.

Kathleen's boyfriend Ryan* grappled with an invisible someone in the guest room.

"You're not welcome here!" hissed the thing. Ryan had been dozing, and he wasn't sure if he was dreaming, or if it was a real person. Then he realized that it was neither and if he didn't overcome it, the thing would haunt him the rest of his life and he would never be happy with Kathleen.

Ryan recalled, "I was not about to let something I couldn't see get the best of me." He felt that the thing was upset by a stranger challenging "his" territory. He must have gotten the best of it because he and Kathleen have been happily married for seventeen years.

The ghostly manifestations didn't confine themselves to family.

"Once when we had some friends visiting from Florida we all watched while a china shoe walked itself off the curio shelf. My friend said, 'We have a whole years' full of cocktail party conversation.' Only we hadn't been cocktailing!"

Even after leaving Dawnview, things happened to Margaret. "My daughter Holly's boyfriend gave me a pair of crystal candlesticks. We were having dinner one night when we heard a crack and one of the pair shattered to smithereens—dissolved into fifty little pieces. I always thought that it was because the boyfriend wasn't right. As it turned out, this was true."

THE HOUSE OF HATE

There is a house near Mansfield that has destroyed at least three families, says Lisa*, whose family was one of the house's victims.

Initially, the house looked like a good buy. It was a substantial 1920s brick house on four acres of land. When Dr. Robert Barry* and his wife Marsha* first looked at the house, Marsha, who had been psychic all of her life, felt a presence, which made her feel very safe and secure when they toured the house.

The Barrys offered the owner, an elderly widow, much less than the asking price. She hesitated, then said that she had to confer with someone. The next day she told them: "*He* said it was OK. He likes you." Marsha had a weird feeling that the widow had cleared the deal with her dead husband.

In June 1971 Robert, Marsha, Lisa, and her two sisters, Patty* and Julie* moved in.

Said Lisa: "The first week we lived there, I wasn't allowed to sleep in my bedroom since it needed wallpaper and paint. They put me to bed in another room, but I wanted to sleep in my own bedroom, and I just had a fit! The next morning I found myself in my bedroom with a blanket under me, a sheet on top, then another sheet, two blankets and a pillow. The bedding was tucked in around me like a sleeping bag. And all the linens came from a hall closet that I couldn't reach. At breakfast my mother asked me how I managed to do it.

'The nice old man tucked me in,' I said.

'Old man? What did he look like?' asked my mother."

Lisa described a large, elderly, balding man with a big smile. He wore a t-shirt with cigarettes tucked into the sleeve and work pants. "He was real friendly and he wanted me to sleep in my own room."

One night Marsha woke up, thinking that somebody was looking at her. There was a man standing at the end of her bed, slowly waving a handkerchief back and forth. She talked to him, but he wouldn't respond. There was some kind of haze over his eyes, but he was smiling. He laid the handkerchief on the end of the bed, then disappeared. Marsha wondered if the waving gesture meant "you're welcome here."

"Soon after that, my Mom took some canning jars that had been in the basement to the former owner. On the widow's mantle, she saw a picture of the man who had stood at the foot of her bed. It was the woman's late husband. That's when Mom realized he was the friendly spirit she felt in the house. She also found that the man's nickname was 'Smiley.'"

One night Robert heard noises outside, and went to Lisa's window, which overlooked one of the garages.

"All the garage doors were going up and down at different times. What was weird was that there was no garage door opener. My Dad thought it was kids and went outside to stop them."

As he approached, the doors were still moving up and down. He managed to slip under one, then the doors slammed down. No one was in the garage.

Soon after that, Norma*, a very good friend of Marsha's, died of cancer. Marsha started "ghost writing," doing automatic writing and typing. She got startling results: letters written in a handwriting identical to her friend's, giving information that nobody knew except Norma—information later confirmed by Norma's husband.

Marsha carefully saved all of her writings and hid them in a cupboard accessible only by ladder. When she went back to get the papers, they had all disappeared.

"The writing apparently drew all the other spirits in the house from somewhere and that's where everything started," said Lisa.

Robert was a doctor who was just starting in practice and he was gone much of the time. There had been strains on the marriage before the house, but after only one year there, Robert moved out, got a divorce, and married a younger woman.

In his haste to leave, he left behind a military trunk in the third-floor attic.

"It was so big that the movers had trouble getting it past the bend in the attic stairs. Mom and a friend tried to move it down so he could take it away, but it kept getting lodged. Mom was upset. She didn't want him coming over, but finally she decided that he'd have to move it himself and went to bed. In the morning the trunk was in the kitchen.

"Mom feels that when my Dad left, he broke the natural shield that we all have around us. When he walked out of the circle, it wasn't complete any more. I sometimes wonder if he released spirits who caused problems for some of the other people who have lived there."

Lisa and her mother and sisters tried to carry on in spite of the divorce and the strange things that happened in the house. Marsha didn't want to scare her daughters so she always had explanations for anything unusual.

"We had a piano in the living room that would play at night," Lisa recalled. "My mother, who was a rhythm and blues singer, would claim that it was her. She'd sing and play R & B during the day, but at night it would be classical music.

"The lights in the house were constantly turning off and on. The basement lights acted as if they were on a sensor. If you were going to check the furnace, the furnace room light came on. If you were going to the laundry room, the laundry room light came on. We used to get blamed for it all the time."

Twice they had to call a locksmith to unlock the front bathroom which stood between two bedrooms. "The locks on the doors could only be locked from the inside and we didn't have the keys. Once my sister Patty, age seven, got locked inside when the door handles wouldn't turn. She started screaming and screaming. By the time the locksmith came an hour later the doors just unlocked themselves. Several other times when no one was in the bathroom, the doors were found locked."

One day as a painter was working in the kitchen, he heard footsteps coming down the back stairway which led into the breakfast nook. The door opened, and a white-gloved hand came out, picked up a can of paint, set it on the inside stair, and shut the door. Just as the door was shutting, the painter yanked it open. No one was there. He stared up the stairwell. There was nothing there except the can of paint sitting on the steps. The painter left and didn't come back.

"But all these stories are nothing!" said Lisa. "When things started getting *really* hectic, I was babysitting my Dad's new baby. My two sisters and my Mom came home from the grocery at dusk. Julie and Mom went into the house to put away the groceries. They were standing at the refrigerator right by the door onto the porch when they heard Patty crying and saying, 'Julie, open the door! That's not funny!'

They tried to open the door onto the back porch, but it was bolted shut, the bolts jammed. They kicked and pulled at the door while Patty stood outside screaming in the dark. Finally the door unlocked itself and they found the screen door on the porch hooked shut from the inside.

The house seemed to hate Patty, who Lisa says was the most sensitive of the sisters. She was sick at home one day, watching TV in her mother's bedroom while Marsha was at the store. She heard the kitchen cupboards opening and closing and assumed her mother was home.

"Bring me up a popsicle, please!" she yelled down. But there was no answer. She walked to the stairwell and looked down into the kitchen. The cupboard doors were opening and closing by themselves. Patty screamed. Then she saw footprints imprint themselves in the kitchen carpet. They moved through the hall, and up the stairs towards her. They were large, like a man's footprint.

Terror-stricken, she crawled under her mother's bed. Staring out from under the dust-ruffle, she saw the footprints come into the bedroom, shut the door, walk around the bed, then into the dressing room, then into the bathroom, and shut the door.

Almost incoherent with fear, she slipped out from under the bed, ran to the neighbors and called her future stepfather. She refused to go back to the house and moved in with her father, only visiting with her mother occasionally. The house got very crowded with spirits about the time they decided to sell the house and get out.

"Mom saw at least twelve spirits in the house. She always felt that the house was a fortress—if the doors were open to the outside, other spirits would walk in. She felt embattled, attacked. We hardly ever used the front door because when- ever you opened the door a cool tingling breeze swept in—it sent a shock through your body. In fact, the house was always very cold."

"Mom was talking to mediums, reading books and trying to learn how to deal with the spirits. Things were starting to scare her."

One night Marsha woke up and heard two or three people talking in her darkened room. She sat up. Directly in front of her was the mirror over the dresser which reflected the wall behind her bed. She made up her mind that this was the night she was going to tell the spirits to leave.

Marsha turned on the light. She sat there in a kind of trance, just looking at herself in the mirror, and she started to see wisps of smoke.

"Who is it?" she demanded. She was answered by a chorus of whispers. Then she saw silhouettes of people moving into the vision. Some were fragments: sleeves, collars, torsos. Some were headless. She couldn't see Smiley among them.

All were different, and each had his own voice. There were ladies in full Victorian dresses. One man had a tall top hat. She mused that it was like walking into a room full of people all painted in a dark smoke color. One ghostly woman was walking in and out of the crowd. One man was shaking his fist, another gestured. One especially terrifying apparition wore a 1950s-style raincoat with a snap-brim hat like a detective in a film noir movie. He alone was not talking like the others. He just stared at her menacingly.

The spirits all rustled and whispered together. Strain as she might, she couldn't make out what they were saying except for an occasional "she" or "her" in a negative tone. Then the whispers began in her head. The voices were grumbling, muttering angrily. The voices grew madder and louder. All night she stared into the mirror, talking to the smoky figures, telling them that Jesus of Nazareth commanded them to leave. They got louder and crueler, jeering at her prayers, it seemed, although no matter how loud they got, she couldn't understand their words. Finally, when she was completely exhausted, they began to fade and melt away like wisps of mist rising off a graveyard dissolve in the morning sun.

The reprieve was only temporary. Night after night the spirits came. In desperation, Marsha tried automatic typing to see if Norma could give her any help in ridding the house of the spirits. But while she typed, she felt a weight on her chest, then on her head. A heavy wind blew against her face. It seemed that someone was trying to enter her, to use her. The writings were terrifying—they weren't from Norma anymore. One of them warned, "while under the street lamp I will take your body."

Marsha brought in mediums and conducted seances in the house trying to get rid of the ghosts. It all helped—for a time. But she wondered if Smiley didn't like the people who had bought the house, that they weren't right for the house. Apparently the spirits were angry too; they saved their most terrifying tricks for last.

Said Lisa, "I was at my Dad's babysitting, early in the evening. My sisters and my Mom were home when the lights started going on and off a room at a time. Mom went to the kitchen for candles and heard a knock on the back door. She thought it was me, so she opened it. No one was there. She closed it, but didn't lock the door. Then there was another knock. Patty and Julie huddled behind Mom as she opened it.

Again, no one was there. The girls ran up to Mom's bedroom and locked the door. Mom called me and told me to stay at Dad's. I could hear the dog going crazy, running through all the rooms, barking its head off."

Marsha went upstairs, packed her bags and called her boyfriend. As she was shepherding the girls out of the house, all the lights went down.

She got the car out of the garage. The electric lights in the house and the gas lantern outside started flickering on and off. Then all the lights, including the car lights and dash light went out. She thanked God that the car itself ran. She drove as fast as she could to her boyfriend's house.

The next day the neighbor called.

"You need to get an electrician," she said. "The lights at your house have been going on and off for twenty-four hours!" Marsha went back to the house with the electrician. She stayed with him as he went to the basement and checked the main breaker switch. He turned it off so there was no power in the house. The lights continued to flicker on and off until the bulbs burned out.

Marsha anxiously kept in contact with the new people. The wife immediately got pregnant as soon as the family moved in. One day as she was alone in the house, she swore that somebody pushed her on the shoulders at the top of the stairs, causing the fall that brought on a miscarriage.

She too found herself locked in the bathroom. The final straw came when she stepped outside the front door to get the paper and the door locked itself behind her. She had left the other doors unlocked, but when she tried them, they were all locked too. She could hear her small children crying inside. Madly she picked up a rock and broke out one, then all fifteen panes of glass around the front door. When her husband rushed home from work, he had to pry the rock from her fingers. The woman had a nervous breakdown, was separated from her husband, and moved back to the west coast.

The next family to buy the house was very religious. Marsha met the woman in the supermarket one day and asked casually, "How do you like the house?"

The woman obviously didn't want to talk.

"All I can say is, I've met your friends who live there with me," she said stiffly.

Marsha tried to smile. "If you want to talk, call me," she said. But she never heard from the woman. She too was divorced from her husband and the house was sold. "Three families broken up in a ten-year period," muses Lisa. "I sometimes drive by the house, just to see how it is. It still looks the same."

And like Hill House, it stands by itself, not sane, holding darkness within.

APPENDIX 1
HAUNTING PEOPLE
Ghost-hunters, tale-tellers, and tours

*Those who dream by day are cognizant of many things
which escape those who dream only by night.*
-Edgar Allan Poe-

See also the Appendix of *Haunted Ohio: Ghostly Tales from
the Buckeye State*

Julia Brown performs spiritual healing through channeling.
180 Red Bud Dr.
Springboro, OH 45066
(513) 748-9417

Let Waynesville Town Crier and Historian Dennis Dalton
show you the invisible sights of "Ohio's Most Haunted Town"
with his "Not So Dearly Departed" Tour. By appointment.
Waynesville Chamber of Commerce, (513) 897-8855
or
Historically Speaking
PO Box 419
Waynesville, OH 45068

Ghost-hunter Paul R. Fraley of Life Directions performs past-
life regressions.
614 771-6818

Mark Francis compiles information on Bigfoots all over the
continent.
North American Bigfoot Information Network (NABIN)
1923 Glenwood Dr.
Twinsburg, OH 44087

Ghost-hunter Anne Oscard is one of the most talented tarot card readers I've ever met. She also does hypnosis and past-life regressions. She's one person I'd like to have along when confronting a ghost.

672 H Residenz Parkway
Kettering, OH 45429
(513) 293-4612

The Reverend Gayle A. Peltz, a medium and ordained Spiritualist Minister, performs work in the area of spirit rescue. She is available for in-depth psychic/spiritual readings either by personal appointment or phone.

(614) 246-4339

Lemoine D. Rice, psychic investigator, hypnotist and past-life regressions by appointment only.

2409 Mechanicsburg Rd.
Springfield, OH 45503
(513) 390-0896

Robert Van Der Velde is a delightful ghost hunter who has traveled all around the United States in his quest for the Unknown. You can book his slide shows on Cleveland-area ghosts, American ghosts, or Dr. Samuel Mudd and other Civil War topics.

7733 Dahlia Dr.
Mentor-on-the-Lake, OH 44060

Chris Woodyard hosts Dayton-area ghosts every October with her "Ghost-bus Tours"®: Drive-by ghost tour of sites like the Victoria Theater, Sinclair Community College, Woodland Cemetery, and much more. Call for dates and times.

You can also book Chris's lectures on the following topics:

Ohio: The Haunt of It All How does a person who is terrified of ghosts become a real-life ghostbuster? Hauntings around the state.

Ghosts of the Dead and Famous A survey of some famous and infamous Ohio people who had encounters with the unseen world, including our haunted presidents. Ghosts and Ohio history.

Buckeye Bigfoots and Other Spectral Animals Bigfoot in Greene County? Black Panthers in Ottawa? Sea serpents in Lake Erie? From giant frogs to ghostly kangaroos, weird and ghostly animals around the state.

What is a Ghost? Six theories and some tentative answers to that age-old question, Also, how to rid yourself of unwanted visitors.

Miami Valley Ghosts Includes the ghosts of the US Air Force Museum, Patterson Homestead, Victoria Theatre, Miami Valley Hospital, Sinclair Community College, Woodland Cemetery, University of Dayton and much more.

(513) 426-5110

APPENDIX 2
HAUNTED PLACES
Sites open to the public

A haunted place it is to me...
-Andrew Lang-

COLUMBIANA CO.
  Harmony Hills Riding Stables, 12243 Sprucevale Rd., East Liverpool, OH 43920, next to Beaver Creek State Park (216) 385-6191

GALLIA CO.
  Our House Museum, 434 First Ave., Gallipolis, OH 45631 (614) 446-0586

GEAUGA CO.
  Punderson Manor House Lodge, off Rt. 44, Newbury Center (216) 564-2279

GREENE CO.

> *Magee Park*, Little Sugar Creek Road north of 725, Bellbrook
>
> *Eden Hall*, 235 E. Second St., Xenia, OH 45485 (513) 376-1274

LICKING CO.

> *The Buxton Inn*, 313 E. Broadway, Granville, OH 43023 (614) 587-0001

MONTGOMERY CO.

> *Sinclair Community College*, 444 W. Third St., Dayton, OH 45402
>
> *United States Air Force Museum*, Springfield Pike (follow signs from Rt. 75 S or 675 S) or Wright Patterson AFB Area B, Bldg. 489, Dayton, Ohio (513) 255-3284

OTTAWA CO.

> *Ottawa National Wildlife Refuge*, off Rts. 2 and 590, Oak Harbor (419) 898-0014

RICHLAND CO.

> *Malabar Farm*, Pleasant Valley Rd., Richland County, 95 N to 603 N (419) 892-2784

SUMMIT CO.

> *Goodyear Airship Operations*, 841 Wingfoot Lake Rd., Mogadore, OH 44260

WARREN CO.

> *Glendower State Memorial*, Rt. 42 near Lebanon (513) 932-5366

WILLIAMS CO.

> *Nettle Lake*, extreme northwest corner of Williams County, near the Michigan border, between 575 Rd. and 475 Rd.

REFERENCES

Chapter One - Women in White

1 Harold Igo, "The Thunderstorm Ghost," *Yellow Springs News,* 3
    June 1943
2 Mary Sherman, *Ghosts and Legends of Bellbrook (*Bellbrook, n.p.)
    "Legends of Bellbrook: 'dark and bloody ground'", *Xenia
    Gazette,* 24 Oct. 1985
3 Betsy Hoffman, *Haunted Places,* (New York: Julian Messner, 1982)
    76-84
4 Jane Beathard, "Pleading spirit looks for help," *The Madison Press,*
    31 Oct. 1991 and personal interview with Dorothy Phillips
    Amling

Chapter Two - Convivial Spirits

1 "Ghostly Presence isn't ghastly at all", *Columbus Citizen-Journal,*
    31 Oct. 1985
2 Mary Bilderback Abel, "Ghostly Guests linger at an inn in
    Granville," *Columbus Dispatch,* 29 June 1979
4 Stephen Kelley, "Lore, Legends & Landmarks of Old Adams,"
    People's Defender Newspaper, [West Union, OH] 16, 23, 30
    Sept. 1982
5 "Beyond Incredible," *Ohio Magazine,* (Nov. 1980) 40-41
6 Pauline Wessa, "Library compiling the chilling history of Fairfield
    ghosts," *Columbus Citizen Journal,* 7 Nov. 1980

Chapter Three - The Choir Invisible

1 Marjorie Burnside Burress, *It Happened 'round North Bend: A
    history of Miami Township and its borders,* (Cincinnati: n.p.
    1970) unpaged
2 Harold Igo, "The Ghosts of Frogtown," *Yellow Springs News,* 13
    May 1943
3 D. Scott Rogo, *A Psychic Study of the "Music of the Spheres." NAD
    Vol. 2,* (Secaucus, NJ: University Books Inc. 1972) 42

4 *Ibid*, 44
5 *Ibid*, 76-77

Chapter Four - Things That Go Bump In The Night

1 Nandor Fodor, *The Haunted Mind* (New York: Signet Mystic, 1959)
   51
2 Letter from Mr. L.M. Austin of Austinburg, Ashtabula County,
   Ohio, dated 4th Feb., 1853 quoted in Emma Hardinge, *Modern
   American Spiritualism*, (n.p., 1869) 393-398
3 *Zanesville Times-Recorder*, 9 April 1978 and *Zanesville Sunday
   News,* 20 Feb. 1916
4 *The McConnelsville Conservative*, 14 Sept. 1869
5 Dr. A. Underhill, *The arrest, trial, and acquittal of Abby Warner for
   spirit rapping, in St. Timothy's church, Massillon, O.,* (Cleveland: Gray and Wood, Plain dealer steam press, 1852)
6 Kate March, "Things That Go Bump In Night Not Necessarily
   Unwelcome," *Price Hill News* [Cincinnati], 25 Aug. 1971

Chapter Five - From The Cradle to The Grave

1 "Cry Baby Bridge," *Haunting Tales from Fairfield County,*
   (Lancaster: Fairfield County District Library, 1980)
2 "Is crying baby ghost gone?", *Oberlin Chronicle-Telegram,* 26 Oct.
   1977
3 "Obituary of Denton Cridge," *Vanguard, (*1 1857) 222 and "Experiences of a Skeptical Medium," *Vanguard* (1 1857) 260 quoted in
   Ann Braude, *Radical Spirits: Spiritualism and Women's Rights in
   Nineteenth-Century America,* (Boston: Beacon Press, 1991) 1
4 F.A. Morgan, *Hants and Hangings: Stories of the Odd, the Bizarre,
   the Sensational in Area Early History and Folklore,* (Quaker
   City, OH: Home Towner Printing, 1976) 1
5 George P. Metcalf, "The Swift's Hollow Mansion", *Pathways of the
   Pioneers,* (Vol. 2 No. 4, June 1968)
6 Morgan, *Op. cit.,* 3
7 "Legend of the Dwarf", *Haunting Tales from Fairfield County,*
   (Lancaster: Fairfield County District Library, 1980)
8 Andrew MacKenzie, *Apparitions and Ghosts,* (New York: Popular
   Library, 1971) 52
9 Robert Dale Owen, *Footfalls on the Boundary of Another World,*
   (Philadelphia: J.B. Lippincott, 1875) 348-9

Chapter Six - Time Warps

1 Helen Meredith, *Ghosts!* (Coshocton, OH: n.p., 1967)
2 *Ibid*.
3 Rick Crawford, "Spirits return to visit house in Utopia site," *Milford [Ohio] Advertiser-Journal,* 24 Oct. 1990
4 Betty Miller, "Small Town Sampler," *Ada Herald,* 24 Oct. 1990

Chapter Seven - Buckeye Bigfoots

1 Roy W. Dixon, "The Crosswick Monster," *Dayton Daily News,* 11 June 1978
2 Janet and Colin Bord, *Unsolved Mysteries of the 20th Century,* (Chicago: Contemporary Books, 1989) 246-47
3 *Columbus Dispatch,* 26 February 1984 quoted in *Fortean Times* 42, 43.
4 Russell Frey, *Rogues' Hollow, History and Legends,* (n.p., 1958) 88-89
5 Interview with Rick Crawford
6 "Stumpy", W.W. Wilson, Ohio Valley Folk Research Project, Ross Co. Historical Society, (Chillicothe, OH, 1962) Ohio Folk Publications- New Series No. 94
7 Louis Bromfield, *Malabar Farm,* (New York & London: Harper & Brothers Publishers, 1947-8) 182
8 *Cleveland Plain Dealer,* 10 Jan. 1990 quoted in *INFO Journal,* (Mar. 1990) 30
9 Janet and Colin Bord, *Alien Animals,* (Harrisburg, PA: Stackpole Books, 1981) 72-3
10 Wessa, *Op. cit.*
11 Harold Igo, "The Jersey Angel," *Yellow Springs News*, 27 May, 1943
12 "The Rushcreek Monster," *Haunting Tales from Fairfield County,* (Lancaster: Fairfield County District Library, 1980)
13 Frey, *Op. cit.,* 82-83
14 Loren Coleman, *Mysterious America,* (Winchester, MA: Faber & Faber, Inc., 1983) 74-5
15 "A Summary of 1988 Bigfoot Sightings by Mark Francis," *INFO Journal,* (July 1989) 24
16 *Warren Tribune Chronicle*, 14 Aug. 1972
17 Marian T. Place, *Bigfoot All Over the Country*, (New York: Dodd-Mead, 1978) 120-21

Chapter Eight - A Gasp of Ghosts

1 Larry Engelmann, "The Ghost Blimp," *Life Magazine*, (July 1982) and C.V. Glines, "The Mystery of the Pilotless Blimp," *Aviation Heritage*, (July 1991) 43-49

Chapter Nine- Death Row

1 Jim Carney, "The matron's ghost," *Akron Beacon Journal*, 29 Oct. 1989
2 Harold Igo, "The Ghost of the County Jail," *Yellow Springs News*, 22 April 1943
3 David Lore, "The State of Ohio's Haunted House," *Columbus Dispatch*, 26 Oct. 1980

Chapter Ten- Ohio's Most Haunted Town

1 Arthur Myers, *The Ghostly Register: Haunted Dwellings, Active Spirits. A Journey to America's Strangest Landmarks*, (Chicago: Contemporary Books, 1986) 293-99
Joe B. McKnight, "Woooooo Waynesville! Does the past haunt it?" *Dayton Daily News*, 30 Oct. 1983
2 Mary Sikora, "The Haunting of Waynesville," *Dayton Daily News*, 4 Aug. 1978
Lawrence Wade, "Listen! They say there are ghosts in Waynesville," *Dayton Journal Herald*, 11 Sept. 1976
Karlene Johnson, "Who's Hoooo In U.S. Haunts? Waynesville!," *The Western Star*, 29 Oct. 1986

Chapter Twelve- Harmful Haunts

1 Janet Romaker, *"A haunting tale, Bumps in the night in Wauseon,"* and "Haunted resident locates her son, still has spirits," *Toledo Blade*, 31 Oct. 1991 and 7 Nov. 1991

MORE GHOSTLY TALES

(See also the Bibliography in *Haunted Ohio*.)

Bord, Janet and Colin, *Alien Animals,* (Harrisburg, PA: Stackpole
     Books, 1981)
     A fascinating look at anomalous animals and *tulpas* around the
world. I love everything these people write.

-*Unsolved Mysteries of the 20th Century,* (Chicago: Contemporary
     Books, 1989)
     One of my favorite guides to the paranormal. A catalog of the
seemingly impossible from ghosts to out-of-place animals to UFOs.

Braude, Ann, *Radical Spirits: Spiritualism and Women's Rights in
     Nineteenth-Century America,* (Boston: Beacon Press, 1991)
     A formidably well-researched and delightfully readable account
of the connection between 19th century female trance mediums and
women's rights.

Coleman, Loren, *Mysterious America,* (London and Boston: Faber &
     Faber, Inc., 1983)
     A wonderfully weird collection including many stories of odd
animals and a state-by-state gazetteer.

Cryptozoology, PO Box 43070, Tucson, AZ 85733
     Required reading for anyone interested in uncanny animals.

Fodor, Nandor, *The Haunted Mind,* (New York: Signet Mystic, 1959)
     The definitive work on the link between humans and poltergeists.

Frey, Russell, *Rogue's Hollow,* (n.p. 1958)
     There are many ghost stories in this history of "the toughest
damn spot in the whole United States."

The GATE, PO Box 43518, Richmond Hts., OH 44143
     Mysteries from all over, plus clips of oddities and reviews.
Highly recommended!

Goss, Michael, *Poltergeists: An Annotated Bibliography of Works in English,* circa 1880-1975

For deeper study of the elusive poltergeist. Somebody bring this up to date, please.

Haunting Tales from Fairfield County, (Lancaster: Fairfield County District Library, 1980)

Some very odd tales collected during an oral history project.

Hoffman, Betsy, *Haunted Places,* (New York: Julian Messner, 1982)

A collection of tales all the more chilling for their matter-of-fact directness of style. Recommended.

INFO Journal, International Fortean Organization, PO Box 367, Arlington, VA 22210-0367

I just discovered the Journal and I'm kicking myself for missing years of stories about spontaneous combustion, showers of frogs, and sea serpents. If you have a taste for the strange, subscribe!

Meredith, Helen, *Ghosts!* (Coshocton: Helen Meredith, 1967)

An interesting pamphlet of unusual local ghost stories.

Morgen, F.A. *Hants and Hangings: Stories of the Odd, the Bizarre, the Sensational in Area Early History and Folklore,* (Quaker City: Home Towner Printing, 1976)

They are indeed odd, bizarre, and sensational. Many taken from Wolfe's History of Guernsey County.

Rogo, D. Scott, *A Psychic Study of the "Music of the Spheres."* NAD Vol. 2, (Secaucus, NJ: University Books Inc. 1972)

A careful, if dry, look at one of my favorite phenomenon.

Sherman, Mary, *Ghosts and Legends of Bellbrook,* (n.p.)

Chilling local tales from "Ohio's Sleepy Hollow."

INDEX
GENERAL INDEX

INDEX OF STORIES BY LOCATION

THEY'LL BE BAAACK!

HAUNTED OHIO III is in the works. We invite readers to send us their stories of apparitions and haunted houses. We are especially interested in spirit photography, haunted art and antiques, haunted highways, ghosts in libraries, hospitals, schools, theatres, and the workplace. Also stories of lake monsters like South Bay Besse.

We also would like to collect ghost stories of any sort from the following counties: Allen, Belmont, Carroll, Clinton, Defiance, Harrison, Highland, Hocking, Holmes, Jackson, Jefferson, Lawrence, Logan, Lucas, Mahoning, Marion, Meigs, Mercer, Miami, Monroe, Noble, Paulding, Pickaway, Pike, Portage, Putnam, Scioto, Shelby, Stark, Trumbull, Union, Van Wert, Warren, Washington, Wood, and Wyandot.

SOME FUTURE CHAPTERS
Code Blue: Haunted hospitals
The Exorcists: Spirit rescues
The Men in Black: Ghostly gentlemen
Tales from the Crypt: More cemetery spirits
Ghosts at Work: Ghosts in the workplace
The Ghost in the Machine: Spirit photography
The Dead Zones: Haunt-spots of Ohio

Some places and creatures we'd like to hear more about: Piatt Castles, Franklin Castle, Loveland Castle, Schwartz Castle (Columbus), The United States Air Force Museum (Dayton), Our House Museum (Gallipolis), Sun Watch (Dayton), The Crosswick Monster and the Loveland Frog

Send your stories to Kestrel Publications, 1811 Stonewood Dr., Beavercreek, OH 45432. Please include an address and phone number. Anonymity will be guaranteed.

NOT SPOOKED YET? HOW TO ORDER
YOUR PERSONAL, AUTOGRAPHED COPIES
OF *HAUNTED OHIO* AND *HAUNTED OHIO II*
(They also make thoughtful gifts for nervous friends.)

Send this order form to:

Kestrel Publications
1811 Stonewood Dr.
Beavercreek, OH 45432
(513) 426-5110

_____ copies of Haunted Ohio @ $9.95 each $_____

_____ copies of **HAUNTED OHIO II** @ $9.95 each $_____

+ $2.00 Book Rate shipping, handling, and
tax for the first book, $1.00 postage for each
additional book. Call (513) 426-5110 for
speedier mail options. $_____

                              TOTAL $_____

NOTE: We usually ship the same or next day. Please allow three
weeks before you panic. If a book *has* to be somewhere by a certain
date, let us know so we can try to get it there on time.

MAIL TO (Please print clearly and include your phone number)

_____

_____

_____

_____

FREE AUTOGRAPH!

If you would like your copies autographed, please print the
name or names to be inscribed. _____

_____

PUBLISHER NOSINESS: Where did you get this copy? _____

_____